"MOON MOTH…SEA SPRITE… LOVELY CREATURE…."

Burke whispered the words against her lips and Allison reveled in their sound. Laughter drifting across the night brought them reluctantly back to reality.

"Come!" Burke murmured hoarsely.

Wanting him with an intensity she'd never felt before, Allison yielded to the strong arm that circled her waist. Moving as one, they slipped into the woods, where moss-hung trees and a screen of verdant undergrowth hid them from prying eyes. There a small ring of ankle-high grass awaited them. In the circle of enchantment he began to undress her.

The two beings who made up the person of Allison Hill locked in an agonizing struggle for control. The rational, clear-eyed self warned her to pull away, but the sensuous side waited a moment too long to obey….

WELCOME TO...

SUPERROMANCES

A sensational series of modern love stories
from Worldwide Library.

Written by masters of the genre, these longer,
sensual and dramatic novels are truly in keeping
with today's changing life-styles. Full of intriguing
conflicts, the heartaches and delights of true love,
SUPERROMANCES are absorbing stories—
satisfying and sophisticated reading that lovers
of romance fiction have long been waiting for.

SUPERROMANCES
Contemporary love stories for the woman of today!

A JENNY LORING
STRANGER'S KISS

A SUPERROMANCE FROM

WORLDWIDE

TORONTO · NEW YORK · LONDON

Published August 1983

First printing June 1983

ISBN 0-373-70074-1

Printed in Canada

CHAPTER ONE

THE LANDWARD SIDE of the island was still shrouded in the deep shadows of early dawn as Allison Hill, struggling stubbornly to stay awake, steered her small boat along the estuary that led into the sea.

In the sweet intoxication of success she had failed to consider how little sleep she'd had in the past twenty-four hours—or, for that matter, in the past week. She'd taken the midnight plane out of New York City. Now, six hours later, her early enthusiasm was lost in full fatigue, aggravated by the long drive down from Savannah after she landed plus the boat ride from the mainland to Ransome's Cay.

Cutting the motor, she let her body slump wearily in her seat while the boat idled, rocking rhythmically on the tide. After a moment she forced herself up from the wheel, stretched her limbs and yawned, her eyes coming to rest on the cool green arc of land that lay before her.

There it was. Ransome's Cay. Her island. How she loved it! Yet with all the money and work she'd invested there during the past weeks she still found it hard to believe the island belonged to her. She wondered if this very disbelief was what had driven her to such immediate feverish activity the moment she'd understood that Ransome's Cay had actually been left to her in the will. There'd been something almost superstitious in the way she'd taken immediate action—as if by putting a large measure of herself into the island as fast as she could she could keep it from being snatched away.

The strong sea breeze caught her hair and whipped it about her face in a dark veil, sharpening her dull senses. What she really needed, she realized suddenly, was a cold shower.

Then she remembered Buttonhook Cove, a small indentation in the shoreline not far ahead and so remote from the island's present-day activities that almost no one ever visited it. The cove's principal charm was a small artificial waterfall, created in some distant past by ingeniously diverting the island's only freshwater stream from its regular course to splash over a head-high, man-made ledge that thrust out of the ancient dunes. It may have served as a shower for its long-forgotten engineer, thought Allison. In any case, that's what she intended to use it for. There was a beach towel in the boat left over from some other outing, and the waterfall offered her as much privacy at this early hour as her own bathroom.

At the cove she secured the boat. Dropping her sandals on the seat, she stepped into the shallows and skimmed barefoot through the water and across the

strip of sand to a small wooded rise where the waterfall splashed out of a bower of sweet bay and cassina
holly. The air was so rich with honeysuckle she could
taste it. The waxy leaves of a magnolia tree, lan-
guorous, exotic and heavy with bloom, shimmered in
the early-morning sun.

Having opted for comfort and packed her city
clothes the previous night in Manhattan, she had
only to peel out of her faded jeans and red cotton-
knit shirt and shed her brief undergarments. Naked,
she hesitated at the edge of the waterfall's pool, then
dipped in an exploratory toe, only to pull back with a
shudder from the cold. With now-or-never resolve
she stepped in all the way and let the water rush down
on her head, over her bare shoulders and thighs.
Sputtering and gasping, she nevertheless held her
ground, conquering a natural instinct to retreat.

After the first shock of chill had subsided she
turned her face to catch the full force of the cascade
and in that moment felt completely, marvelously,
alive. Her flesh tingled and firmed. Exhilarated, she
was suddenly more intimately aware of her own body
than she'd been in a long time. She took new pride in
the rise of her breasts, the slimness of her waist, the
clean round curve of her hips—pride common to her
at eighteen, not so common at twenty-six.

Wide awake now and feeling wonderful, she had
just stepped forward out of the flow to reach for her
towel when her eyes caught a flash of movement in
the near distance. She looked again and stood hyp-

notized by what she saw racing toward her from out of the ocean.

It was a man! Or was it a man... or some perfectly carved creation, splendidly proportioned, who moved swiftly, surely, through the foam like a Michelangelo sculpture rising out of the sea? She pressed her hands to her eyes to dispel the improbable mirage, but still it remained before her.

Her eyes followed avidly. Streaming water, horse and rider came out of the waves, splashing through the shallows to explode onto the beach in a burst of sand and foam. The huge animal lifted his forefeet, fighting the air, until he stood nearly upright. The man leaned close to the horse's neck, welding his muscular body and denim-clad legs to the bare-backed mount. In the golden haze of the morning man and horse seemed one.

Lost in the sheer beauty of the unexpected tableau, Allison had no thought for anything else. Her own nakedness forgotten, and with it whatever embarrassment she might have felt, she watched and caught her breath, her throat filled suddenly with an exquisite bittersweet pain as horse and rider charged across the beach at full gallop all the way to the magnolia tree near the waterfall. There the rider pulled his mount to such a sudden halt the great beast rose bolt upright once more and pawed the air.

She felt her gaze drawn to meet the pair of eyes that looked down at her from the lean strong face, bronzed, like the sinewy, half-naked body, by the sun. Below a wind-tossed thatch of sun-streaked hair, eyes gray green and iridescent, as darkly mysterious as the sea, held hers until she felt as if she were caught in some strange phantom riptide in which she might willingly drown.

When the front hooves of the stallion came back to earth, the horseman's eyes released hers and moved coolly, shamelessly, down her body, unhurried, clearly savoring what they saw. Allison, strangely frozen to the spot, stood for a long moment as the rider's masterly hand on the bridle ordered the impatient stallion to stand. A long arm rose lazily, muscles rippling under bronzed flesh, to pluck a great cream-colored blossom from the tree overhead.

At last Allison roused herself. She picked up her towel from the ground and wrapped it around her, summoning as much dignity as she could under the circumstances.

"Whoever you are," she declared angrily, "will you please get off my island!"

The two dark gold wings that were the man's brows shot up in quizzical arches. He laughed, an amused throaty laugh.

"So the island belongs to the water nymph. And here I thought it was mine! Well, we'll not quarrel about it. Go on back to your bath, sweet Venus." The sensuous mouth curved into a gently sardonic smile. With wicked aim he tossed the magnolia blossom. It landed at her feet.

The horse wheeled suddenly on a signal from the

rider and thundered away across the pale ribbon of sand, weaving between clumps of palmettos until at last, far down the beach, the two turned inland and disappeared into the dark, moss-hung woods. Allison had a driving urge to call after them, but her voice caught in her throat.

She knew the horse! It was Cherokee, the renegade stallion from the island's small band of palominos. He belonged to Burke Ransome, a cousin of her late husband, Tyler Hill. Unlike the rest of the herd the stallion had the run of the island. Because of his owner's long absences, the animal hadn't been ridden regularly and had gradually reverted to the wild. The island people left him strictly alone, convinced the creature would kill anyone who tried to get on his back but Ransome.

In spite of herself Allison felt a sneaking admiration for this audacious marauder who had slipped onto the island and overcome the great half-tamed beast. Still, she must report the matter to Bunker, the caretaker, to make sure it didn't happen again, although by the time she reached Plantation House and actually found Bunker it might be too late.

She pictured the mysterious bronzed horseman, at that very moment racing the stallion through the woods to the other side of the island for a mad swim across to the mainland. It was some distance, but the horse was powerful, she thought with satisfaction. He had a good head start. He would never be caught.

With a sudden catch of breath she remembered the

man's eyes. Ah, those iridescent... *brazen* eyes! She knew she should be enraged and had the grace to feel guilty she was not. She saw herself for a moment riding behind the bold intruder in his daring escape, the wind in her face, her body molding itself to the splendid sinewy back, her arms encircling the muscular waist she clung to precariously.

Why not, she asked herself dreamily. She owed the absent cousin no loyalty. She'd never even seen the man. Tyler had refused to discuss his cousin during the four years of their marriage except to hint darkly at some vendetta between them. Why, then, should she be obliged to look out for Burke Ransome's blasted horse?

Sternly she answered her own question: *because the island is yours.* The responsibility for the horse came with the territory.

Towel-dried and respectably clad, she was about to return to the boat when her eyes fell on the magnolia blossom. There it lay on the sand near her feet, as insouciant and exotic as an ivory silk hat. She hesitated but an instant. Half-sheepishly she bent down and picked up the flower, then in a show of indifference tossed it on the seat when she reached the boat and stepped in behind the wheel.

With ruthless discipline she wrenched her thoughts from the disturbing donor to consider the irony that had given her possession of Ransome's Cay.

Though it was here that she'd spent the first idyllic weeks of her marriage, Allison had never imagined that the lovely water-locked piece of land might some day belong to her—least of all that it was to be willed to her by the long-absent ex-husband for whom she now felt nothing but a mildly contemptuous pity.

The gift seemed almost as improbable as the unquestioning adoration she'd wasted on the charismatic guileful Ty during the last years of her waning adolescence.

R. Tyler Hill. Even when it came to his name Ty had been impelled to tamper with the truth, claiming to be a direct descendant of the tenth president of the United States. What ancestral connection, if any, the Hill family had with John Tyler, the president was remote and nebulous at best.

But no matter, thought Allison. The important part of the name was the introductory *R*, which stood for "Ransome." Here Ty's lineage was on a plumb line straight down from the first colonial Ransome. It had entitled him to Ransome's Cay.

Nonetheless, when Ty's longtime friend and lawyer, Herb Canby, had called, after Ty had been killed in the crash, and said she'd inherited the island under a will Ty had made at the time of their marriage, she simply hadn't believed him. She was wary of Herb. He seemed more interested in jetting around the world than in the practice of law.

Yet when Herb swore he'd discussed the will with Ty only a few days before the accident and had been told to let it stand, she had to believe him. For all

Herb's eccentricities, she didn't doubt he was to be trusted when he gave his word.

Actually, until Herb showed it to her that day she'd never really believed there was such a will. Oh, there'd been the romantic "share-and-share-alike" flimflam Tyler had given her early in their marriage, of course. He'd flashed a piece of paper in front of her and said it was a will leaving all he owned to her if he died. Later she had come to understand it for what it was—a ploy for Ty to get her own small inheritance in joint tenancy so he would have access to her funds. In her adoring schoolgirl innocence she had left custody of the checkbook to her husband.

After the day she found out what a lot of her money he had squandered carelessly and without her knowledge she was never again such a fool as to imagine he'd given her any claim to the island in return.

That was the day four years ago when Allison had walked out of their posh Manhattan apartment on Park Avenue and moved into a fifth-floor walkup in the West Seventies, the day she had discovered they were about to be evicted for nonpayment of rent, and that the generous personal and household allowance he gave her each month came solely from her own funds. It was the day she learned too, that Tyler's frequent absences had nothing to do with his "business," which in itself turned out to be hardly more than a myth, and everything to do with a blond receptionist on Madison Avenue and before that a hostess for Air France. The mystery of it was that after all the pent-up bitterness she poured out on him that day he hadn't changed the old will in which he'd given Ransome's Cay to her. Maybe being Tyler, it never occurred to him that some dark day he might drive his high-powered car through the guardrail on a faraway freeway at a hundred and ten miles an hour and not survive.

On the other hand, maybe Ty had really intended her to have the island, unlikely as that seemed. How like him to think willing her Ransome's Cay would wipe out all that had gone on previously, she thought wryly. There was no bitterness now, though bitterness had nearly consumed her before she quit feeling sorry for herself and saw their parting as the best thing that could have happened to her.

Then, too, there was the fact that Ty's only living blood relative was Burke Ransome, an even more unlikely candidate for heirship than his ex-wife.

Dismissing the matter with a shrug, Allison turned the boat into deeper waters and headed down the shoreline toward Plantation House, pushing the throttle forward in sudden impatience to get home. She wanted above all to see Peg's face when she found out Allison had come back from New York with guarantees for a full house the crucial week of their grand opening July 4, the week Ransome's Cay would become a retreat for paying guests.

Her laughter burst on the morning air. For the first time she really half believed her great gamble might pay off. She'd risked everything on it—the last of her money, her job, the security of a coterie of amusing friends, including Bob Birch, the investment counselor who had been squiring her about town.

They'd all advised her strongly—even heatedly, in the case of Bob—to sell the island. She couldn't afford the taxes and upkeep, they pointed out. And in all fairness they were right. If she sold the island and invested the money in gilt-edged securities, they all agreed, she'd have enough to live on comfortably for the rest of her life.

All, that is, but Peg Crewes, who had managed a small resort hotel in the Adirondacks for years after her husband's death. She was the one person who hadn't told Allison she was crazy when she let it be known she intended to keep the cay and turn it into a vacation island for paying guests. It was a great idea, Peg said. Risky, yes. But—in Peg's own words—Allison had the "moxie" to pull it off, and she could count on Peg's experienced help.

Edwin Barron, senior vice-president at Carston and Ames, the accounting firm where Allison worked, had taken her proposed venture in stride. He was more than a boss. He was her mentor and friend. He had hired her after she'd left Tyler and had shown a paternal interest in her career. She would have hated it if the move had earned his disapproval. It was Edwin Barron who had suggested she take night-school classes to become a certified public accountant and had shown confidence in her by giving her executive responsibilities, tacitly urging her to aim upward in the firm. Without his encouragement she might not have discovered that the challenge of cold impersonal facts and figures was good therapy, that she handled them well, or that she had a real aptitude for administrative work.

She smiled as she recalled his remark the morning she told him what she proposed to do with Ransome's Cay.

"You're an able sensible young woman, Allison," he said. "If that's what you want and you have confidence you can make a go of it, go to it, my dear. I must confess I hate to see the firm lose good executive material, but as I see it, the very worst that could happen to you would be to lose a piece of property you didn't really expect to own in the first place. And you can always come back to Carston and Ames as long as I'm in the company."

She realized suddenly that those words had been the deciding factor. Edwin Barron and Peg Crewes outbalanced the lot of her nay-saying friends.

How good it was to be returning now from her business trip to New York with the news for Peg that one of the top credit-card companies agreed with her judgment enough to do a cover story on Ransome's Cay and its authentic plantation house for an upcoming issue of the company's monthly travel magazine.

In the next instant all thought of Peg fled Allison's mind. The little boat was approaching the point where she'd seen the palomino and its rider disappear.

What a brazen woman you are, Allison Hill, she told herself, a bit shocked that she was not more embarrassed when she looked back on the remarkable encounter. She realized with shame that the warm rush of blood to her face at the recollection came not so much because a stranger had caught her dressed in nothing but a golden chain as because she'd had no control over the situation. It had been all in the hands of the man.

Pulling in close to shore, Allison could see in the pale sand the shallow, crescent-shaped, water-filled wells made by the stallion's hooves as he charged down the beach. Before her mind flicked an image of the rider, his bare trunk rising up from the horse's back erect and virile like the quintessential symbol of all that is male. Deep within her body leaped a sudden, almost forgotten flame.

A delicious shiver shot up her spine, and she raised her eyes without hope from the beach to follow the bridle path into the moss-hung woods, knowing her golden centaur was long gone.

With a sigh she lowered her eyes and pulled a tight rein on her flightiness. The faint smile that played on her face was tinged with irony as she looked back to the moment she'd first known and understood the nature of that sweet hot pain. It had tricked her into a wrong marriage at nineteen with a year of college yet ahead. Once she recognized it as her betrayer, something inside her turned cold. No man she'd met since had ever rekindled the flame. She had begun to fear that for her it had been forever snuffed out.

At least the pilot light still burns, she thought in a flash of self-mockery. But why did it have to flare so inappropriately? Why wouldn't it light up for someone she could count on? Someone like Bob Birch instead of a...a—

She broke off, aghast. Was she out of her mind? That golden godlike rider was a horse thief and nothing but!

With a scornful laugh she revved the motor and swung the boat away from the telltale hoofprints in a sharp, precarious turning that took the boat back into deeper water, trailing an angry wake.

By the time she pulled within sight of Plantation House the peace of the seascape had gradually worked its way with her, and she drew in a deep breath of contentment. The big, three-story mansion stood white and majestic on the crest of the green slope rising up from the beach. The golden light of the early-morning sun cast a halo on the gracious old beauty.

Around the south wing of the house Allison spotted Peg, her short plump body draped in a cerise-and-green muumuu splashed with tropical flowers. Atop was a shock of burnt-orange hair and a rosy face graced by a small, amazingly flawless nose, which, Allison knew, was in some stage of sunburn, that being its usual state. Peg made a brilliant spot on the landscape as she crossed through the shade of the giant magnolia tree that overhung a corner of the south veranda, and walked out into the full sun.

Easing into the piling, Allison tossed her suitcase up on the plank deck. When she had anchored the boat, she scrambled aboard the landing. There she retrieved her bag and ran lightly across the sandy beach to the lawn.

"Peg! Halloo! Hey, Peg!" she called out.

The other woman turned her head and stopped. With a wave and a quickening of her steps she approached, puffing heavily. "Boy, am I glad to see you!" she gasped, struggling to catch her breath.

"And have I got good news for you!" chortled Allison.

"I've always got an ear for good news," said Peg with a grin. "Let's have it." She listened, nodding with satisfaction as Allison hurried through a breathless, abridged account of what she'd accomplished during her ten-day stay in New York. Details could wait till later.

"With a couple of friendly travel agencies on our side, some great free publicity and a sellout opening week it looks like we're off to a very good start," she finished.

"Good for you," Peg cried delightedly. "I knew you'd do it! Shall we break out the champagne now or wait for the sun to climb over the yardarm, if I may coin a cliché?"

"To tell you the truth, Peg, all I want to do is crawl in bed and sleep for a week."

"Go on up to the house and tuck in, then. We'll pop the cork when you wake up."

"Wait a minute," Allison said as her friend turned on a purposeful heel and started off across the lawn toward the beach. "You haven't told me what's been going on here since I left."

Peg stopped and turned back. "Nothing that won't keep till you've had some sleep," she said. "Oh, one nice bit of excitement. A big yacht anchored off the lagoon last night, the boys tell me. The whole island's agog this morning." She gave an exasperated sigh. "I know as well as anything Hoddy and Max have gone up to look at it. And I've got a job for them at the house. Drat that pair! I'll round them up if I have to chase all the way to the end of the island."

Allison watched her friend start off again in search of her teenage twins, resident handymen at Plantation House. Peg was a relentless taskmaster. Allison half hoped she wouldn't find them this morning. Her mouth gaped unexpectedly in a cavernous yawn that brought tears to her eyes and told her she was much too tired to run interference for them as she often did. She picked up her bag and started on to the house.

DEEP IN THE WOODS some distance beyond, the rider slowed Cherokee to an easy canter after another plunge into the sea. His body accommodated itself to the rhythm of the palomino as if they were one. Strong-boned and muscular, his tall frame was as supple as a sea otter's. When he moved, it was with a spare effortless grace that came from seagoing years. The lean, strongly hewn face was marked by a generous slash of mouth and a full lower lip that spoke of the lover within. It was a mature face, as well seasoned by life and the world as by sun and sea, the face of a man who had survived the callowness of youth and in surviving had come to know himself.

Laugh lines at the corners of the gray green eyes were etched there permanently by long hours of watching the distant edge of the sea. Otherwise the face that squinted through the sun-dappled shade was youthful and scarcely lined.

Ransome's Cay! After ten years he was home at last on the sickle-shaped swatch of land that was one of the dwindling number of the South's celebrated Golden Isles still in old-family hands. A card-playing Ransome had won the island two hundred years earlier on a lucky draw and had made the Ransome fortune there growing long-staple cotton and indigo before the boll weevil put an end to the cotton and chemical dyes made indigo obsolete. Now the island belonged to him, Burke Ransome, last of the Ransome line.

The racing beat of his own homecoming heart had matched the throb of the small ship's engine the night before as the *Ulysses* sailed into the shelter of the island's lagoon to anchor—at the end of its long ocean voyage through the canal and up the Atlantic coast.

" 'Home is the sailor, home from sea,' " he had

murmured into the wind, fully aware of the irony the line from Robert Louis Stevenson's poem held for him. How little Plantation House had resembled a home that long-ago night when he had stormed off, swearing never to return.

Had he flirted again this morning with that same old danger down there at Buttonhook Cove? "My island," she'd said, the azure eyes shot with fire like an opal. *"My* island," which meant, of course, that she was a child of one of the island's families, grown into disturbingly beautiful womanhood during the years he'd been away.

No matter, he told himself angrily as he exorcised the image from his mind. It was because of a beautiful woman that he had abandoned Plantation House and Ransome's Cay ten years earlier. He would not let himself succumb to that danger again, nor was he about to get involved, however superficially, with any woman, even a simple island girl, the first day after he reached home.

Margo had been no simple island girl, he recalled ruefully. As if it were yesterday, another image thrust itself unwelcomely into his mind—an image of the hotheaded young lord of the manor he'd been at twenty-four, exploding out of Plantation House that black night and swooping off in the company's single-engined plane, swearing he'd never come back.

With an acute sense of shock Ransome realized now it was a good thing he'd stormed away. If he'd stayed, he'd have killed his cousin, Tyler Hill, then and there.

"Don't look so scandalized," Ty had muttered shakily, all the while fumbling himself back into his clothes. "She was mine before you ever saw her. She's never been yours."

It was like a blow to the face. He started for his cousin's throat. Then through the blood-red anger that clouded his sight he saw the secret pleasure in the expression of the beautiful naked woman reclining on the rug like a smug satiated cat. She made no effort to cover herself. *Good God! She wants us to fight,* he remembered thinking.

"Is that true?" he demanded.

"I thought you knew," she said provocatively, the sloe eyes egging him on. "Everybody else does."

Half suffocating from disgust, he gasped, "But why?"

"*You* should ask!" she replied in her sullen silky drawl. "You know it's not fair that all the family money went to you."

A terrible revulsion spread through him. "You were lovers when you married me," he said dully. His voice was not accusing; he was simply stating the newly learned fact, as if to hear it aloud would make it the lie he wanted it to be. "You're lovers now."

"You wouldn't take away the only fun I've ever had?" she pouted, still baiting him. "You don't know how to play like Ty. You may have inherited the money, Burke, but Ty and I know how to have fun!"

Margo...his wife of less than a year. For that woman he had left his island, moved to Atlanta and taken his place in the corporate structure of the family's milling company. How it had bored him—that multimillion-dollar business with its chain of management that went back three generations and stoutly resisted all change.

He had stormed out of Plantation House that grim night and returned to Atlanta. The next day he went back to work at the company, but this time as a laborer in the mill. In a vain effort he strove to dilute his anger and disillusionment with his own sweat.

Wild horses couldn't drag him back to the island, not as long as he and Tyler, the last surviving members of the clan, owned it in equal shares. Nor would either of them sell to the other, though Lord knows his cousin was more than willing to sell to anyone else who could come up with cash. The catch was, of course, that no would-be buyer would go for half ownership and Burke had no intention of selling his share.

Who knows how long the stalemate might have gone on if Ty—who spent money as if the United States Mint had issued him his own private set of engraving plates—hadn't married an expensive wife. Ransome hadn't even known that Margo had moved on to other prey and his cousin had married until a day four years ago, when Ty came begging to him to buy the other half interest in the island, because one more time Tyler was in dire financial straits.

The irony of his cousin's predicament had escaped him at the moment, Ransome realized now with a tight smile. He'd been too besotted with triumph over the unexpected turn of events to note it. Total ownership of the island meant everything to him. He knew exactly what he would do from that point on— had known it most of his adult life.

For generations the island families had supported themselves from the sea. Then, some years back, a devastating tropical storm had caused the nature of the great lagoon at its northernmost end to change. The oysters and shrimp that had been their livelihood gradually disappeared. Fishermen could no longer bring up catches worth hauling over to the mainland.

After his first year in college Burke had come back to the island for summer vacation to find most of the friends he'd hung around with all his life gone. Ollie Joe Fritter and Brick. Catfish Miller. Esau, who would show up at the back door at Plantation House with a bushel basket of oysters after everyone said the lagoon was dead. All had gone to the mainland to find jobs.

In those long humid summers when there was nobody left to talk to but Bunker, the caretaker, and his wife, Effie, he'd made a vow that if he did nothing else with his life he would turn his share of the family's considerable fortune into helping the handful of families on Ransome's Cay make a living, so the Esaus and the Ollie Joe Fritters would have reason to stay. To this end, along with his Harvard business degree, he'd managed to tuck in a fair amount of knowledge about the business of farming the sea.

His first move when the island was his had been to buy the *Ulysses*, the sturdy, sixty-five-foot craft lying out there at the edge of the lagoon. He'd had it converted into a research vessel and handpicked a crew of sailors who for the most part were also scientists.

Beginning with the great landlocked Bay of Arcachon in France, where five hundred million oysters are produced each year, he and his ship moved on from ocean to ocean, wherever there was any form of sea farming or aquaculture. They visited places as far-flung as Port Erin, England; Guaymas, Mexico; and Hawaii's Paradise Cove. For more than a year the ship sat at anchor off the coast of Japan while skipper and crew studied prawn farming and man-made oyster beds.

When word finally reached Ransome that Tyler had been killed some weeks earlier, the ship was tied up at San Diego, where Ransome was finishing a study with the Scripps Institute of Oceanography and observing a bait-shrimp operation in San Diego Bay. If it weren't for his cousin's death, he wouldn't be back here now, thought Ransome. It was almost as if news of the fatal crash had been the signal he'd waited for.

Not that he hated Tyler, though he had for a long time. The sea had washed that poison out of him, thank God. No, it was simply that he'd spent too

much of his life bailing his cousin out of one financial scrape after another. The two of them had never
much liked each other, even as kids. He'd felt no sorrow at his cousin's death. Just a terrible sense of
frustration at the wasted life and an unreasonable
anger at the wife who'd had a chance to save Ty from
himself if only she hadn't been so selfish, an extravagant woman who chose to exploit her weak husband's natural fecklessness.

What was her name, the wife? *Allison*, he recalled
after a moment's thought. He didn't want to meet
her. He didn't even wonder what she was like. On
those increasingly rare occasions when he thought of
Margo, he saw not her face but the calculating predatory eyes of a sleek jungle cat. And that was the way
he imagined Tyler's widow, that faceless Allison—
calculating, predatory, out to use every man as
served her best.

He knew from firsthand experience what cousin
Tyler Hill's women were like. This Allison had taken
Tyler to the cleaners. What else did he need to know?

The mask of the cynic on his face, he told himself
he should thank Ty's high-spending Allison. Had it
not been for her extravagant whims he still would
just half own Ransome's Cay. Only on the brink of
ruin would Ty have sold to him, and if he hadn't....
Ransome grimaced. As Tyler's widow, Allison Hill
would no doubt own the other half interest in the
island.

Ransome came out of the deep shadows of the

woods into the bright clearing of the field where the horses were kept. Spotting Bunker, the caretaker, on the far side, he touched a heel to Cherokee. Except for an exuberant welcome in the early morning they'd hardly talked. They had some catching up to do. He had a great fondness for Bunker and his wife, who had almost grown up in the Ransome household.

The caretaker looked up from where he hunkered, examining a horse's hoof. Seeing Ransome, he rose and came to meet him, reaching to take Cherokee's rein. "After all these years, don't look like he can throw you yet," Bunker remarked dryly.

"He's wild as a boar, but a few gallops in the surf reminded him who his master is," said Ransome with a laugh as he swung down off the palomino's back.

Bunker slipped off the bridle. The animal's huge frame shuddered, and he was away in a cloud of dust.

"It's been a long time, Bunker," Ransome said seriously. "Tell me...how're things going, and how's Effie?" Assured that Effie was in good health, he inquired about Jimmer, their adored son and only child. He was disturbed to see a cloud of sadness darken the older man's deeply tanned and weathered face.

"We lost Jimmer," the caretaker said.

"You mean—" Ransome started in a voice of shock, but Bunker interrupted with an apologetic humorless laugh.

"No, no. Nothing like that," he said. "He ain't dead, God forbid. Maybe Effie and me better remember to be thankful for that. No. There just wasn't no work for him here, and he's a man with a wife and a child. He's got to make a living. He and his family moved up north. He got himself a job in a tire plant. Pays right good, but they're sure homesick, and Effie and me, we sure do miss them."

"Well, get him home," ordered Ransome cheerfully. "I need him here on the island. Tell him I'll pay him at least what he makes up there."

For an instant Bunker's face lighted up. Then he shook his head.

"'Twon't wash," he said. "There ain't nothing for him to do here, and he ain't even about to take no make-work job you cook up for him, Burke. I know you mean well, but Jimmer don't take charity, and me'n Effie wouldn't be proud of him if he did."

"I'm not in the charity business," Ransome told him. "This is the real McCoy. I'm starting a project that'll put the whole island to work and make money for all of us."

Briefly Ransome explained to Bunker his plan for cultivating the lagoon and was rewarded with a light of pure happiness on his old friend's face.

The caretaker reached a gnarled hand into a pocket and brought out a bandana to wipe his eyes. "Lordamercy, Burke, that's the best news I've heard in near all my life. Wait'll I tell Effie." Shamefacedly he blew his nose.

"Tell you what, Bunker," Ransome said. "I'll go back to the ship and take care of a few things. Then I'll come on up to the house and pay my respects to Effie. It'll be good to sleep in a bed again. . . get back in my old room."

Was he imagining it, or did he see something uneasy in the caretaker's eyes as he turned away? Ransome turned back on an afterthought.

"Oh, by the way, which one of the island girls changed into a smashing beauty while my back was turned?" This time he saw nothing but puzzlement in his old friend's eyes. In spite of himself he had to go on. "Tall, dark hair, well built. . . ."

Suddenly Bunker nodded his head. "Oh, that ain't one of the island girls," he said nervously, almost defiantly. "I reckon Mrs. Hill's got back from New York. Mrs. Hill—your cousin's widow."

Ransome's face set suddenly in a hard unyielding line. "Mrs. Hill! Mrs. *Allison* Hill? What the hell is *she* doing here?"

"Well. . .it looks like she's kind of took over Plantation House, her and her friend. They're. . .well, they're kind of, you might say. . .converting it."

"What do you mean, converting it? Converting it into what?" Ransome exploded. He didn't wait for an answer. "That woman doesn't have a right even to visit this island without a personal invitation from me. It'll be a cold day at the equator before she gets it."

"Well, it seems she kinda thinks the island belongs to her," Bunker informed him reluctantly.

An expletive burst from Ransome's mouth.

"Now, Burke..." Bunker began, his tone cautionary.

But Ransome would have none of it. "Save your breath, Bunker. The island is not and never will be hers," he said, his voice harsh with disdain. "Send her and her lover packing. I don't want to see her. Get her out of here. I'm going back to the *Ulysses*. Get word to me when she's gone."

"Now, Burke..." Bunker ventured again, and this time when Ransome started to break in, the caretaker held up his hand to be heard out. The younger man yielded out of respect.

"In the first place, nobody said nothin' about a lover," Bunker said firmly. "I said she had a *friend* up at the house. The friend's a woman with a good head on her shoulders and a couple of smart near-grown orphaned sons that've been workin' like spawnin' shad to get that old house back in shape."

About to interrupt, Ransome was stopped again. "That's in the first place, Burke," said Bunker. "In the second place, if I understand it, your daddy left half interest in the island to your cousin. The way your daddy saw it, both sides of the family had the same right to the island, even though th'other side's never been worth a peck of peas. Now don't Ty's widow get his—"

This time Ransome had his way. "Tyler's widow has no rights here whatsoever because neither did Tyler when he died. I bought him out four years ago, just as my father bought out his. I don't know if my cousin had anything to leave to his widow or if she'd already managed to strip him clean, and frankly I don't give a damn. In either case the island belongs to me," he finished grimly.

After a moment Bunker, visibly shaken by what he'd just heard, said in a subdued voice, "I didn't know. I don't reckon Mrs. Hill—"

"To hell with Mrs. Hill! You don't think I would have set up that account to take care of the island if half of it belonged to Tyler?" asked Ransome truculently.

"How d'ya expect me to know, since I wasn't told?" Bunker bridled. "It was *you* who always wrote the checks for the place, wasn't it, even before he sold his part to you?"

Again Ransome swore. "You know anytime my cousin had money he wasn't about to spend it on Ransome's Cay," he reminded Bunker. "If I'd waited for him to pay his share of the expenses, the place would have crumbled around our feet years ago. What's more, you wouldn't have got paid. Get this straight, old friend. I don't intend to have any dealings with that woman Tyler married, so it's up to you to get rid of her, and I don't give a damn how you do it."

"It ain't all that simple, Burke," Bunker told him unhappily. "She's been here for quite a piece. She's made a lot of improvements at the place, and the money's all come out of her own pocket. She and her friend, Mrs. Crewes, and those two big strapping boys just took over. They never asked me to pay for nothing, not even the workmen who come in from outside.''

Ransome gave a resigned sigh. "All right, all right," he said angrily. "Pay her. Get someone to figure out what she's put into it and pay her off, but not one cent more than she's got coming, y'hear? Tell her to get the hell out once she's been paid.''

"She's fixin' to stay," Bunker said doggedly. "They've got the house set up to take in guests for the summer. Paying guests.''

"What!''

"She's hired island folks to help in the kitchen and dining room and the three Harris girls and their ma as chambermaids," Bunker told him. "Scarce as jobs is around these parts, I don't reckon none of them folks is going to be right happy at being beat out of cash-money employment.''

"Forget the jobs," Ransome told him coldly. "There'll be plenty coming up. You go tell this Mrs. Hill I don't want her on my island. If she doesn't know it's mine, you can tell her that, too.''

The caretaker squared his shoulders and looked his employer straight in the eyes. "Not me, Burke," he said flatly. "You go tell her yourself.''

They stood for a long moment, their eyes locked in combat. Had Margo, after all, left him a cripple, Ransome wondered in sudden shame. His mind swung back to a time when he'd used women badly,

as if by encouraging their infatuation and then walking away he could somehow get back at Margo.
For a moment, remembering, he was filled with self-
disgust. He knew there was no way to mend it. At
least it had just been a phase.

There'd been other women since, women he'd admired and enjoyed and maybe been a little in love
with, but there'd been no talk or thought of marriage
on either side. Of that he was cured, just as he was
cured of Margo.

So why was he trying to saddle Bunker with his
own hatchet job? Was he afraid to meet the test of
Margo's successor—Tyler's calculating wife?

A wave of self-contempt swept over him. He gave
Bunker a sheepish grin and laid an apologetic hand
on the older man's shoulder. "I'm sorry, old
friend," he said quietly. "I've got a helluva nerve
bellowing at you like a bull."

The caretaker eyed him uncertainly for a moment.
Still bristling a bit, he said, "I meant it, Burke. I ain't
going to tell her. She's a nice lady. You can tell her
yourself."

"I know. I know. I don't expect you to do my dirty
work. I'm going back to the boat."

But Bunker waited to hear him say more.

Ransome sighed and gave in. "Don't worry. I'll be
over to talk to the beautiful Mrs. Hill this afternoon," he said with heavy irony.

CHAPTER TWO

"WAKE UP, ALLISON!" It was Peg touching her shoulder. "Tyler's cousin, Burke Ransome is downstairs and says he won't go till he sees you."

Allison fought her way up from a deep dreamless sleep to stare stupidly at her friend. "Tell him to go away," she groaned, squinting at her bedside clock with sleep-drugged eyes. She saw she had been asleep for nearly six hours.

"Do you think if I could get him to leave I'd be up here waking you now?" asked Peg crossly.

Although she was scarcely awake, Allison could see her friend was genuinely upset. "What's wrong?" she asked, sitting up in alarm.

"There's something real fishy going on," said Peg, her brow furrowed with worry lines. "That boat down there in the lagoon is his."

Suddenly wide awake, Allison gasped. "You mean Burke Ransome's been on the island since last night?" At Peg's nod a terrible feeling of helplessness swept over her. "Oh, my God!" *Cherokee... the bronze-bodied horseman!* "What does he look like, Peg? Tell me! I've got to know."

Peg considered a moment. "Tall and strong and terribly virile-looking, with lots of muscle and good bones under a great tan," she said. "Plus a thick head of hair about the same color as his skin. Gives you the feeling the man's golden brown all over."

Allison, holding her breath as she listened, let it out in a small sigh.

"Does that ring a bell?" asked Peg, suddenly curious.

Allison hesitated, not sure just how much of her early-morning encounter she wished to share with her friend. "He was riding Cherokee in the surf up near Buttonhook Cove as I came in this morning," she said after a moment. "I never thought it could be Burke Ransome. I was going to report him to Bunker, but I was so sleepy I forgot. I thought someone was stealing the horse."

"You're sure that's who it was?"

"From your description how could I miss?" asked Allison dryly. "You seem to have taken a pretty good look. You got everything but the eyes."

"Gray, with flecks of green and amber . . . and long thick dreamy eyelashes . . . bedroom eyes," Peg told her promptly. "But don't let the marvelous laugh lines fool you. The man's used to being in charge. There's authority and toughness in that face. You can bet he's here on Ransome's Cay for something, and he's out to get it. I just hope it's not the island."

"Oh, Peg, don't be such a pessimist," Allison said in a voice more positive than she felt. "What good would it do him to want the island? Ransome's Cay belongs to me, and I don't have any intention of selling it, if that's what he has in mind.''

A whisper of excitement thrilled through her at the prospect of meeting him again... only this time she'd be the one in control. This time she'd be fully clothed.

''Go tell him I'll be down shortly,'' she said as she stepped out of bed and headed for her closet.

She slipped into a fresh pair of jeans and a soft blue, collarless shirt with long sleeves, which she turned up loosely at the cuffs, aiming for a careless but no-nonsense look. When she had combed out the tangles, she brushed her dark hair until it took on a satin sheen and left no reminder of its earlier dousing. A discreet touch of makeup hid the shadows of weariness under her eyes and brought out their natural blue. As an afterthought she dabbed a light gloss of rosy lipstick on her mouth.

A last glance in her full-length mirror satisfied Allison that she looked crisp and businesslike. Except for the veil of dark hair that hung to her shoulders and curled softly around her face. She eyed herself anxiously. It wouldn't do for Burke Ransome to mistake her for that wanton nymph he'd seen in the waterfall at Buttonhook Cove.

Reaching quickly for her brush, she pulled her hair back severely from her face and fastened it in a short ponytail at the base of her neck. She studied the effect with satisfaction. It gave her the look she wanted—very much on top of things.

A moment later she was descending the broad three-story staircase with its carved walnut balustrade that led to the great hall. There, below, not sitting properly in one of the side chairs placed for guests but standing imperiously, one hand on the newel post, the other on his hip, waited Burke Ransome.

Ominously her heart missed a beat, then thundered on. She laid a steadying hand on the balustrade, her chin high. Glacial eyes watched her come.

As she walked down the stairs to meet him, Allison had the strange feeling she was not moving under her own power but rather was being drawn by a magnetic force across the separating stairs and into Burke Ransome's unfriendly waiting arms.

He made no move to withdraw to the reception hall from which the stairs rose. The stairway was much too spacious for him to block her way, but his position would force her to pass too closely in front of him for her own peace of mind. For the moment it was something she wasn't prepared to do.

Three steps above him she stopped, tightening her grip on the balustrade for support at the flare of recognition she saw in the wintry eyes. She felt the rush of blood to her face, her own image as he'd seen her that morning at the falls mirrored vividly in her mind.

In spite of an incipient inward flutter that threatened to give away the state of her emotions she managed to say, "I'm Allison Hill, and you are...."

"You can forget the amenities, Mrs. Hill. We both know who we are. The less time we waste on small talk, the sooner you will understand why I'm here."

He glared at her with eyes of granite, but she would not be intimidated. She looked down on him with the hauteur of a dowager empress, while inside she trembled.

"If you've something on your mind that concerns me, Mr. Ransome, I'm willing to listen, in spite of your unfriendly tone," she said formally. "However, I prefer to discuss it sitting down. If you will please join me."

Without waiting for an answer, she steeled herself, took the remaining steps in swift flight and left Ransome facing the empty stairs. As she sailed past him, an inner thrill of danger swept through her, and she half expected a sinewy arm to reach out and pin her to the wall like a specimen butterfly. Securely seated in one of the straight-backed side chairs, chin high, her own back as rigid as the chair's, she fought for composure and waited for Ransome to turn.

If only he weren't so positively overwhelming, she thought, unable to ignore the flame that sprang to life within her as she watched the muscles of the man's upper back grow taut under the brown cotton-knit shirt.

Her tactics had worked. He continued to face the stairs for a bare instant, as if taking charge of himself. Then, with the merest suggestion of a shrug, he dropped his hand from the newel post and turned to cross the parquet floor to where she sat, his face expressionless.

Instead of taking the other chair, he stood looking down at her, forcing her eyes to raise to his. She met steel with steel and felt again his magnetism. This time he was setting the ground rules, bidding her to rise and stand before him like a culprit child. She stayed put. There was no way she'd play puppet on his string!

With a grunt of annoyance Ransome took the matching chair after a moment and jockeyed it irritably until he faced her, his expression grim. "Bunker tells me you've made changes at Plantation House," he began accusingly. "By what authority, may I ask?"

"By my own," retorted Allison with asperity. "And may I ask what concern it is of yours?"

"You hardly need that spelled out, I should think," he said harshly. "You know I'm Burke Ransome. You also know, I presume, that I'm the last member of a family that's owned Ransome's Cay since colonial times. Isn't that enough to make it my concern? I want no changes, but first and foremost I want you and your people out!"

Allison's mind reeled under the onslaught. What could she reply to this crazy man? The implications of what he'd just said were staggering. Surely he must know Tyler had left the island to her.

"I'm sure you can have no objections to what we've done," she said, stalling for time. "We've

made no structural changes and our first consideration has been to preserve the historical integrity of
the house. For the most part it's been painting and
papering. We've put in some badly needed plumbing
and done some rewiring to make the old building
safe."

She could see he was not listening, merely biding
his time to break in. "Why the sudden interest in
Ransome's Cay, Mr. Ransome?" she interrupted
herself in an unexpectedly acid voice. "It's my understanding you haven't set foot on the island for at
least ten years."

For a moment the strongly hewn face looked almost gaunt. The eyes that surveyed her beneath thick
golden brown lashes were dark with secrets.

"My absence was for personal reasons," Ransome
replied tautly. "It had nothing to do with my feelings
for this place."

The conversation was totally frustrating, thought
Allison. Did he think he could swoop down on the
island like some huge predatory bird and seize it now
that he no longer had Tyler to contend with?

"If you'll excuse me," she said, rising suddenly to
her feet, "I have a lot of things to do. I hope you will
enjoy your visit." This time the arm reached out and
a strong hand seized her.

"Visit?" thundered Ransome. "I'm not here to
visit. I'm here to stay. Just who the hell do you think
owns this island, Mrs. Hill?"

"I do!" she snapped.

In an aura of white heat they faced each other, only a pace or two apart.

"The hell you do!"

"Tyler left it to me in his will," Allison said flatly, her voice choked with anger. "Surely you know he'd never leave it to you."

"And surely you know that my cousin couldn't leave the island to anybody," Ransome retorted in brittle mimicry. "He didn't happen to own the island. Not any part of it."

"I don't believe you!"

A muscle twitched at the corner of one of his eyes. "Nevertheless it's true. Now let's cut out the subterfuge, Mrs. Hill."

Striving to control her fury, Allison said bitingly, "I see now why he disliked you so. The island was all in the world Tyler ever got from the Ransome clan. Now that he's gone you think you can sail up in your private yacht and take over. Well, I'm here to tell you you can't! Isn't the family money you inherited enough? Are you determined to have Ty's island, too?"

Some of the heat was gone from Ransome's face when he spoke again, this time more quietly. "Is that what my cousin told you?"

"No, but you don't have to be psychic to see that's the way things stood. Tyler Hill never had enough money to buy a canoe, much less a yacht."

"You're wrong about the rest, but you're dead right on that point," said Ransome caustically.

Though she had no doubt Burke Ransome's sole purpose in coming was to intimidate her, Allison could feel her facade of composure crumbling under the weight of the anxieties he'd stirred. She must get away from him until she had Herb Canby to back her up.

"I think we understand each other," she said abruptly. "Consider yourself my guest. As a member of the family you're welcome to stay—as long as you accept the fact the island was willed to me. It belongs to me and nobody else."

She made a step toward the stairs, and again the strong hand shot out and closed tightly around her arm. She was whipped about and found herself face to face with the formidable glowering presence of Burke Ransome.

She stood before him, tall, well-rounded, yet slender as a willow branch. She held her head high, proudly, and her blue eyes, slanted upward at the corners like a startled doe's, were only inches away from the sea-green iridescence of his. The two pairs of eyes locked in a new contest of wills. *Bedroom eyes,* Allison remembered irrelevantly, obsessively aware of the full curve of the sensuous mouth so close to her own. Peg was right! She felt a sudden trembling inside, and in spite of herself was the first to look away.

"Make an accounting of what you've spent on the house," Ransome ordered, his voice hoarse with anger. "When I've had it checked out, you'll be paid in full. Then I want you and your friend and her sons packed and ready to get out. With Tyler's death you ceased to be a member of the Ransome family, and you definitely are not my guest. Do I make myself clear?''

"Quite clear," Allison replied. Her voice threatened to break, but she managed to control it and went on, "Now I'll make *myself* clear. I think you are a consummate liar. I'm staying. The island belongs to me.''

"Not one magnolia petal on Ransome's Cay belongs to you, Mrs. Hill," Ransome said scathingly.

"No?'' The word shot, unbidden, out of the morning's memory like a fiery arrow and hit its mark. Even as she wished desperately it could be recalled, the man before her was again the golden horseman. He pulled her body to him, bending her head back as his mouth came down like a bird of prey.

Anger forgot its way. What began as an attack grew soft. Lips met and clung; tongues touched in wanton exploration. Within her those most tactile secret recesses swelled in sudden tumescence. The hand that entwined her hair moved with excruciating slowness down her back until finally the fingers spread and firmed, cupping her body to his. In response her own hands slipped shamelessly around his waist, pressing fiercely against him as if to make the joining complete. From the moment he became to her the sea rider of Buttonhook Cove she never thought to struggle, aware only of the fullness of his arousal and the exquisite white-hot pain that suddenly burned inside her.

Even when he groaned and shook himself free like an angry lion she clung to him. Dazed as much from the flame that leaped hungrily inside her as from the unexpectedness of their embrace, she looked up at the man before her with bleak questioning eyes. There were no answers in the sullen pools she gazed into, though for the first time the stern face seemed almost vulnerable.

"I would have done that this morning, but I thought you were one of the island girls," Ransome murmured.

The gratuitous statement brought Allison smashing back to reality. "If you mean by that you think the island girls are beneath you, that was a despicable thing to say," she snapped.

"You draw unfortunate conclusions on the most specious grounds." The sensuous mouth slanted obliquely into the suggestion of a smile, but there was no humor reflected in his eyes. "I merely meant I respect the young girls who grow up on Ransome's Cay. Their parents are my friends. I'm the last man to intrude upon their innocence."

"Such admirable sensibilities do not apply to your cousin's widow, it appears."

"Correction, Mrs. Hill," replied Ransome coolly. "My cousin's *women*. I've known them well. I've seen them come and go. I don't know how you suckered him into marrying you, but—"

The sharp crack of her palm as it came across Ransome's cheek brought the words to a sudden stop. His hand rose involuntarily to the point of contact, then shot on to seize her wrist, his eyes blazing with fury.

Overhead the persistent hum of a small plane coming in low over the house impressed itself vaguely on Allison's consciousness as she pried, in a vain effort to break away, at the unyielding fingers that gripped her.

"You really are contemptible," she gasped. But even as she said it she saw that her captor did not hear. His head lifted. There was a listening look in his eyes. Slowly he relaxed his grip.

"We'll finish this another time," he said grimly, and released her.

Half stunned, Allison watched him stalk across the broad expanse of parquet floor and through the front door. From where she stood she heard the motor of the island's utility jeep come to life a moment later and roar off in the direction of the lagoon.

As if to free herself from the scene that had just taken place, she gave her head a vigorous shake and started slowly up the stairs. Still seething, she had just reached her room when Peg, fairly twitching with curiosity, appeared out of nowhere. Allison groaned inwardly. She wasn't ready at the moment to discuss the recent conversation with anyone, and in any case she wasn't sure how much of it she wanted Peg to know.

"Well, that didn't take long," said Peg. "What's he like? What's he got on his mind?"

"He's...impossible!" Allison burst out. It had been a long time since frustration or anger had caused her to dissolve in tears, but she knew she was close. "Nothing I want to talk about now. Don't worry about it—I'm just too tired. I'll tell you what he said tomorrow." She whisked past her friend, hoping Peg had not seen how upset she was, and hurried into her room.

"You'd better eat something," Peg called after her. "You haven't eaten all day."

As she closed the door to her room, Allison mumbled something over her shoulder to the effect that she would rather sleep than eat. But her friend paid no attention. She arrived shortly with a tray of food. Allison picked at it while Peg dropped little conversation starters, ignored for the most part by Allison.

If Peg had hoped Allison would confide in her over the supper tray, she was disappointed. It was not until late the following evening, after a sleepless night and a miserable day spent trying to reach Herb Canby in New York, that Allison finally decided to tell Peg the gist of the conversation she'd had with Burke Ransome twenty-four hours earlier.

"And then he had the unmitigated gall to say he'd *pay* me for what we've spent here at Plantation House, after which we're supposed to pack up and leave," she finished. Only sheer willpower kept the growing tension within her from mounting into hysteria. "The arrogant beast!" she added between clenched teeth.

Peg's face had paled until her small pink nose shone out like a signal light. "Oh, Allison, I'm afraid he means business. Hoddy and Max were up at the end of the island today and they say it's a regular construction camp up there. Some high-powered marine biologist flew in late yesterday in an aquaplane, and they've got a crew of men from the ship working on a kind of anchored barge in the lagoon. There's no doubt about it—Ransome's here to stay until you figure out how to throw him off."

"I don't even know how to begin," admitted Allison.

There was a long moment of silence before Peg ventured cautiously, "Now listen, Allison...don't get mad...but are you sure this island belongs to you?"

"Of course I'm sure! You don't think we'd be here if I weren't, do you?" The answer was sharp but spoken with affection. "The question is not if the island's mine. It's how I get rid of Ransome short of calling the marines down from Parris Island."

"Take my adivce, Allison," said Peg. "Don't tangle with that man again until you've talked to the attorney who's probating the estate. Just make sure everything's in order and then let him handle Mr. Ransome. If it were me, I'd be on the phone to that lawyer right now."

"I've already tried today," Allison told her unhappily.

"What's the guy's name?"

"Herb Canby...but I don't know where to reach him," Allison replied in a worried tone. "I tried to see him when I was in Manhattan, but all I could get was a recording of his voice saying he would be out of town for a time, to leave my name and number and he would call when he got back. It was the same today."

"When was the last time you talked to him?"

"When he told me about the will. He was leaving the next day for the film festival in Cannes, but he promised he'd get everything rolling as soon as he came back. I'm the executor and only heir so I guess he doesn't feel pressed."

"Sounds to me like a pretty freewheeling way to probate an estate," said Peg in disgust. "Still, a film festival doesn't go on forever."

"I know, but Herb sort of strings along with the international set. I'm afraid he's rather casual about time."

"But he is probating the estate?"

"Well...I suppose he hasn't actually filed the probate papers," Allison confessed. In response to her friend's look of tight-lipped disapproval she hastened to add, "It's really not all that unheard-of, Peg. It happened just as he was about to take off for Europe and...well, at least he did get in touch with me before he left. That's something."

"Just what do you know about this character, Allison?" Peg persisted grimly.

"Oh, Herb's all right," Allison reassured her hastily. "He's not the slippery shyster type, if that's what you're worried about. Good old Southern stock. He and Tyler grew up together...roommates in college, all that. I've known him for years." Nonetheless a frown creased her forehead. "Herb's really bright, but he's got a well-heeled family who subsidizes him. I'm afraid sometimes he tends to play at practicing law."

"Good!" exploded Peg. "It's great to know you've got somebody on your team who's really dependable!"

"No, it's all right, Peg," Allison insisted. "Actually it's my own fault. I probably should have made him get the probate started before he left or turned it over to another lawyer. But I never dreamed he'd be gone so long. It was all so sudden and unexpected I wasn't really thinking straight, and by the time I was Herb was gone."

The older woman shook her head in dismay. "That's unbelievable!"

"Except for the squatters down in the lagoon there's nothing to worry about," Allison told her, regaining confidence as she talked. "I hate to see Burke Ransome get so firmly attached, but Herb will know how to handle it when he gets back. He's honest, and he knows his law. He assured me I could do whatever I like with the island except sell it. That would have to wait until he got back. It's mine, and there's no one to question since I happen to be the only heir."

"You're sure of that?"

"That's one thing I'm *really* sure of," Allison insisted impatiently. "I saw the will with my own eyes, signed by Tyler and properly witnessed. Herb gave it to me to read. Not only that, Herb discussed it with Ty a few days before the accident and Tyler told him he had no reason to change the will."

Peg's eyebrows arched in astonishment.

"It was pretty magnanimous of Ty, considering everything I said to him the day I finally walked out," Allison said with a rueful grin.

"It sounds all open and above board," her friend agreed reluctantly, "but I don't like the fact Burke Ransome obviously has designs on your island. You'd better get your hands on that playboy lawyer and get him primed for a fight."

CHAPTER THREE

THE LARGE, OLD-FASHIONED KITCHEN at Plantation House was constructed of white plaster, with timbered walls, brick-red tile and polished copper and brass. Above its huge cookstove and ovens hung pots and skillets of all sizes and shapes. This was the realm of Effie, Bunker's wife. Effie held a special place in Allison's affections, and it was here Allison came for breakfast early the following morning after yet another restless night.

Watching the ruddy-faced woman with her work-lined face and sandy, gray-streaked hair hover over the stove, Allison thought of that honeymoon summer years earlier. Troubled and bewildered, she'd fled to this room and the motherly comfort of its chatelaine more times than she liked to count. In those early days of her disillusionment she'd found in Effie an artesian well of mothering, and in Allison's teenage life mothering had been in short supply.

Looking back, she was amazed at how childlike and vulnerable she'd been that first summer of her marriage. It was inexperience, she realized now. She had missed out on the usual boy-girl encounters that adolescence was all about, and this had left her exceptionally naive.

The accident that had taken her father's life when she was thirteen left her mother an invalid, and when she wasn't in school she was urgently needed at home. Even at university in her hometown in Connecticut she'd lived under her parental roof and spent all her free time with her mother. The shadow of her mother's impending death had hung heavily over her, and she'd had neither time nor heart for dating games.

When her mother died she felt an intense sense of loss, and the home that had sheltered her since birth seemed hauntingly empty. It was to escape the emptiness that she accepted a scholarship for her third college year in the Deep South, which she'd only read about, at a university she had never seen. There she met and fell ridiculously in love with Tyler Hill.

A plate of feather-light scrambled eggs thrust in front of her by Effie brought Allison's wandering mind abruptly to a halt. "Ooh! Hot Sally Lunn bread and scuppernong jelly," she exclaimed with pleasure. "Effie, you spoil me."

With a grunt Effie turned back for the coffeepot. "What's wrong with spoilin', honey?" she asked in her sorghum-smooth country drawl. "We all got a ration of spoilin' comin' in a lifetime. What makes y'all think yours is already used up?"

Allison grinned. "C'mon, Effie. Sit down and visit. Have a cup of coffee with me."

"Now who's spoilin' who?" grumbled the big woman, but she lumbered back across the kitchen for another cup. Watching her, Allison wondered about her son, Jimmer. He had taken his wife and little girl from Ransome's Cay and moved up north, where he'd found work in a tire plant. She hesitated to ask. Too often when she did, it brought a shadow of sadness to the pale blue eyes. Effie had told her sadly that Jimmer and his little family "like to perish every time they think of the island, they're that homesick!"

Bunker and Effie mourned their absence continually—hopelessly, Allison feared. The real money for the islanders had come out of the sea, and those days were over, everyone knew. Except for the few blue crab still to be caught, she'd be obliged to ship in seafood from Chesapeake Bay to the north to keep the Plantation House table supplied when they opened for guests.

As the older woman settled her bulky body down at the table across from her, Allison detected a new brightness in the blue eyes. She felt encouraged to ask, "What do you hear from Jimmer these days?"

A flash of pure joy lighted Effie's worn face. She looked at Allison knowingly before her eyes darted shyly away. "My land, honey, y'all know what we hear from Jimmer!" she exclaimed.

"You've got good news, I can see!" Allison cried with pleasure. "I don't know a thing about it. Remember, I've been away."

"Aw, stop foolin' with me, honey—y'all are just

playin' like you don't know Jimmer's bringin' his family back home for good in a few days," Effie said, half laughing as she spoke but plainly uneasy with the game the other had chosen to play. "You know that! You'n Mr. Burke. Why, if it weren't for the both of you there wouldn't be nothin' for Jimmer and the rest of the young island folks to come back to."

"Mr. Burke?" The name caught in Allison's throat. For a moment she couldn't go on. She took a deep breath. "I know he's here, but I can assure you I don't know what he's up to, Effie."

"I thought you and him. . .Mr. Burke and you were in it together." The pale eyes clouded with uncertainty and her lids dropped down to hide them. When they lifted again all expression was erased.

"Please, Effie. . ." Allison began, then stopped. It was no use, she knew. She said instead, "I'm sorry I have nothing to do with whatever it is, if it means something good for your Jimmer. I'm happy for all of you, but I've nothing to do with your Mr. Burke." In spite of herself she could hear the sound of her own resentment in her voice, not at Effie but at Burke Ransome and the position he'd put her in.

Effie looked at her a long moment in agonized indecision. Finally she shook her head. "Nobody told me nothin'," she said uncomfortably. "I just reckoned it was all part of what's going on here at Plantation House and that the two of you was in the whole thing together now that Mr. Tyler is gone and you own half of the island with Mr. Burke."

Allison's eyes widened, and for an instant she could make no sound come from her mouth. "Half of the island?" she repeated in a choked voice.

"Well, that's the way Burke's daddy left it, y'know—half to Mr. Burke and half to Mr. Ty," Effie said, once more clearly uneasy with the conversation. "Because they both come down from that first Ransome, y'see, and they was the only ones that was left. That's the way old Mr. Ransome was. He had to do what he saw was fair."

"But you're saying Tyler's father never did own the island at all."

"Land, honey. Colonel Hill didn't own nothin' he didn't spend. No, that ain't right for me to say. That's gossip," Effie hastened to add, dampering her tongue. "It was Mrs. Hill who was the Ransome. The colonel was up in Congress, you know. What I shoulda said is he never come here a lot. Mr. Ty, either...even after he was give a half share in the will. Guess the longest he ever spent at Ransome's Cay was on your honeymoon, and you know how restless it made him then."

From out of the cauldron of emotions that seethed inside her, Allison made herself ask, "Ransome's Cay didn't really belong to Tyler even then, Effie?"

Effie's pale eyes begged forgiveness for the hurt her words were about to deliver. "Just the half old Mr. Ransome left him in the will. Mr. Burke owned the other half."

"But why did Tyler..." began Allison dully, but

there was no need to finish. She knew why. It was typical of Ty. As long as Burke stayed away he could carry on a ruse that made him feel important and made his material wealth far greater than hers. It was just like him to carry the lie even into his will.

Tight-lipped, Effie pushed back her chair and struggled to her feet, her face flushed from the effort. "I reckon I talk too much," she muttered sorrowfully. Unexpectedly she leaned down and gave the slender shoulders before her a hug. "I know you still love him, honey. He could charm the birds off the trees, but let's face it—he wasn't no good."

Allison looked up at her in a kind of daze. "Please don't talk like that, Effie," she remonstrated absently, almost automatically. "You know how it bothers me." Too bound up in new worries to move, she remained seated, staring unseeingly out the window as Effie cleared the table and started back across the kitchen with the dirty dishes.

"Go on back to your business, honey," Effie said gruffly from the sink. "I done too much shootin' off at the mouth already."

Allison left the kitchen and went to the phone in the morning room. There she placed a call to Herb Canby's office in New York. Herb's cheerful voice came to her once more with his now familiar message on the answering machine.

She hung up in despair

SHE FELT LIKE A BIRD that had tried to fly through a plate-glass window.

"What on earth am I going to do, Peg?" she asked hopelessly. She had spent the rest of the morning wandering restlessly through the house, and this was the first time her path had crossed that of her friend's.

"Beats me," Peg murmured in sympathy. Then on a practical note she said, "We've got a welcoming party to arrange for a houseful of people July 4 and five days to do it in, Allie. As I see it, we'd better keep right on doing what's to be done until someone stops us."

"I know, I know," said Allison, though at the moment she was aware that she was quite incapable of dealing with even the simplest chore. The stunning realization she was doomed to share ownership of Ransome's Cay with a man who threatened to run her off the island had frozen her ability to act. Her mind thrashed about furiously in a cage of frustrations, reminding her with deadly frequency that she hadn't the foggiest notion what she could or could not do as joint owner of the island.

"You don't suppose he could bring this whole operation to an ignominious halt, do you?" she asked Peg, seeking reassurance yet aware her friend had none to give.

"I don't know, and you won't either until you run down that cockamamy lawyer and find out what's going on," Peg told her impatiently.

Allison caught her lip in sudden dubious inspiration. "I know the club he belongs to in Manhattan, but it's one of those male citadels. Even if they knew how to reach him they wouldn't tell!"

"Well, for lack of anything better, give it a try."

It took no more than this slight verbal push from Peg to send Allison to the phone. She was passed to three different voices before she was connected with a fourth, who said he knew Herb Canby well. She explained she was a client and had been trying to reach Canby regarding an inheritance. To her surprise the man she spoke with assured her Herb would be back at least by July 7 because they were to have dinner together that night at the club.

It wasn't all Allison had hoped for, but at least now she had a date to focus on. In the meantime she intended to call Herb's office daily and try to catch him before then. Beyond that, all she could do was carry on as if Ransome had never appeared on the scene and make sure she didn't run into the man. Although her common sense told her he had no more power to throw her off the island than she had to get rid of him, the last thing she wanted was an encounter that could force her to discuss their joint ownership. It would be foolhardy until she talked to Canby and learned exactly where she stood. Perhaps in the long run she would be wise to have the attorney do all the talking with her late-husband's cousin.

Talk to my lawyer! she could hear herself saying

imperiously to Burke Ransome. The sound of it made her grin and lightened her anxious mind.

At the same time she was consumed with curiosity to know what was going on at the north end of the island where Ransome had sailed into the lagoon and invaded its shore. To go up and see for herself would mean running a risk of meeting the very person she hoped to avoid, and though she was sure Bunker knew exactly what Ransome was up to, she hesitated to ask him. Effie's erratic behavior earlier that morning told her that Bunker, too, would not take to being quizzed.

For a moment she was stumped, and then she smiled. Of course! The Crewes twins knew as much about what was happening on the island as Bunker. The cay had been their turf since the day they set foot on it. They hadn't missed a thing that had gone on since. Peg complained that their interest in activities up at the lagoon interfered with an endless list of chores she had lined up for them at Plantation House in preparation for the July 4th opening. They'd be only too glad to share the benefits of their in-depth study with her.

Darn that elusive Herb Canby, thought Allison crossly as she set off to look for the pair. If he hadn't left her high and dry when he went off to Europe she would have known all about the hazards of her inheritance before she'd become so deeply embroiled. It would have been nice if he had at least kept in touch. Still, if she couldn't have the bird in hand, there was some satisfaction in knowing he would soon be in the bush.

ALLISON WOULD HAVE BEEN the first to say that without the twins, Maximillian and Hodding Crewes, she would have scuttled the Plantation House project that first month, when she learned that the labor costs for a contractor to do the needed work were nothing short of staggering. What she planned to do was simple enough. She'd never intended to build a posh retreat on the opulent scale of the fabulous Cloister, Sea Island's luxury hotel. She wanted to keep the historic colonial structure much as it had always been—she'd simply refurbish and restore it. Not much, really, but when the bids came in she'd seen at once she couldn't swing it.

At that point sheer desperation drove her to give in to Peg's urgent recommendation that she call in the twins. It was a lone last straw. Allison hadn't the faintest hope the two nineteen-year-olds, just two years out of high school, could do the work of a high-priced crew of expert workmen.

As it turned out it seemed there was hardly a thing in the world that Hoddy and Max couldn't do.

They were good-natured, tenacious, stubborn, tractable, funny, exasperating and, above all, curious and independent. Their mother did everything she could to thwart this last trait, though they continually outsmarted her with a delightful deviousness. It was a rare issue against which they openly rebelled.

Not the least in their sizable list of assets was the fact that they possessed the combined strength of a small tractor and the energy of a pair of young bulls.

As Allison neared the carriage house a strident rock beat from a tape deck on the far side led her around the building. There she found the pair bent over one of three ancient electric cars that provided much of the utility transportation around the island for Plantation House. Even in the shade of the building she could see the strong trace of Peg's carrot red in the two brown heads, though the sturdy young bodies above and below their cutoff jeans were the color of saddle leather, affirming an affinity for the sun not shared by their mother's milkweed skin.

Coming up unnoticed behind them, Allison was startled by a sudden sharp crackle and a shower of fireworks from the motor they were working on. A scatological expletive exploded from young Hod's mouth.

"You knothead," yelled Max cheerfully above the persistent throb from the tape deck. "You know better than to stick a screwdriver on a live wire."

Not wanting to be taken for an eavesdropper, Allison hastened to make her presence known. "Hi, guys," she broke in, shouting to be heard over the cacophony of the rock tune.

The Crewes twins looked around. Max reached over and turned off the sound. Hoddy gave her a sheepish grin in apology for the four-letter word. "Sorry about that!" he said.

Allison grinned back. "I didn't hear a thing," she replied, then went straight to the point. "What's going on up there at the end of the island?"

"You mean in the lagoon?" asked Max. The two bright open faces were suddenly blooming with excitement. "Wow! You wouldn't believe it! They're starting an oyster farm."

"An oyster farm!" she repeated incredulously. "What in the world does Burke Ransome know about oyster farming?"

The youths looked at each other. "A lot, it looks like," one of them said. "And if there's anything he's missing, there's this marine biologist he's got. Doc McGinnis. He's a real neat guy. He flew in a couple of nights ago."

So that's who she had to thank for rescuing her from her stormy encounter with Ransome, Allison thought.

"As soon as we get this old clunker humming again we're going up there," Max told her. "They brought in a barge yesterday and anchored it in the lagoon. Burke's out there working today. He said if we could get a boat and come on out we could watch them scuba dive."

So it's "Burke" already, Allison noted sardonically. Aloud she said, "Maybe I'll go up to the end of the island and take a look at what's going on myself." Why not, she thought. If Ransome was on the barge she wasn't likely to bump into him. "Are any of the carts in running condition yet?"

"We've got the other two purring like kittens," Hoddy told her.

"They don't look all that great, but when we get done painting them and put on the new awning tops you got and new cushions, they're gonna look as good as the Sea Island golf carts."

Allison stepped into one of the rusty carts and steered it around the carriage house and out into the oyster-shell road that led to the lagoon.

It was some distance to the upper end of the island. For the most part the land was wooded. Here and there Allison passed a clearing with a stand of corn, a few rows of peanuts or a garden patch. Wherever she found someone working outside one of the aged dwellings, she stopped to visit for a moment.

These were the people of the island; many of their families had lived on these same farm plots since before the Civil War. Allison had come to know most of them during that honeymoon summer with Tyler. In his restlessness her husband had often gone off to the mainland and left her to fend for herself. The discreet kindliness of the simple warmhearted islanders had imprinted itself on her heart for all time.

Falling out of love with the man she'd married, Allison had come to love Ransome's Cay, little dreaming as she left that when she returned another Ransome would shatter her peace of mind—a far more dangerous, more powerful, more threatening Ransome than the weak man she'd married.

Damn the Ransomes, she muttered under her

breath. It wasn't enough that Tyler had never owned more than half of the island. She was going to be obliged to put up a fight to keep even that.

Suppose Burke Ransome took her to court in some tricky legal maneuver to seize it from her. She could never match his money for legal fees. Could he win her share of the island by default?

Never! she vowed defiantly. The island meant too much to her. She'd found strength in the courage and perseverance of its people, peace in the quiet of its woods. Here she had learned to cope with her own disillusionment.

She felt it now—a sense that it was here she belonged. She would not give it up without a struggle. She'd fight for it to the last cent she could lay her hands on.

Coming out of the woods onto the sand, Allison saw at once that Ransome had wasted no time in establishing a beachhead. Two oversize mobile units, apparently brought in by barge, had been set up a short distance down the shore and back from the water under a giant live oak tree. On the deck of the barge, moored across the lagoon, she could see men moving about. One, she presumed, was Ransome himself.

Nevertheless she cut the cart's motor at the edge of the woods and surveyed the building cautiously just to be on the safe side. Though neither mobile unit showed any sign of life at the moment, it was with a sense of daring that she continued on. As she neared the structures a moment later a screen door on one of them swung open unexpectedly and a man stepped out. To her instant relief she saw he bore no resemblance to Ransome but was stout and balding, his face amiable.

All the same, Allison couldn't be sure the man she wished to avoid was not inside, and she came to a halt several yards away while she considered how she might gracefully retreat. The man gave a welcoming wave and came down the steps and across the sand to greet her. She watched the door from which he'd emerged uneasily, at the same time shamefully aware of a quite irrational half wish that Ransome might himself appear.

"Welcome to the Ransome's Cay Marine Laboratory," the man spoke out as he approached. "My name's Doc McGinnis and yours has got to be either Mrs. Crewes or Allison Hill."

Surprised, Allison stepped out of the cart and reached to meet the hand he extended in greeting. "You're right on the second guess," she said with a smile that reflected her puzzlement. "I must say, since you no doubt heard of us from Burke Ransome, the warmth of your welcome surprises me."

Candid blue eyes gazed at her quizzically from out of a round, deeply tanned face. "Not from Burke," he said with a grin. "My friend happens to be in a silent mode. No...I heard about you from the Crewes twins. A remarkable pair of young men."

"What would I do without Hoddy and Max!"

Allison agreed heartily. "They've also mentioned you to us. They tell us you're a marine biologist and 'a real neat guy.'"

"Well, that's what I am—a marine biologist," replied McGinnis. "I don't know about the 'real neat guy,' but I'm glad they say so," he added with a slightly embarrassed laugh, though he looked obviously pleased. "Since you're here, would you like to take a look at our lab?"

Allison hesitated. "Are you alone?" Realizing at once the implications in the question, she hastened an abashed addendum. "I didn't mean that the way it sounded!"

This time McGinnis's laugh was an easy one. "You mean you're not afraid this plump, middle-aging marine biologist is trying to lure you into the laboratory to make improper advances? I have to confess the double intent of the question didn't occur to me—and I am quite alone. Everyone's out on the barge today."

It was Allison's turn to grin. "In that case I would love to see your laboratory. Thanks for offering to show it to me. Hop in. I'll give you a ride over and park this thing in your shade."

With McGinnis beside her she drew the rusty cart up into the shade of the oak tree. They sat for a moment while he explained the layout before them, beginning with the barge across the lagoon, intended as the anchor for oyster frames eventually but currently the base for underwater explorations.

He turned then to the spacious mobile units, one of which they were about to enter. This was the laboratory. The other was to serve as living quarters for McGinnis and Ransome when they were not aboard the small ship that lay at anchor in the lagoon. It was not the pleasure yacht Allison had thought but a research vessel that had traveled over half the world's waters and could be self-sustaining for long periods of time.

"But why the mobile units when you've got it all out there?" she asked.

"This one's because we needed more lab space for the operation," the scientist told her. "As for the other, you can probably give me a better reason for it than I can give you."

Allison looked at him blankly and shook her head.

"No? Well, Burke gave me a complete history of that big house down there as we came up from the Panama Canal," McGinnis said. "From the way he talked, the minute he hit Ransome's Cay he intended to take up permanent residence in the room that was always his. He was willing to give me the choice of the dozen or so others." She knew he was watching her for the effect of his words.

After a moment, when she said nothing, he went on. "Between the time I left the ship at Key West and flew in here the other night something went haywire—and I'm darned if I can find out what it is. There's no more talk of moving into Plantation House. The truth is, Burke ain't sayin' nothin' about nothin'. Home is that mobile unit, and he's pretty poor company when he's awake. My guess is, Burke's staying away from Plantation House has something to do with you."

"Mr. Ransome can stay at Plantation House whenever he likes and he knows it," Allison said stiffly. "I've told him that myself." Then in a warmer tone she added, "You're welcome there anytime, too, Dr. McGinnis."

McGinnis thanked her with another of his infectious grins. "It's Doc—and that doesn't answer my question."

"Mr. Ransome might at least have told you what's going on," she said. "Fortunately I have no such scruples. You certainly have a right to know. The truth is, Ransome's Cay doesn't completely belong to him, as I'm sure you've been led to believe. It happens to be half mine."

McGinnis watched her curiously as she went on to explain her marriage to Burke Ransome's cousin, his death, the inheritance and how she and Peg and the twins had come to the Cay and set about turning Plantation House into a small vacation resort.

"In resort terms it will be modest, of course," she told him. "The house can only accommodate sixteen to twenty people at any one time. We're trying for the atmosphere of a private house party in a gracious country home." Even as she spoke, the delicate balance they sought between the quiet elegance of Plantation House and a casual house-party ambience came to mind, and she felt a passing moment of doubt.

"I promised myself I'd never make any drastic alterations to the old house," she told McGinnis. "Like adding on rooms to bring in money or knocking out walls—things that would change the intrinsic nature of the place. We'll keep it small. It's such a gem as it is it would be a sin to let it get big and touristy."

"You tell me Burke owns half the island," McGinnis said after a thoughtful pause. "I take it you own the half that includes Plantation House."

For an instant Allison felt as if someone had hit her in the face with a cold wet sponge. *Oh, no!* something inside her cried out in strident panic, and she imagined for a moment she'd said the words aloud. Somehow she'd never thought of it like that. She'd thought only in terms of an exceedingly difficult partnership wherein each would have to compromise and adjust to the other's demands. It had never occurred to her that dual ownership of Ransome's Cay could mean cutting the beautiful island into his and hers.

It was like King Solomon and the baby—they could never cut it in two. Yet if that was the condition of ownership, the house might very well belong to Ransome and the lagoon to her. What possible use could she make of the lagoon without the house? She could give it up in the interests of peace to make a trade, but Ransome would never give her the house.

She could count on that. If the island was thus divided, how could they compromise?

A discreet throat clearing from McGinnis brought her out of the morass of her speculations.

"Well, now, how about the lab?" he suggested, and they moved inside.

As he showed Allison through the compact, splendidly equipped marine laboratory, he briefly explained the science of aquaculture—systems designed to produce seafood in places where mollusks and crustaceans had disappeared or previously never existed. She learned from him that Burke Ransome's concern for the island families had impelled him to rebuild a shellfish industry to provide jobs for the natives, most of whom were descendants of people who had come to Ransome's Cay more than two centuries ago.

Impressed as she was with both the lab and the biologist's running commentary on how it all worked, Allison still found it hard to believe that under the aegis of a Ransome the visionary project could ever become a viable enterprise. She suspected instead that this elaborate and costly operation was simply a new game yet another hedonistic member of the land-owning family would soon tire of.

There was a strong possibility in her mind that the magnificent gesture would turn out to be more of a curse than a blessing to the island folk. What of the Jimmers, who had left the security of jobs on the mainland because of Ransome's promises? Once their benefactor grew bored with the project and

moved on to some new diversion, would he continue
to provide capital and expertise to keep the enterprise
afloat? Not if he were anything like his cousin,
thought Allison grimly. Tyler's attention span had
been that of a lightning bug.

Aloud she said, "Max and Hoddy mentioned you
had a laboratory, but I had no idea it would be so
complex and complete."

"By the way, I told those fellows I'd teach them to
scuba dive, but only with their mother's permis-
sion," McGinnis told her. "They don't seem to think
they can get it. I like them and they're bright kids,
but I'll be damned if I let them snow me into taking
them down until I'm sure it's okay with her. I'd like
very much to meet the lady. Maybe I can persuade
her myself."

"We'd love to have you come to the house," said
Allison. "I know Peg would like to meet you. But I
may as well warn you, I don't think she'll go for the
diving. She's plain silly about water—something that
happened when she was a child. She almost took the
twins out of the school they went to because it was
compulsory for the kids to learn to swim. They took
to the water like a pair of otters, but she still worries.
They'd love scuba diving. I wish you would work on
Peg."

As they stepped through the door of the lab onto
the small landing outside, Doc glanced down the
shore. "There's Burke," he remarked. "I thought I
heard an outboard motor."

Quickly Allison's head turned to follow his gaze. To her dismay her heart quickened its beat.

From a small dinghy beached on the sand stepped Ransome, his bare, sun-browned torso glistening in the late-morning sun. For a moment he was the golden centaur of Buttonhook Cove. The next instant he was the tough unbending man of the previous night.

She took the first step down as if to flee, then stopped, completely aware there was no way she could escape with dignity. With the sun in his eyes and the mobile units still in deep shade he could not see her from where he stood, but at that moment he came forward. He was only a short distance away, and in a moment she would have to cross directly in front of him in the noisy cart to reach the path. She wasn't about to be caught in that kind of humiliating hasty flight.

"It looks like we have a chaperon after all," Doc said lightly.

Allison couldn't fail to note the poorly hidden curiosity in his eyes. Summoning all her poise, she moved on down the steps, McGinnis behind her. She was not without a plan. She would pause just long enough for a polite word to acknowledge Ransome's presence before walking on past him to the cart, head high.

She turned to say goodbye to Doc and saw Ransome come into the shade. He looked up for the first time. She imagined she saw him falter and then regain his stride, a new air of determination on his face, a hard set to his jaw.

"I do thank you for showing me around," she said to McGinnis. Though it came out warmly, she said it with only half her mind. "It's been a pleasure meeting you. I hope you'll come up to Plantation House and see Peg. We'd like your company anytime, even if you can't work out anything for the twins."

"Thanks, Mrs. Hill, the pleasure has been all mine," the biologist said gallantly. Then he turned to Ransome. "We have a visitor, Burke. I've just been showing her around."

As if McGinnis hadn't spoken, Ransome directed his harsh words to Allison. "I trust you are here about the accounting."

Allison stared at him in disbelief.

"Accounting?" she said.

"Accounting! The money you spent for materials and work at Plantation House," said Ransome unpleasantly. "I can't think of any other reason for you to be here."

"Hey, Burke!" the protesting voice of Doc McGinnis broke in.

"Stay out of this, Doc." Though he spoke with respect, Ransome's tone was chilly and firm. "Mrs. Hill was married to my late cousin and has taken up squatter's rights on my island on the spurious ground he left it to her in his will."

"Look, Mr. Ransome, I have no intention of playing games with you," Allison said frigidly, determined not to let him drag her into a wrangle about who owned the island.

Before she could excuse herself and leave, Ransome continued. He completely ignored her words and spoke as if she weren't even there, directing his remarks to McGinnis.

"The fact is, I am quite willing to pay for any work she and her crowd may have done at the old house—though I wasn't consulted and have no doubt much of it will have to be done over."

"Of all the self-righteous—" Allison broke off in mid-sentence, appalled she'd been about to subject the biologist, who had nothing to do with the problem, to a full-scale argument.

Again Ransome took up where he left off, as if she had not intervened. "There must be an accounting, of course—it wouldn't do to cheat my cousin's widow," he said caustically. "When I've had her figures checked out I'll see that she and her crew are adequately paid for whatever it appears they've done."

"And after that magnanimous gesture, Mr. Ransome?" she asked with heavy irony. "What other arrangements have you in mind for my life?"

"Just one thing, lady," Ransome answered in a voice that would freeze fish. "Get off my island. Go back where you came from."

"Back to the rock I crawled out from under! That's what you'd like to say," she snapped, the presence of Doc McGinnis quite forgotten in the heat of her fury. "Don't waste your energy trying to bully me into leaving Ransome's Cay, Mr. Ransome. It won't work." Pulling herself together, she continued with icy calm. "I only learned this morning that I do not own the whole island. If that's what you meant when you called my claim spurious, may I remind you I do own half of it. By the same token, your claim is spurious, too. Just how we're to work out this sticky matter remains to be seen. My lawyer will be in touch."

In less than a dozen steps she reached the cart and stepped into it. The motor started without a splutter, thanks to Hoddy and Max. Allison pushed forward on the control and, leaving a wake of sand behind her, headed for the oyster-shell path.

CHAPTER FOUR

HE'D STAYED AWAY too long, Ransome told himself glumly as the cart took off toward the woods. He should have taken the first plane out of San Diego the day he'd learned of Tyler's death and let the *Ulysses* make its way leisurely through the Panama Canal and up the coast to Ransome's Cay without him. He might have guessed that if the island were left unguarded Tyler's widow would get there first and dig in.

During the last nights of the voyage up the coast from the gulf he had fallen asleep in his crowded quarters to the satisfying thought that before the week was out he would be back in his spacious old room at Plantation House. There he would stretch his six-foot-two frame to its full length in the over-sized four-poster bed his parents had had built for him when at twelve he'd been pushing six feet and showed no sign of stopping. There he would stay, in the big east bedroom with the balcony overlooking the sea, above the morning room at Plantation House.

How was he to know that when he returned he

would find his cousin's widow firmly entrenched in his childhood home? And his two meetings with Allison still had left him with no illusions that she would be an easy one to get out.

Plantation House! He thought of it now as he had first seen it the other afternoon from the deck of the returning *Ulysses*—a great, white-pillared, neo-Grecian structure at the crest of a sloping lawn, proud and haughty as a begum.

He was thankful he could look at the house and see it as his long-loved home—and not Margo's trysting place. It was a measure of his cure. His years at sea had restored him to a sound though wary man.

Ransome was not unaware that McGinnis had walked away and was standing on the porch of the lab watching him with disapproving eyes. His own bristling aggressiveness faded into a restless dismay, his eyes following the straight line of Allison Hill's back as the electric cart disappeared down the oyster-shell path. He had to give this much to Tyler: his late cousin had possessed an infallible eye for beauty.

For a moment his departing adversary—proud, spirited, fully clothed—was lost. In her place, through a transparent veil of rushing water, he saw a pair of firm, rosy-budded breasts rising up from a waist so slender he could span it with his own two hands; glorious curved thighs sculptured for a man to stroke; long, slender, elegantly proportioned legs. He sighed.

What was there about this unsettling woman that

turned him into an irascible bull the moment she came in sight? A reminder of Margo?

But he had no feeling left in him for that long-ago wife. All that remained was a certain wariness that came from knowing the depths of deception that could lie hidden beneath a facade of feminine allure.

It was that wariness, learned at the hands of Margo, that told him this incredibly attractive woman was harboring some slippery scheme to get his island. The fact that he couldn't figure what she was up to played havoc with his normal control.

Take the way he'd overreacted just now, he thought uncomfortably. He'd come on like a battery of field artillery, and he didn't feel good about it.

He turned impulsively to say as much to McGinnis, but the frank look of disapproval and astonishment on his friend's face caused him to get his back up unreasonably. His moment of candor was lost as he cast about for arguments in his own defense.

"Would you mind telling me what that was about?" McGinnis demanded. "It was a friendly visit until you stepped ashore. In my book she's a lovely young woman."

"You're entitled to your opinion," said Ransome coldly. "You know who she is, I suppose."

"Your cousin's widow, of course. But that's no excuse for treating her as if she'd just stolen your gold inlays."

"Look, McGinnis, I don't have any use for any woman who's been mixed up with Tyler Hill," Ransome said harshly.

"Mixed up with and married to are two different things," Doc continued.

Suddenly all the bitterness against Margo and his late cousin, buried for years and long forgotten, surfaced anew in Ransome, embodied now in the person of Tyler's widow.

Remembered pain of the old betrayal clouded his reason and he struck out blindly. "I can think of only two kinds of women who would have married the scoundrel," he said, his voice tight as a fiddle string. "One who's too dumb to see through Tyler, or one who plays his game. Whatever flaws the beautiful Mrs. Hill may have, stupidity is not one of them."

"Of course she's not stupid," agreed McGinnis, "but what about naive? Innocent?"

"Naive! Innocent!" Ransome threw the words back at the other man scathingly. A muscle in his hard jaw twitched ominously.

The stubborn defiance in Ransome's eyes dared McGinnis to go on in Allison's defense, but he was not to be intimidated. "She must have been very young. Has it ever occurred to you that marriage to your cousin might have put a swift end to naive?" he asked dryly. "As for innocence—I could bet she was a very innocent young girl at the time she married him. She couldn't have been more than eighteen—a child. She's a mature woman now. Twenty-one's the cutoff age for innocence. Everyone's entitled to give it up then. In this day and age you're in a lot of trouble if you don't.''

"That doesn't give her a license to try to pull off this hocus-pocus about a will," flared Ransome.

McGinnis gazed at him soberly for a moment. "From the little you've told me, Burke—and from talking to the lady myself—I think you've got the situation sized up wrong," he said. "Allison Hill appears to me to be a straightforward decent young woman, and I think you owe her an apology for that senseless attack on her just now."

"Traitor!" Ransome exploded accusingly. "First Bunker and Effie. . . now you. She ingratiates herself with you all. Next thing I know—"

He stopped, at a loss for words, appalled by the heat that was building up between them. This was McGinnis—friend, confidante and colleague through a good many experiences over the course of a good many years, the man he'd come to admire and respect both professionally and personally above most other men. And with reasonable confidence he felt these sentiments were returned.

There stood McGinnis, looking at him as if he were a creature from outer space—yet another cause for resentment toward the absent Mrs. Hill. Indirectly she was at the bottom of all this fuss. Ransome felt a compelling need to make his friend understand there was indeed reason behind the harsh words he'd rained on Allison Hill.

He lined up his arguments carefully, and his voice was quiet when he spoke. "Let me tell you about this Allison Hill you and the Bunkers look on as such a paragon of virtue," he began, almost on a pleading note. "The minute she knew there was no one around to stop her—Tyler dead, me gone—she moved fast. She slipped in and established herself at Plantation House with her entourage. If you'd ever had any dealings with my cousin, you'd recognize it as a typical Tyler Hill trick. He learned it at the knees of his daddy, that old past master, Colonel Stanfield Hill. It's quite obvious Mrs. Hill has used the same tactics once again."

"You seem to forget she believed the island belonged to her by right of inheritance, Burke," McGinnis reminded him. "Even now her understanding is that she still owns half of it."

"Damn it, Doc, you don't really believe she hasn't known all along that Tyler sold that half to me?"

"I most certainly do," McGinnis replied emphatically.

Burke scarcely heard him, so intent was he on developing a theme that had started out as a mere suggestion but was now taking rapid shape in his mind.

"When Tyler leaves her without a cent, the first thing she does is start looking around for something she can parlay into cash," he speculated coolly. "Plantation House is empty. I've been off on the *Ulysses* for a couple of years, so she figures I'm no more interested in Ransome's Cay than Ty was. She doesn't have the papers so she can't sell it, but as long as I stay away she can make money off it as a summer resort. And she really doesn't expect me back—maybe not for years. So in the tradition of her late husband she finds a patsy with two robust sons to do all the real work and moves in."

"If you mean Mrs. Crewes and her twins..." McGinnis tried to break in.

But Ransome, experiencing a certain grim satisfaction in finding that the scenario he was putting together was making a vague sort of sense, refused to let himself be deterred.

"Those kids," he persisted, "I bet she's got them working for little more than their room and board. No doubt their mother gets paid a little cash and a lot of promises. If I'd been a month later getting back to Ransome's Cay, Plantation House would have been running full speed ahead as a summer resort when we arrived and it would take a court order to close the place down and force her out. If I walked in on a fait accompli, that wily widow no doubt assumed I'd agree to some kind of a deal rather than take it to court. Whether I stayed away or came back, with any luck she could walk away from here with more money than she had when she came."

"You're talking about extortion!" Doc intervened angrily. "It's not like you to make a brutal prejudgment like this, Burke. It doesn't take a psychologist to see that whatever went on between you and your cousin turned you sour where women are concerned. But don't try to make an innocent woman take the rap for it. How about hearing what she has to say?''

Not waiting for Ransome to reply, he continued snappishly, ''Your cousin victimized his wife at least as much as he ever did you, I'll bet. She honestly thought for a while that she had inherited Ransome's Cay. When she found out her husband had never owned more than half of it, she didn't try to hide it. It was just like Tyler to let her think it was all his— that's what she told me. And there wasn't even any bitterness when she said it. Made me wonder if she isn't still in love with the guy. . . .''

Burke found the last words strangely disturbing. They implied a kind of gentle enduring passion undeserved by a man like Tyler and quite out of character with the woman he'd just finished describing to McGinnis.

Unexpectedly his ire was spent. He gave in with a bit of amiable teasing. ''You always have been a sucker for a pretty face, haven't you, Doc,'' he observed but his peace-making grin was lost on McGinnis, who remained preoccupied.

''That lady's in for a helluva shock,'' Doc said sadly after a moment.

The remark swept Ransome unwillingly back into the fray. ''Stop worrying about the woman,'' he said brusquely. ''She knows, I tell you! She has to know. About the first thing a lawyer checks into when he opens a probate is the value of the estate so he can estimate the inheritance tax. When the attorney in this case found out my cousin didn't own even an oyster shell on Ransome's Cay, you can bet he told Allison Hill. He certainly wouldn't hold back that kind of information from the one named in the will, if that's what you're thinking.''

''Hardly.'' Doc's voice was dry. ''But the truth's even more mind-boggling. I was about to tell you. The probate was never started. The lawyer's out of the country. Didn't leave word when to expect him back.''

Undeterred by Ransome's open skepticism, McGinnis repeated everything Allison had told him about her many frustrated attempts to locate an attorney who was basking in some unspecified watering spot halfway around the world.

''She tells me he was a friend of your late cousin,'' the biologist informed him coolly. ''Understandably Mrs. Hill was too overwhelmed by the unexpected inheritance to get down to the nitty-gritty immediately. By the time she was ready to ask questions the lawyer had taken off for Europe. All she's been able to get since is his voice on an answering tape.''

Ransome remained unconvinced. ''You're telling me he vanished into thin air without even starting the probate? C'mon, Doc! Who ever heard of an attorney who would pull a stunt like that?''

''Well, you've heard of one now,'' said McGinnis grimly. ''The name of the guy is Herb Canby.''

Ransome's eyes widened in a look of dawning

comprehension. McGinnis continued his account of the legal problems of Allison Hill, but Burke heard none of it.

Herb Canby! The name echoed and reechoed in his mind. Now there was a rogue! Canby had never been known to let the practice of law interfere with his fun and games!

For the first time since he learned that his cousin's widow had moved into Plantation House a trickle of doubt seeped in to dilute the perfect confidence Burke Ransome had in his theories.

IF THE STEAM generated by the white heat of her fury had been harnessable, it could have powered the cart Allison steered down the shell road toward the haven of the old mansion.

Her anger was directed first at the man who had ordered her off the island with contempt as if she were some lower order of being, but a share of it was also turned on herself. Hadn't she let curiosity lure her off her own turf, knowing she shouldn't risk an encounter with Burke Ransome until Canby came back to rescue her from the limbo he'd left her in? What she got she had asked for, she told herself with disgust.

Still, it was not the humiliation of the encounter that disheartened her, she realized after a time. It was the awful knowledge that the man who had lashed out at her with bitterness a few minutes earlier was the same golden, mistakenly mythical being who had splashed out of the morning sea and started an exquisite half-forgotten budding deep within her, a stirring of joy she had feared lost to her for all time.

For a moment she saw him as he'd been then, hard muscular torso glistening in the sun; she saw herself standing rapt, quite unconscious of her own nakedness as she watched him approach. An involuntary shiver coursed its rapturous way down her spine at the image. Not since the embers of her misguided passion for Tyler had cooled to ashes had any man lighted the secret jet flame deep within her or bathed her in the sudden warmth of hungering hope as this man had. This man who was not Ty, who was so unlike him, yet more dangerous, more devastating, in fact.

In the last moment before she left the cart with the Crewes twins and walked on to the house to find Peg she hid her terrible feeling of desolation behind the mask of a cheerful face.

Back at the house she found her friend at the small desk in the pantry poring over one of those endless checklists she insisted on keeping, crossing off missions accomplished, making new lists of work still to be done. Thrusting the unsettling encounter to the back of her mind, Allison joined Peg once more in preparations for the grand opening less than a week away.

Bent over the desk together, the two women matched the assortment of expected guests to the rooms offered at Plantation House. The information provided in the reservation requests was sketchy, forcing them to depend more on instinct than judgment in carrying out the task.

Satisfied to let her friend take charge, Allison did little more than nod agreement to Peg's suggestions, while her mind engaged in small winning battles with the enemy. At the same time she half expected Ransome to descend on them momentarily with a crew of men to load her and Peg and the twins into a dory and deposit them bag and baggage on the mainland across the estuary. Could he really do it, she wondered. And what could she do about it if he tried?

Escaping from these apprehensions back to the job at hand, she would find Peg eyeing her with curiosity and reproach. But Allison pretended to be unaware of the clear invitation to confide. Why upset Peg? Besides, was there any real reason to think she had something to worry about?

"Sorry," she would murmur contritely.

With an offended sniff Peg would then pick up where she'd lost Allison's attention. "I said, why not give the rooms off the east balcony to the couple with the two young girls? And what about Bob Birch? Where do you want to put him?"

And so it went, Peg firming her plump chin to invoke patience, Allison struggling to keep her thoughts from wandering off into limbo. Both were clearly relieved when they came to the end of their shared chore.

Throughout an afternoon spent hanging curtains,

planning menus, consulting with Effie on available island talent for the Fourth of July beach party, Allison's mind kept returning uneasily to Burke Ransome.

"Get off my island!" he'd ordered peremptorily. His angry words hung over her like an ominous shadow, seeming to threaten her every move.

Finally sundown came. Dinner was over, the workday at an end.

"Mah-jongg anyone?" Peg called out from the library as Allison passed the open door on her way upstairs to her room.

They had become a nightly thing, these mah-jongg sessions. Hoddy had found an exquisite set of the tiles from another age and world in an unexplored drawer, and Peg, the only one who knew the game, decided they must all be taught.

As a game it had not captured Allison's interest, but its aesthetic appeal had turned her into a devotee at once. Fashioned from gemlike fragments inlaid in ebony by some ancient, Far Eastern artisan, the delicate translucent pastel chips were so perfectly fitted into each tile her exploring fingers could not detect the joinings. She loved to feel the smooth satiny markers and study the mysterious artistry of their designs. She loved the faint spicy scent of sandalwood emanating from the box that held them; a scent that lingered with her for a time after she played.

But the day's anxieties, imagined or real, had built up too much turmoil within her for enjoyment of such subtle pleasures. The cheerful pretense she'd managed to maintain in the face of Peg's curiosity was worn thin. She had to get away by herself.

She paused in the library doorway to answer Peg. "Sorry, not for me tonight. Bunker says Godiva needs to be ridden, and I could do with some fresh air myself."

Upstairs Allison pulled on an old pair of jeans and sneakers and one of the new green-on-white Ransome's Cay T-shirts she'd had silk-screened in New York as check-in gifts for incoming guests. A moment later she stepped through the front door into steamy heat that felt like a Turkish bath.

It was one of those oppressively humid evenings that drained one of all vitality. Allison was tempted to escape back into the cool haven of the air-conditioned house. Only the prospect of having to fake more hours of good cheer sent her doggedly on her way.

The best she could hope for was that the temperamental mare wouldn't choose this evening to play coy and run her halfway around the field before allowing herself to be caught.

But Allison was to be saved from this fate by Bunker, she discovered gratefully. When she stopped by the paddock to pick up a halter and a bucket of oats for bait she found the horse standing placidly in her stall, saddled, with only the cinch to tighten and the bridle to be put on.

Even these slight exertions sent a trickle of perspi-

ration spilling across her brow. When she reached up
to mop it away she discovered that the new T-shirt
was already beginning to cling to her sweaty shoulders.

Except for Plantation House the only cool spot
that night was the ocean, she thought glumly as she
led Godiva out of the stall. Across the screen of her
mind flashed an instant picture of a man and a horse
in the sea. Suddenly a burst of adrenaline spurted
through her body and burned off her languor.

"Why not?" she whispered under her breath.
"Why not, indeed?"

Alive with an unexpected burst of energy, she un-
fastened the cinch. She pulled off the saddle and
hung it back on its rack, then, grasping the horse's
mane, took off from the ground with a leap that sent
her shinnying up on the animal's back. She nudged
Godiva sharply with sneakered heels to get moving.
A moment later she was cantering briskly along the
path that led to the sea.

Godiva was a gentle mare, but she had a skittish
streak, inclining her to shy unexpectedly at common-
place objects that turned up along her path. Allison
was not at all sure how the mare would react to bap-
tism, but as she galloped eagerly toward the plunge,
the shiver that raced up her spine had nothing to do
with fear.

Until that morning two days earlier when she had
arrived back from New York, it would never have occurred to her to go swimming on horseback. Now as

she urged the palomino swiftly toward the beach, she realized that from the moment she'd watched Burke Ransome rise up out of the waves on Cherokee, somewhere in the back of her mind she had known it was something she was bound to do.

Planning her strategy as they flew down the path, Allison decided her best bet was to get Godiva submerged before the beast had time to react. Forcing the animal into a fast canter as soon as they reached the sand, she headed directly for the incoming waves and hit the water's edge at top speed. There Godiva came to a sudden stunning halt that caused Allison's back teeth to clench. Only the quick reflex action that brought her heels pressing hard into the animal's belly and sent both hands to clutch Godiva's mane kept her from being thrown.

Even at the edge of the water the air around was sultry. By the time Allison prodded and coaxed her mount far enough into the cooling surf for the hooves to lose touch with the ground, the horse's flanks were lathered and the rider bathed in sweat.

Once under, the battle was done. Clinging to the mane, Allison leaned forward along the mare's neck and reveled in the cool salt water that washed them, feeling herself a part of the swimming beast, as if the powerful muscular system that carried her through the water were an extension of her own.

Splashing in and out of the surf, they galloped across the sand. Where the ground gave way with the tidal ebb, they were forced to swim, the horse no longer fighting the water, until once again they reached solid beach.

By the time Allison tired of the game, the anxieties that had turned her into a bundle of raw nerve endings had vanished. They had not been really washed out to sea, she knew, but were more likely floating in some eddy of her mind, still around and bound to come back. At the moment, though, relaxed and exhilarated, she didn't give them a thought.

Dripping water, horse and rider set off up the beach at a leisurely canter, the evaporation from Allison's drenched hair and clothing cooling her body as they went. She lifted her face to the warm evening air, which felt as soothing as a caress.

In time they came to the point where the sea cut into the island and formed the lagoon. There she pulled up on the reins. Across the water the white hull of the *Ulysses* seemed etched in bas-relief against the dark background of the shadowy wooded shore. She let the mare rest for a moment, her eyes fixed on the small ship, and thought of the enigmatic Burke Ransome.

Eventually, she slipped down from Godiva's back and brought the bridle reins over the animal's head. Holding them with a light hand, she made a seat for herself on the wild grass, then sat down to rest her chin on her knees and stare out at the endless hypnotic movement of the sea.

Why should she think of him as an enigma, she

wondered suddenly. Except for that single, swiftly passing moment at the cove the other morning, there'd certainly been no mystery about him at any time. Clear unadulterated unpleasantness was all he had ever shown to her.

There was no mistaking his dislike for her—a dislike colored by an inexplicable trace of bitterness, even a shadow of contempt at times. He'd shown himself to be an avaricious vindictive man who had inherited his family's fortune, its business and a half of Ransome's Cay yet was still not satisfied. He wanted more.

Without considering herself a poor helpless widow, it seemed contemptible to Allison that this man should try to threaten and bully her into giving up the only recompense she'd ever seen from Tyler, the only acknowledgment really of all he'd squandered of hers. She felt a certain sadness for the shallow young man who had been her husband. It seemed a pity that Ty's most decent gesture in their whole relationship was in danger of being negated by his unprincipled cousin.

In her mind she tried to picture Ransome as he'd been that afternoon when he confronted her at the sea lab and ordered her from the island they were obliged to share. But try as she might, the golden apparition of that splendidly sinewed horseman rising from the sea in the early dawn erased all other images. For a long moment she forgot to breathe as she daydreamed the almost mystical tableau again—

from the rider's first appearance to the magnolia blossom at her feet.

For all its bravura there was a careless sweetness about the performance, a certain gallantry in the man who played out the scene with a delicate concern for the innocence and modesty of the island maiden he'd thought her to be, had surprised in her bucolic bath.

There the dream ended. A wild whinny and sudden jerk of the head by Godiva yanked the bridle straps from Allison's hands. Lunging forward in the sea grass, she scrambled desperately to retrieve the reins, but in the same instant the horse was off.

"Whoa, Godiva," she yelled frantically as she rolled to her feet and took off after the animal at a dead run.

"Godiva!" she called out again. She pushed for more speed, knowing that to call was fruitless but calling nonetheless. "Come back, Godiva, whoa!"

Her final "whoa" came out no more than a breathless grunt as her toe caught in an exposed root and she sprawled full length on a thatch of grass that cushioned her fall.

Recovering, she rolled over and sat up. The action brought such a wrench of pain to her ankle that she could do nothing immediately but sit where she was in a half-dazed slump. It was a second or two before she fully realized the seriousness of her situation. She'd lingered far longer than she had intended. The long shadows of dusk were beginning to close in. She made a halfhearted attempt to stand on the injured foot but knew from the pain it cost her that it wouldn't carry her far.

Lowering herself to the ground, she seriously considered for the first time the possibility that she might be obliged to stay there all night—a prospect she viewed with alarm. It would never occur to Peg to check her room when they finished the mah-jongg game. She would assume Allison had come in while they were playing and slipped upstairs to bed. Even if they knew she was missing, how would they know where to look in the dark?

She thought nervously of the wild creatures of the island—the deer, the wild boar, the big-horn sheep. Except for an occasional passing glimpse they were seldom seen. There wasn't a predator among them, she reassured herself, her eyes casting about all the same for a heavy stick that might be used as a weapon just in case. And then a small flicker of memory caused her to pause.

In that dreamy instant before Godiva bolted there had been a sound on the periphery of her fantasy... the distant trumpeting whinny of a stallion on the scent of a mare.

Raising herself to her knees, she cupped her face with her hands to form an amplifier and called out as loud as she could, "Help! Help!" She rested a moment then called again and again, disheartened that she heard no answering sound. The island horses were not left to run about but kept in pasture. It was reasonable to hope there had been a horseman as well as a horse.

She was about to shout one last time when a horse and rider came crashing out of the woods a short distance from where she sat. A small involuntary cry of relief broke in her throat. It died the next instant as she recognized in the gathering dusk the least welcome of all rescuers—Burke Ransome on Cherokee.

"Oh, God," Allison groaned softly. She might have guessed this would be the team to cause that silly Godiva to bolt.

On they came, to pull to an abrupt halt not far from where Allison sat, steeling herself to rise.

"What's the trouble?" Ransome shouted. "You called for help?"

Ignoring the pain it produced, Allison brought herself stubbornly to her feet. Ransome dismounted and led Cherokee to where she stood. She raised her chin in a defiant lift and met his eyes coolly.

"Don't bother," she replied distantly. "I'm quite all right."

"You did call for help?"

She detected a stiffening in his voice when he'd seen who she was, but as he drew near the wide expressive mouth seemed unable to suppress a slight twitch of humor.

"If I may say so, you look as though you'd been dunked in a watering trough," he said.

His words were an unwelcome reminder to Allison of her appearance. The humid air had done little to dry her wet T-shirt and sodden jeans. They clung to her like a second layer of skin, accentuating every line and curve of her body. She was uncomfortably aware that she looked more naked than if she actually were. It was all she could do to keep her hands from flying up to cover her firm round uptilted breasts and the rosy brown aureoles she knew were only too clearly defined through the flimsy cotton of the T-shirt and transparent lace of her bra.

She would not let herself glance down but kept her eyes squarely on Ransome's face. She saw that he did not share her constraint. As if in spite of himself, his eyes traveled slowly, completely, over her body, returning to her face with clear reluctance.

For a long moment he didn't speak but seemed to be assessing the situation.

"You're on foot," he observed at last. "Lucky for you I happened to come along."

"If you hadn't come along on that damned stallion and caused Godiva to bolt, I wouldn't be in this position," Allison shot back.

"Don't blame Cherokee," said Ransome. "That mare's always been flighty. She'll bolt at her own shadow."

The matter-of-factness in his voice inflamed Allison's anger to the blazing point, but before she could respond, Ransome continued, his tone annoyingly impersonal. "Obviously you can't stay here all night. The best thing I suppose is for me—"

This time Allison would not let him finish. "Forget

it!'' she snapped. "The best thing you can do for me is go away and leave me alone." It took all her concentration to contain the note of hysteria she could feel creeping into her voice. "Correction. That's the next best thing. The best thing would be for you to get completely out of my life!''

It was a speech to be followed by a grand exit, but her first step away from Ransome brought a revealing cry of pain she could not hold back. Had the man not reached out and caught her, she would have stumbled to the ground.

"There may be differences between us, Mrs. Hill, but that's no reason for martyrdom," he said in that same infuriating contained tone. "If you'll quit thrashing about and sit down, I'll take a look at that foot.''

Allison glared angrily, warning him with her eyes that should she decide to do as he'd asked, it did not mean she yielded one ounce of her spirit. Even in her defiance she wondered if she could give in to him on any single point without compromising in some unsuspected way what he called their differences.

She hesitated. He would not wait. Ransome brought to play his considerable superior physical strength, picked up her wet body in his arms and set her down on the ground.

In the action her breast was pushed for an instant against his bare chest. She was acutely aware of the clean male smell of his skin and the slight teasing prickle of the hair on his chest through the moist fabric of her shirt. As he let her go, the wet shirt pulled away from her breasts with a sighing sound and clung for an instant to the bronzed flesh against which it had been pressed.

"Hold the reins," he ordered brusquely, handing them to her as he knelt down to look at her foot. "And this time hang on to them or we'll both be stranded."

She took a quick glance at her ankle, which bulged out in an obscene-looking band between the top of her sneaker and the bottom of her slim-legged jeans, then turned away, biting her lip to hold back the cry of pain as he unlaced the soft canvas shoe.

"Sorry," he said, though he handled her foot with surprising gentleness. "This shoe's got to come off."

When she looked again, she was astonished to see that he was reaching into a pocket of his jeans to bring up a Swiss-army knife. Without bothering to ask if she minded, he slashed her pants leg down the outer seam to the hem some ten inches. With the lessening of the pressure she felt immediate relief from the pain. It seemed only fair to swallow the protest that rose to her lips.

"Can you wiggle your toes?" he asked when he'd bared the foot. This time she obliged at once by wiggling them. "Good," he said, "it's just sprained. If you'd cracked it, I'd have to leave you and go get the jeep."

"How can you be sure? You're not a doctor."

"I've had a little experience—no big deal," he answered with seeming embarrassment, as if he felt rather foolish having to explain such a thing. "The ship's doctor on the *Ulysses* had a problem with mal de mer. Every time we hit rough weather the poor devil got seasick, and sure as Satan some guy would slip on the deck or get slammed into a bulkhead. It was up to me to pinch-hit for the doctor. Between up-chucks the old boy taught me how to tell a fracture from a simple sprain. This is a sprain, believe me. Now let's get you up on the horse."

Allison raised herself on one elbow to look him full in the face, her apprehension reflected in her eyes. "Not on your life," she said in a voice thick with alarm. "You're not going to get me up on that crazy nag!"

"Don't be unreasonable. The quicker you get that ankle packed in ice, the sooner you can walk on it again," said Ransome testily. "Come on. Come on. It's the early treatment that counts." He waited as if for a sign of agreement. When it failed to come he said firmly, "I'm taking you to Plantation House on the horse and that's final. You'll just have to trust me."

"Trust you!" Allison exclaimed, finding it hard to believe he would use such a word. How could he ask her to trust him? But then she shouldn't really be surprised. He was Tyler's blood cousin, wasn't he? Was it any wonder he was as blindly insensitive as Tyler?

"You must think I'm really stupid or terribly naive," she said, her voice quiet and controlled while still betraying a hint of her utter dismay. "Do you expect me to trust the man who is trying to bully me out of what Tyler left me? You—the man who ordered me off this island today? I don't know how you squeezed Tyler out of a share in the family's fortune, Mr. Ransome. I never wanted to know. But I've wondered sometimes if bitterness over what you did made him the way he was."

"Are you blaming me for what my cousin made of himself?" Ransome demanded savagely.

Hearing the unspoken rage in his voice, Allison rallied her defenses. "Well, no one would ever blame you for his charisma Mr. Ransome," she said. In spite of their thrust the words came out less sarcastic than wry. "There's no denying he had that."

Impulsively she repeated Effie's remark from the day before. The housekeeper had never wasted any love on Allison's late husband. "'He could charm the birds off the trees,'" she commented. "That's hardly your style."

"If there was something in it for him I've no doubt he could and did," Ransome replied caustically after a long pause. "I must admit I never saw that side of him."

"Considering how he felt about you, that hardly comes as a surprise," Allison said bluntly.

"Exactly how did my cousin feel about me?" His words sparked like static in the air.

"Just as *you'd* feel if you'd been maneuvered out of your share of your family's inheritance except for half ownership of a rundown island," Allison remarked with asperity.

"Is that what Tyler told you?"

She hesitated a moment, then honesty forced her to add, "He only said it obliquely, but he didn't leave much room for doubt."

"And you? Do you believe it?" asked Ransome harshly.

"What reason do I have to believe otherwise, Mr. Ransome?" said Allison formally. "You've made it quite clear you intend to use every means possible to seize Tyler's share of the island."

There was frustration in the mangled expletive Ransome gave as his only reply.

"Maybe we both have some misconceptions that need to be untangled," he began after a moment, "but this is hardly the place or the time. What's urgent is getting some ice on that ankle." He arose from where he'd hunkered down beside her.

Sprawled on the thicket of sea grass where he'd placed her, Allison watched as he stood to tower over her in the eerie light of a giant, apricot-colored moon rising out of the sea over the eastern horizon behind them.

From her perspective on the ground at Ransome's feet the tall, well-built body silhouetted darkly against the moon seemed to possess heroic proportions. Why argue something that could be decided by physical strength alone when you knew before you started you had only to lose?

She held her peace and watched his shadowy figure approach the horse. With a hand on the stallion's neck, the man spoke quietly, urging the animal nearer to where Allison lay, until she cried out in alarm. From ground level the creature looked huge and menacing.

"Stop!" she yelled.

"Sorry. He's not going to step on you," he assured her.

"Do you expect to hoist me up on that beast?" she asked in alarm.

"Why not? Just do as I say and it'll work," said Ransome, clearly chafing to get on with it. "I won't promise it won't hurt a little when I move you, but I will promise it will do you no lasting harm."

"I can stand the hurt," snapped Allison. "I just don't want to be killed. That stallion won't let us ride him double. Until you came back he hadn't had a leg over him in years."

"You malign Cherokee," said Ransome impatiently. "Come on now! Cut out the nonsense. Put an arm over my shoulder and keep the weight off the foot. I'll bring you up."

He leaned down to support her, and Allison panicked. This was insane! She'd seen others try to ride Cherokee. It was bad enough to have a sprained ankle. She wasn't about to try for a broken neck.

In a sudden movement that brought a screaming

pain to her ankle she rolled away from the man bending over her. Determined not to let her go, he flattened out beside her.

Pinned to the mat of sea grass, Allison fought the sob that rose in her throat. For the first time since childhood she found herself crying real tears from pain.

"Of all the damn-fool stunts," Ransome muttered from where he lay spread-eagled on the ground.

"Go away!" sobbed Allison, destroyed finally by frustration, exhaustion and pain.

"Oh, God, don't cry!" groaned Ransome. "You're not crying are you, Mrs. Hill? Are you hurt?"

"Of course I'm hurt!" wailed Allison. "Please go away!"

There was a moment of silence. Then to the astonishment of the distraught woman bent on regaining her composure he did just that. He rolled over and got to his feet, retrieving the bridle reins he'd dropped as he went scrambling after her.

"Steady, Cherokee," she heard him say quietly. She felt a fleeting surprise that the horse had stood still all through their noisy tussle. Was this the terror of the island—that renegade stallion every man on Ransome's Cay was afraid to mount?

Ransome remained there, stroking the animal's neck for a moment before he came back to where she lay. He studied her curiously as if she were a kind of puzzle he was obliged to solve.

"I don't have much use for the guy who uses superior physical strength to get what he wants, whether from a woman or another man," he said in a prickly voice from where he stood looking across at her. "It wasn't my intention to take up the practice just now."

Dropping to the ground beside her, he continued in a reasonable tone. "My experience with women in crises has been limited, I'm afraid. It looks as if I've gone about it all wrong this time. All I'm trying to do is convince you it's for your own good to ride back to the house on Cherokee. If I can't do that I'll go get the jeep."

The change of pace came as such a surprise to Allison she could only stare at him. It was then that she became acutely aware of the strong male presence so close to her. She had merely to shift her position slightly to bring her thigh in solid contact with him.

The realization stirred a shameful quickening of her pulse. From the moment of their first meeting she'd noticed in herself a disconcerting susceptibility to his sheer physical magnetism. The knowledge that she responded so sensuously to a man she mistrusted deeply disturbed her each time it came to mind.

Without any movement from her, the full length of her body was suddenly touching his as Ransome unexpectedly stretched out on his stomach beside her. Leaning on one elbow, he looked squarely into her moonlit face.

"Ah, that's better," he said. "Now I can see

you.'' He was silent for a moment, then continued. ''About Cherokee. Would it reassure you to know that when I was eighteen I spent the entire summer trying to teach that horse to do Spanish Riding School stunts—and failed miserably. What I did succeed in doing was turning the rascal into the best disciplined horse on the island—as long as I'm the one on his back.'' For the first time Allison heard Burke Ransome laugh. It was a soft baritone rumble that brought a grin to her face in spite of herself.

''Just ask anyone on the island,'' he said. ''I wouldn't let them geld Cherokee. Some say he's a good horse for me because he's grateful. Others are less charitable. They say it's extortion, that he figures he could still go under the knife. In either case that horse knows when he's well off. You needn't be afraid of Cherokee,'' he reassured her again.

Allison responded with a small chuckle.

Leaning close to her, Ransome reached across and turned her face more directly toward his own. ''Look at me, Allison.''

The sound of her given name from him was strangely seductive. In spite of herself her eyes were drawn to his. Then, unexpectedly, as if there were a magnetic pull between them, his head came down. In the last second before his mouth took hers she felt the whisper of his breath on her lips, caught its fresh clean scent with her nose.

The hand that tipped her face slowly traced the line of her cheek and neck. He probed softly at her breastbone a moment. Then his hand strayed down to cover the still damp mound of her breast, his fingers curving lightly around the soft sphere before tightening over the small firm bud that sprang up to meet the solid flesh of his palm.

She made a single effort to protest, but it came to nothing as his hand lifted and thumb and forefinger played tentatively with the small erection. A deep exquisite pain quivered at her very center, overriding the ache of the injured ankle for the moment.

Her body was at once ripe with hunger. In an instant of release as his mouth pulled away from hers, her tongue spread its moisture over the full curve of her hungering lips.

A heavy agonized sigh escaped from Ransome. He rolled away from her once again and pulled himself to his feet. Half dazed, Allison struggled to a sitting position, and the sweet lingering pain of the moment was lost in the steady throb of the injured ankle. All that was left to her of the enraptured interlude was a pervasive heaviness within her breast, a feeling of desolation and shame.

"I'm sorry. That was the *last* thing I expected to do," Ransome said heavily. "Let's get the hell out of here before...." He left the remark dangling.

Leaning over, he lifted her as impersonally as an ambulance attendant until her weight rested solidly on the uninjured foot. He jockeyed the horse around to her side.

After all the fuss the act of mounting was anticlimactic. Cherokee moved not a muscle as Ransome lifted her with great care to a position where she could ease the sprained ankle over the animal's backbone and down on the other side when she was seated. He then handed her the reins and leapfrogged over the horse's rump to seat himself behind her. Slipping his arms around her, he took the reins.

"You'd better get that foot elevated," he advised, his voice still tight with constraint. "Lift it up and cross your leg in front of you as if you were riding sidesaddle. Hold it steady with your hand and let the ankle rest on the other knee."

"I'll fall off," she protested.

"No, you won't," he assured her, speaking more easily now. "I won't let you. Lean into me with all your weight. I won't let you fall. Come on. Let's go."

At a cluck of Burke's tongue the improbable Cherokee moved off as sedately as the old gray mare, in a rocking-chair gait that carried them homeward at a fairly rapid pace. Ransome's body formed a human saddle around her, enfolding her firmly within its perimeters. Allison was left only to cleave to the strong male body and struggle against a shameful preoccupation with the play of muscles she felt through her clothing.

With each pull he gave to the reins she could feel the flex of his arm muscles against the outer curves of her breasts. She could sense the tendons tighten in his inner thighs as his legs changed grip on the horse. She could feel the rhythmic rise and fall of the flat hard surface of his frontal torso pressing against her back.

An uncontrollable excitement swelled in her. This was hardly the wild escape ride behind the bold intruder she'd fantasized the morning after Buttonhook Cove, but it had its charms.

CHAPTER FIVE

ALLISON WAS TEMPTED to hold her back stiffly aloof, to remind her rescuer that in spite of her temporary dependence on him she hadn't suffered a change of heart, but she discovered early in the ride that she would be smart to put off their vendetta till another day. For her own safety and comfort she let herself ease back and conform to the planes of the broad chest and muscular limbs that scissored around her.

Securely enwrapped in Ransome's firm sure embrace, their bodies moving together in time with the horse's rocking-chair gait, she relaxed into a sensible acceptance of the circumstances and put aside contention for the duration of the ride.

With a sort of mindlessness she gave herself over to the luxury of the temporary moratorium on hostilities. Except for when some slight change in the stallion's rhythm sent a stab of pain up her leg, she lost touch with the steady throb of the injured ankle. Locked together like puzzle pieces they rode in silence, as if each feared words might break the silken spell.

Up ahead the lights of Plantation House signaled

that the end of the ride was at hand. Allison was suddenly aware that her body pressed more closely against the man behind her, unexpectedly reluctant to leave his strong protective embrace. She felt his thigh muscles tighten involuntarily in response, and a shiver of pure sensuous pleasure raced down her spine. She closed her eyes and for a moment savored the full delight of their closeness.

Then the stallion took a sudden sidestep to avoid a fallen branch. The lurch threw her off balance and back to her senses. Pain radiated up from her ankle, and Ransome steadied her with a tightening grip.

Shocked at her own eager participation but a moment earlier, she stiffened and straightened herself into an upright position, resisting the magic pull of his body.

Ransome seemed not to notice her abrupt withdrawal. He made no effort to urge her back into his arms, though without the support of his upper body her perch was precarious. And as they rode on, she was racked with pain. She gritted her teeth and endured.

When they reached the house, Ransome steadied her with one hand while he dropped easily to the ground. He lifted her off Cherokee and in spite of her vigorous dissent carried her into the house and up to her room. There he turned her over to Peg—but not before he had given specific instructions on how to prop up the foot and pack the ankle in ice bags.

Still, it was not the sprain or Peg's comings and goings to change the ice packs that filled the hours of
the night with fitful dreams and half awakenings.
Something had happened to Allison in the course of
the rescue. A strange mixture of thoughts and emotions whirled within her. Her head felt like a child's
snowflake globe after it's been shaken.

Why had he bothered? The Burke Ransome she
had known up to that point would have loaded her
on the horse and hauled her grudgingly home without
ceremony, impatient to get the job over with fast.
Her fears and pain would have meant nothing to
him.

Unpredictably the man she'd pegged simply as the
enemy had turned out to be a decent considerate
human being. He'd met her prickly resistance with
patience and—in fairness—more good humor than
her own unpleasantness deserved.

Nothing was simple anymore. Her bitterness had
lost its edge. In the sleepless intervals she wished...
for what? Not his friendship. With all that lay between them it was too much to expect they might ever
be friends. For his respect, maybe; to know she could
meet those sea-deep eyes and see something in them
other than a withering contempt.

It had been easier, she decided, when she'd felt
nothing for Ransome but anger and distrust. And yet
even then there had been something more.

There was no denying the strong physical attraction she felt in his presence from the first moment

she'd watched the splendid figure of the man come riding out of the sea in the golden light of the morning sun.

Nor could she deny her keen disappointment when she'd learned who the rider was. She could handle all that. Physical enthrallment was an exciting fact of life but a passing thing. She simply told herself, "Watch it!"—and in the case of someone named Ransome that shouldn't be hard to do.

Only nothing was simple now. Something new had slipped in to complicate things. She felt strangely vulnerable. Inexplicably her thoughts flew back unbidden to the time long past when she first met Tyler Hill, and suddenly she was afraid.

So went the night. She dozed and wakened and dozed and wakened again to such kaleidoscopic thoughts, until her clock said 7:30. Easing herself gingerly up on her elbows, she assessed the situation to determine how best to extricate her foot from the swathing of towels around it. Before she could move further, her bedroom door opened and in marched Peg, carrying a covered tray.

"For heaven's sake, Peg, get me out of this mess," she begged. "My leg feels like a Popsicle."

"Hold your horses," said Peg, setting the tray down on a nearby chest and moving to the bed to peel off the towels. "Let's take a look at it. How does it feel?"

"How should I know?" said Allison crossly. "It's numb from the cold. Between Burke Ransome and you I'll be lucky if I don't lose my foot from frost-bite.''

"Don't criticize your Good Samaritan, honey. Never mind what other complaints you may have about the man, he does know what to do for a sprain.''

As she laid aside the ice bags, Allison leaned forward to examine the ankle more closely, surprised to see that it had returned to its normal size. She moved it tentatively and could feel only a small reminder of the previous night's pain. She pivoted herself in bed and was about to ease to a standing position when Peg laid a detaining hand on her shoulder.

"Not so fast, dear girl,'' Peg said. "Mr. Ransome said absolutely no weight on that ankle until it's firmly wrapped in an elastic bandage. Here's your breakfast. You can eat it in bed, and then I'll work on your leg.''

To show she meant business, Peg pulled a roll of bandage from a pocket of her flowered smock.

"I can't eat breakfast until I wash my face,'' Allison complained.

"Okay. I'll give you a hand into the bathroom, and then it's back to bed with you, chum.''

"If you say so, sergeant,'' Allison said with a relenting grin as she submitted meekly to using Peg as her crutch.

DOWN IN EFFIE'S KITCHEN at that moment Burke Ransome arrived bearing gifts.

"Effie, love... '' He greeted the plump little

housekeeper with a bear hug that swept her off her feet, her short legs waving frantically. "Time's been good to you. You look great!"

The woman's round cheerful face beamed on him fatuously. "Well, it's about time you got down here to see me," she scolded playfully. "What took you so long?"

"I couldn't come empty-handed," he said, laying a tissue-wrapped bundle across her arms. "Bunker's told you what we've been doing up there at the lagoon, I suppose, so you know why I haven't had a chance to dig into my chest before. I brought you a trinket or two from my wanderings."

"You didn't have to do that, Mr. Burke," the little woman protested, her hands working at the gold seals that held the package together. Under impatient fingers the bits of foil came away. She cried out in delight as a richly embroidered, red silk kimono un-folded in her hands. "Oh, lordy, lordy! Y'all don't mean this for me! It's the prettiest thing I ever did see."

"Of course it's for you, Effie," Ransome told her, his eyes reflecting his delight in her pleasure. "Who else would I buy it for? Aren't you my favorite lady? Here...put it on. Let's see how it looks."

Taking the garment from her hands, he slipped it over her cotton house dress in spite of her protests and tied the slender silk sash around her plump mid-dle.

"Hey! You look gorgeous," he told her with satisfaction. "Wait'll Bunker gets a look at you in that. You'll drive him crazy."

Effie's cheeks turned rosy.

"Mr. Burke!" she admonished, but her eyes sparkled, and she couldn't hold back an embarrassed giggle.

Ransome reached into a pocket of his light cotton Windbreaker and brought out an oblong box. He was about to hand it to the delighted woman, then held it back and fumbled in another pocket, from which he withdrew a second box somewhat similar in size and shape.

"This one's for you. It's genuine French perfume I bought for you in Paris—it's guaranteed to make you smell like a courtesan," he informed her with a wicked grin. "The other is a pipe for Bunker. But I'll give that to him later myself. Now you've got to sit down with me and have a cup of coffee. We've got some catching up to do."

At the kitchen table a few moments later Effie, still wearing the red silk kimono and liberally splashed with her wicked French perfume, filled her visitor in on the happenings on Ransome's Cay during his long absence. She was fairly bursting with joy over the expected return of their son, Jimmer, and his family, and embarrassed Ransome with a tearful effort to express her gratitude to him for making the return possible.

Ransome was so undone by the combination of tears and gratitude—two things he never knew quite how to deal with—that he was at last impelled to plunge headlong into the single subject he had really come to talk about with Effie that morning. He'd hoped for a more subtle approach, but he had no choice.

"About Tyler's widow—" he asked abruptly. "What do you think of this Allison Hill, Effie?"

Effie made a final dab at her still moist eyes and gazed on him speculatively from across the table for a moment. "I'm glad you asked," she said. "Bunker says you've got her all wrong and you wouldn't listen to him. If you really want to know what I think, Mr. Burke, you got to listen to what I say, even if it's not what you want to hear."

"I'll listen," Ransome said grudgingly, knowing that except for the previous night's events he would not have been willing to heed Effie's words.

He had a deep affection for this peppery little woman who had given him what mothering he'd had since his early teens when his own mother had died. He respected her innate canniness and judgment.

"How long have you known her?" he asked.

"Ever since she married that darned cousin of yours," Effie told him. "I guess you didn't know he brought her here on their honeymoon—if you can call it that. She was here for maybe three or four months. That's when you were up there in Atlanta working like a common laborer in the mill your daddy left you, trying to play like there wasn't no such place as Ransome's Cay."

For a long time after that ugly night he'd walked in on his wife stretched out naked on the floor beside Tyler, he'd stayed in Atlanta and tried to forget there'd ever been a Plantation House. The memory had long ceased to pain him. He dismissed it now with a passing dismay that he had let the ugly tableau cast such a pall of bitterness over his life for so many years.

"Bunker never told me they were here," he said, half apologetically.

"As far as I know you never asked. Besides, it was half Tyler's, you know."

"It was then," conceded Ransome.

Effie turned curious eyes on him. It was clear to Ransome that Bunker hadn't mentioned his own later purchase of the other half to his wife. Still, she didn't ask.

"She was as fresh and sweet as honeysuckle and just turned eighteen when she come here as a bride," Effie told him. "She took to the island like she'd been born and raised here. I reckon if it'd been up to her they never would have left. But you know that cousin of yours. He never come here except when he was broke and didn't have no place else to go."

With Ransome her attentive listener, Effie gave a full account of a strange honeymoon wherein the radiant adoring bride soon found herself abandoned on the island for days at a time, with only the Bunkers for company, while her bridegroom took off for the mainland on "business."

It hadn't taken long for the Bunkers to learn through the domestic grapevine on Ransome's Cay that during these absences Tyler was in Savannah or Atlanta, gambling or making the social scene with a high-flying party set. Meanwhile the young bride, whom Ty had falsely led to believe would be mistress of Plantation House, spent long hours with Effie, learning the mysteries of cooking and caring for the house "to surprise Ty," or with Bunker, who taught her to ride the island horses. When Tyler came back from the mainland one day to announce they were moving to New York at once, Allison and the Bunkers cried.

"God, what a rotter!" muttered Ransome as Effie wound down. "Makes you wonder why she ever married him. Maybe she thought he was rich."

Effie's warm eyes were at once angry and reproachful. "I bet he told her he was, but that wouldn't have made any difference," she said hotly. "This lady is not that kind. She was just a sweet kid, head over heels in love with a good-looking, no-account guy. The world's full of 'em. Can't you understand that, Mr. Burke? What's come over you? You didn't used to look at things like that when you were an island boy."

"Trouble is, Effie, you've known me too long." Ransome gave her a wry grin. "I've taken a few lumps since those days. They've turned me into a bit of a cynic, I'm afraid."

"Well, in this world there are Margos and there are

Allisons," retorted Effie sagely. "Just remember this, Mr. Burke, they're not one and the same."

The housekeeper leaned back in her chair and paused a moment to let her pearl of wisdom sink in. "To get back to what you said," she continued, "money wasn't a problem with her—at least not then it wasn't. She'd inherited enough from her folks. I reckon that's what they lived on. I know this for a fact, though—it was real love as far as that bride was concerned, and in spite of how bad he treated her, I'd bet anything she's still in love with the guy."

A wave of unreasonable anger swelled suddenly in Burke. "That's sick!" he retorted. "What makes you think so?"

"Well, in the first place she don't let anyone put Tyler down," she told him. "That's the one thing she gets snappish about. Just try and breathe a word of criticism and she cuts you off."

"That doesn't mean a thing," he said with a strange sense of relief. "Pride, loyalty...simply the fact that he's dead. It seems a rather admirable way to behave."

Effie thought about it. "Yeah. She'd do that anyway. It's the kind of person she is. Forget that. When I mentioned something, awhile back, though, about how she ought to get married again, the look she gave me was as deep and dark as the grave. You know what she said to me? She said, 'After being married to Tyler? I couldn't! I don't think there'll ever be anyone again.' Them were her exact words."

Ransome had heard enough. As he mounted Cherokee and rode away from Plantation House he thought bleakly, *here we go again!* Being the senior member of the family after his father's death, it seemed as if he'd spent most of his adult life making amends to people Tyler Hill had used.

A fierce resentment toward his cousin's widow rose in his breast. The sense of freedom he'd felt from such obligations since his cousin's death was suddenly shattered by the discovery of this new and most poignant victim of all.

If Allison had entered into the marriage with money of her own, as Effie seemed to have reason to believe, it left him little room for doubt that his cousin had got his hands on some of it—enough, for certain, to finance the wedding and his gambling-partying forays to the mainland during that farce of a honeymoon.

The whole situation was deeply troubling to Burke. He didn't question his own obligation to make proper amends on behalf of the family honor even now that the culprit was dead.

Just how much of his bride's resources had Tyler Hill managed to squander, he wondered. Even as she watched him fritter it away, she must have felt some sense of security in the belief that Ransome's Cay and Plantation House were there to return to when everything else was gone.

How must she have felt in these last days to have half that belief destroyed? And what a blow it would be when she discovered, as soon she must, that it had all been a mirage—another of Ty Hill's lies. Would the loss of the island leave her destitute, he wondered, and once again the old sense of helpless fury he'd foolishly imagined had died in him with his cousin's death rose to confound him.

He felt an almost overpowering compassion for this beautiful woman he was so strangely attracted to. Yet he wanted no relationship with her. He would work out some kind of fair material compensation for whatever Ty had taken from her, but the less actual contact they had, the better. He was acutely aware of the strong physical attraction between them—an attraction he was sure she was aware of, too. It would take all his power of resistance to avoid an alliance in its way more fraught with danger than his marriage to Margo.

With Margo he'd known almost from the first that the restless passion he'd felt had little to do with love, though he'd never admitted it to himself until long after that fateful night. In the end the wound he'd suffered had been to his manly pride, not his heart.

With this Allison Hill it would be different. After all his years of believing he was long past any serious affairs of the heart he had met a woman with whom he might conceivably fall in love. Except for one thing: she was a woman herself in love with the memory of his dead cousin. Even that might be understandable if Tyler hadn't cheated and mistreated her when he was alive.

Damn it! The woman suffered from a self-punishing neurosis. That's what it was! She knew Ty was rotten to the core. To worship at that same shoddy shrine even after he was dead was a basic character flaw he didn't want any part of. If he let himself fall in love with this woman he would put in jeopardy far more than his silly pride, more than his heart...as much, perhaps, as his soul.

CHAPTER SIX

BACK AT HIS QUARTERS at the edge of the lagoon, Ransome was surprised to find both the housekeeping unit and the lab deserted. The dinghy was tied at the edge of the water, indicating McGinnis was still on land. Ransome tossed his jacket inside and was about to head for the dinghy to go out to join the workmen on the barge when the sound of an electric cart commandeered from the Plantation House shop told him McGinnis had returned.

"Hey, what's the matter, friend," Doc called out as he brought the cart to a stop and left it to join Ransome in front of the lab. "Something wrong on the barge? You've got trouble spilled all over your face."

"Sorry," grunted Ransome. "I didn't know it showed. It hasn't anything to do with the barge. You might as well know, I guess, that I'm through playing the heavy in this inheritance mess my late cousin left me as a token of our mutual admiration and trust. The only trouble, McGinnis, is I'm damned this time if I can see how I'm to make amends."

McGinnis rubbed the flat of his hand over his bald

pate and gave a sympathetic nod. "I take it something has made you change your mind about the
character and motives of your cousin's widow. I'm
glad you've seen the light."

Ransome grinned wryly. "I had a cup of coffee
with Effie Bunker this morning," he said. "She
didn't leave me much choice." He went on to give
McGinnis the highlights of what he'd learned from
the housekeeper.

"So it looks like Tyler took the lady for everything
he could lay his hands on," Ransome finished, his
brows pulling together in a puzzled frown. He was
finding it increasingly difficult to reconcile the sweet
submissive child-bride described by Effie with the
mature independent young woman he'd matched
wills with in two separate meetings the previous day.

"She defends the memory of my late cousin
against the slings and arrows of unkind tongues, says
Effie," he added gloomily. "The woman must be
some kind of masochist to still be in love with a worm
like Ty."

"Has she found out about the island?"

Ransome groaned. "Not that I haven't told her!"
he said. "She accused me of trying to bluff her out of
her inheritance. Looks like I'll have to send for the
plane and bring her the deed from my safety box in
Atlanta. She'll never believe me without it. I'd better
do it before she wastes any more of her money on
Plantation House."

"You're too late, I'm afraid," Doc said. "I went

down there this morning to see her friend, Mrs. Crewes, about teaching the boys to scuba dive—without much luck, I might add. But she gave me a guided tour of the old house. She tells me Mrs. Hill has already sunk everything she had left from her family inheritance into the project.''

Ransome stared out across the lagoon in silence.

''Any suggestions?'' he asked gravely, turning back to his friend after a time.

''If it were me, I'd lay low for a while,'' McGinnis said flatly. ''It's not going to do anybody any good to throw a monkey wrench into the works at this point. They're booked solid through the Fourth of July—they either make money or go in the red. A little red ink might convince Mrs. Hill it's a losing proposition. She might even be relieved to have you buy out her equity.''

''Suppose they make money.''

''They deserve the rewards, I'd say.''

''How I'd love to get my hands on Herb Canby!'' Ransome exploded suddenly. ''If he'd started probating that estate, she would have known where she stood from the first. It's going to be a lot harder on her now. She's had time to reorganize her life around this phony inheritance.''

''In any case she won't be in the dark much longer,'' Doc volunteered. ''According to Peg Crewes, Canby's due back right after the fourth, and Mrs. Hill's all set to nail him down.''

''Good!'' said Ransome morosely. ''I've lost all

inclination to tell her myself. I'll gladly leave it to him. Maybe he can get me some figures on what she actually spent there at Plantation House in money and labor—she and Mrs. Crewes and the sons. But that's not the half of it, I'm afraid.''

"You're probably right. I gather she gave up a good job in New York—against the advice of everyone but Mrs. Crewes—to set up this business at Plantation House.''

For a long moment Ransome gazed at his friend without really seeing him. Money would never take care of the anguish and worry the mix-up had cost the woman, but money was all he had.

Whatever the compensation he offered, it must be enough. He would not have her think he placed a low value on what she'd suffered at his cousin's hands. Nothing would inflame the proud Allison Hill more than a bad guess on the value of what she'd lost because of a member of the Ransome family.

It occurred to him then that this couldn't have come at a worse time. There were unusual financial demands to be met in connection with starting the oyster farm. It might mean he'd have to liquidate some solid investments. Under the circumstances that was irrelevant. A family debt was a family debt. He shrugged the thought aside.

A blink of his eyes brought his mind back into focus, and he turned his attention to his friend, realizing suddenly that McGinnis had been speaking to him.

"Remember how you used to talk about setting up some kind of an experimental center for aquafarming here at Ransome's Cay, Burke?" he asked.

The dark shadows passed from Ransome's eyes. His face took on a faint musing smile. "How could I forget?" he replied. "The whole time we were banging around the world watching the way different people in different places farm the sea it was on my mind as a means of pulling it all together for the benefit of everyone."

His sea-green eyes looked almost wistful. "I'd lie on the deck at night and think about what a natural this island with its deep lagoon and sheltered coves would be for a study and research station. Creative people from all over the world with practical know-how would come to us—scientists, technicians, men and women working and experimenting in the field."

"How did you plan to lure them here?"

"By offering them a working vacation," Ransome explained. "A lot of these people are too tied up in their work for normal vacations, and Plantation House has horses and beaches and boats. They could bring their families. They'd all be headquartered at the house and take their meals there together. There could be music, discussions, movies—whatever they wanted to do in the evening hours."

"And who's going to pick up the tab?"

"The Ransome Foundation could supply some of the funding but not enough of it," he replied. "One of the big foundations that's concerned with world food supply has agreed to fund fellowships, but we might as well forget about that." By this time Ransome's enthusiasm was spent. "Unless we go full speed ahead now," he said dismally, "we'll lose out with them...and I don't have the money to do the groundwork until this Allison Hill thing's cleared up."

"What money?" asked McGinnis. "Between the *Ulysses* and the land lab and the barge you've got all the basic equipment to start out with, I should think."

Ransome nodded impatiently. "Equipment, yes, but the old house has been going to seed for years. I can't invite these people here to leaky plumbing and blown fuses every time someone plugs in a shaver."

"You haven't been listening," the marine biologist reprimanded his friend. "What on earth do you think those two women have been doing there at Plantation House all this time?"

"Converting the place into a resort, I've been told," Ransome said sourly.

"Which is pretty much what you mean in the ways that count," McGinnis pointed out. "A difference of people, but the accommodations are the same. If it's plumbing and wiring you're worried about, I happen to know both systems have been redone and passed inspection."

Ransome interrupted, his voice growing testy. "Well, I can't do anything about it until they're out of there, and from the look of things that could be awhile. Under the circumstances I'm not about to rush them.''

McGinnis would not be deterred. ''You'll need an administrative staff at Plantation House to keep that end of the operation running smoothly,'' he continued. ''You're not going to want any part of that.''

''For God's sake, McGinnis,'' exploded Ransome, ''we'll cross that bridge when we come to it. The first order of business is to see that my cousin's widow gets relocated and reimbursed.''

''Maybe she doesn't need to be relocated,'' Doc said blandly. ''Maybe the two women could be persuaded to stay on and run Plantation House for the research center.''

''Why would I do that?'' Ransome asked, not bothering to hide his annoyance.

''It might be one way to lessen some of the obligation you feel toward Mrs. Hill,'' his friend explained. ''You could suggest they run Plantation House for your guests for whatever profit they can make out of it. You'd retain title, of course, and regularly write off an agreed amount of your indebtedness in lieu of rental they'd otherwise have to pay.''

Ransome eyed him thoughtfully, his first reaction a recognition that such an arrangement would mean unavoidable meetings with Allison Hill.

For a moment his mind was overwhelmed with memory of her from the previous night—the melting defiance in her eyes as his mouth came down to play upon hers; the firm mounds of her breasts, rising tumescent against his hands; the sensuous thrust of her hips in those provocative, water-soaked jeans; her scent; her voice; the ever-present crosscurrent of sexuality between them.

Filled with her image, he knew the sudden hot rise of desire and wondered how long he could be alone with this woman without taking her in his arms...a woman who was in love with the memory of her dead husband.

It would never work.

He shook his head to drive out the pervasive presence of the water nymph.

"No!" he thundered.

McGinnis blinked, clearly surprised and troubled by the violence of the response.

"Do as you like," he said shortly. "Are you going to let Canby break the good news?"

"Why not? She won't believe me. She doesn't believe anything I say."

Doc eyed him sternly. "You know, of course, that they've been sitting down there for days, expecting you to arrive with the sheriff to try to run them off—or at the very least show up with a restraining order of some kind."

"I guess I did come on a little strong at first," Ransome said, his voice uneasy. "Maybe I'd better go down this afternoon and do what I can to calm their fears. She may as well know I'm not doing anything until she's talked to Herb Canby. By then maybe I can figure what to do about the whole mess."

"Yeah? Well, what about Plantation House?"

Ransome grunted. "No reason they can't run their resort for the rest of the summer without interference from me. With the research center on the shelf I don't have a lot of use for the house myself. The mobile unit here has all the comforts of home. I don't have any good reason even to go down there."

"About the research center, Burke. I still think—"

"Forget it!" Ransome cut him off sharply. He turned and headed for the mobile, shutting the door behind him with a snap.

AT PLANTATION HOUSE Allison sat at the kitchen table, grumpily making lists, her bandaged ankle propped up on a footstool. Peg's anxious face suddenly appeared in the door.

"You wouldn't happen to know where the twins are, would you?" she asked.

"Hardly," replied Allison. "You need them for something?

Peg blinked rapidly, belying her surface calm. "We-ll, no. Not right this minute...but I could need them. You know how things go around here."

Under Allison's critical eye she backed down. "Well, to be perfectly truthful, Ally, I'm afraid they're up at the lagoon. That marine biologist—McGinnis—has got them all steamed up about scuba diving. He came down this morning to see if I'd let him teach them. I told him no! You don't think he would on the sly, do you?"

"Of course not!" Allison said. "He's not like that. He told me yesterday he wouldn't think of taking them on without your consent."

She looked at her friend's anxious face. "Don't worry, he's tough enough to withstand even Hoddy's and Max's wheedling." The sound of voices toward the front of the house turned her head in that direction. "There they are now."

"Where in the world have you two—" Peg began angrily as her sons burst into the room, but she got no further.

"Fireworks!" sang out Max.

"Nothing doing," his mother said firmly. "Too dangerous. Allison and I decided against it. Can't take a chance on some kid losing a hand or an eye."

"Not firecrackers, mom," explained Hoddy. "Fireworks. You know—showers and fountains of colored lights. The flag. Stuff like that."

"Sorry, guys," said Allison. "That's out, too. It costs too much. I've already checked it out in Savannah. In addition to their price, which is staggering, they're not something for a bunch of amateurs like us to fool around with."

The twins started to protest. "Not that I think you fellows couldn't handle it," Allison added quickly, "but it's still no go. We can't afford to hire an expert."

"Doc McGinnis is an expert," Hoddy insisted. "He bought tons of the stuff when they were in the Orient—rockets and Roman candles like they use in those big Fourth of July displays."

In a sudden burst of interest the two women looked at each other and then, with new eagerness, back at the twins.

"What makes you think he might like to share his treasures with us?" asked Allison cautiously.

"Because he said so," Hoddy replied. "It's kind of like a hobby. He'd like to put on a show. He used to shoot the stuff off the ship deck when they were at sea, but that's not the same. He says if you're interested he'll be down to talk about it later today."

"Of course we're interested!" said Allison.

"Well, what are you waiting for? Go tell him yes," urged their mother briskly, shooing her sons on their way. Her mind was clearly distracted from Allison's injury. Without a parting glance at her friend she followed the boys out the door, peppering them as they went with questions about the remarkable marine biologist and his extraordinary hobby.

Her job finished, Allison set her papers aside and stood up, determined to get on to more urgent matters before Peg reappeared on the scene with additional work to keep her shackled to the desk. She touched the bandaged foot to the floor cautiously and was pleased to find that, just as she'd thought, except for a certain tightness under the constraining bonds of elastic the ankle felt almost normal.

Even when she let her full weight rest on the foot it didn't actually hurt; there was merely a residual tenderness that warned her she was not yet ready for gymnastics. She walked gingerly across the carpeted library and on to the polished inlaid hardwood floor of the reception hall.

A slight sound from the drawing room beyond brought her head around guiltily as she collected her wits to do battle with Peg. To her astonishment, across the distance of the room she found herself looking into the bronzed face of Burke Ransome.

"Who let you in?" she demanded, remembering too late that Ransome undoubtedly felt no need to be let in by anybody. He'd made it unmistakably clear he considered the place his. For all she knew maybe it was, she admitted with a tremor of panic.

"And who let you up?" Ransome asked in return, moving toward her, a quizzical look on his face. "I thought I told your friend Mrs. Crewes to see that you stayed off that foot today."

"And who appointed you and my friend Mrs. Crewes to tell me when my foot's well enough to stand on," she asked crossly, but there was a new look in the luminous eyes that took the edge off her sharpness. The rancor she'd seen so clearly through most of their brief encounters was gone.

Far be it from me to stir up sleeping dogs, she thought wryly. "Thanks to you, it's practically well," she continued in a more amiable tone. "Anytime you want a testimonial I'd be glad to give you one."

Ransome responded with a grin. "Always glad for an opportunity to play doctor," he said. "I hate to spoil a compliment, but you didn't have a very bad sprain. Between your sneakers and the bottom of those skinny pants your ankle had nowhere to go but out—which is why it looked so ugly. Still, you'd be smart to stay off it the rest of the day. You'll have a fat ankle again before the day's over if you go frisking about like this."

"With twenty strangers arriving at Plantation House in four days there's no way I can sit around with my foot propped up," she protested. Then unexpectedly she found herself confiding anxiously, "You'd think that after all the time leading up to this opening we'd be ready. It's not as if it comes as a surprise. There are just too many last-minute things that have to be done and not enough of us here to do them."

"That's what the Crewes twins tell me," Ransome said. "I came down to see if we could help." He was watching her closely, as if uncertain how she would react. "We're waiting for some equipment to come, so we're pretty much at a standstill up at the lagoon until after the fourth. No reason we can't give you a hand."

Allison found herself completely unprepared for Ransome's overnight change of face. She received his offer with a look of surprise and suspicion she made no effort to disguise. "I hardly think—" she began, her voice sharp with distrust.

But Ransome broke in. "Wait!" he said. "Don't say anything until you hear me out. You and I have a problem about the island, but as you've already suggested, it might be better left for your attorney to clarify. It's my understanding he won't be available to you for consultation until sometime after the fourth.''

"That's right," Allison was obliged to agree.

The dark gold wings of his brows arched, and the broad mouth curved into a disarming smile.

"Then how about an interim cease-fire?"

"Frankly, Mr. Ransome, I find it hard to believe in this change of heart," Allison said bluntly, a full measure of honest skepticism in her voice.

"Let's not say 'change of heart'," he said quietly. "More accurately, my perspective has changed."

With a trace of the old bitterness creeping in he added, "Regardless of what you may have been led to believe, Mrs. Hill, I do not go around swindling people out of property that is rightfully theirs."

Gazing into the clear depths of the gray green eyes that held hers, Allison could almost believe him. Still she hesitated, unconvinced that this wasn't simply a new ploy to ease her out—though for the life of her she couldn't see how his gratuitous offer of help could serve him in any way.

At the same time she could see definite advantages to being on a friendly footing with this co-owner of the island if they were to work out a desirable division of the property in the end.

Ransome held out his hand.

"Is it a deal, Allison?"

As on the previous night, her pulse raced to hear

her given name on his lips. She hesitated a moment longer, looking earnestly for answers in the strong inscrutable face but finding no more than a certain sense of reassurance. A tentative smile from her brought a broad answering grin. On impulse Allison extended her hand, to have it swallowed up in the man's strong callused grip.

"It's a deal, Burke," she agreed.

CHAPTER SEVEN

EVEN IN ITS EARLIEST HEYDAY the old house could never have looked better, Allison thought with satisfaction the morning of the grand opening. The downstairs public rooms—reception hall, library, drawing room, dining room—were for the guests to use as if they were in their own homes. Here the faint tangy smell of lemon oil and rich perfume hung sweet and spicy on the air. Diligent polishing had enhanced the luster of the fine old hardwood, and huge bowls of island blossoms splashed color throughout the rooms. Under the loving hands of Effie and her crew the crystal and silver gleamed, and the darts of light the delicate prisms from the dining-room chandelier threw out were as brilliant as a cluster of stars. Upstairs the scents of lavender, freshly ironed linen and fragrant soaps pervaded every room.

The Plantation House fleet of surrey-topped electric carts, newly painted white with green cushions and fringe and manned by members of the island staff, lined up at the boat landing to meet the first load of guests arriving from the mainland by chartered launch. With two guests crowded in each cart the procession looked as festive as a carnival parade. The jaunty vehicles followed the oyster-shell path that skirted the two-acre slope of freshly cut lawn up to the broad veranda, where Allison and Peg waited to greet the arrivals in person.

Following the train of glistening white carts like an oversize caboose came the household jeep, laden with the guests' luggage. Hoddy and Max rode in full command, and between them sat a nubile teenager with long blond hair. Her bright blue eyes, round and clear as two glass marbles, peered out of a pretty, sun-tanned face.

"Oh-oh, here comes trouble," muttered Peg to Allison as her eyes moved down the line and came to rest on her sons and their passenger.

In the next moment the first cart unloaded its pair of passengers. They were greeted by the two women, then moved on to make room for the next couple. By the time the guests were all assembled on the veranda Peg was too occupied with welcoming them to comment further on what Allison took to be a hunch. Yet even she couldn't miss the new air of rivalry between the twins as the jeep came to a halt and they piled out on either side, all but falling over each other to help the young lady out.

The actual arrival of the guests seemed almost an anticlimax after the three days leading up to it. One crisis had seemed to follow another, ranging in gravity from petty annoyances such as a balky starter on the jeep to a threatened major disaster when the mainland market Allison had counted on to supply shellfish for the July 4 shore supper on the beach—the weekend's crowning event—backed out two days before the date.

Within the hour Burke Ransome had heard of it from the Crewes twins and was at Plantation House assuring Allison and Peg they had nothing to worry about. He'd already arranged for live oysters, mussels, shrimp and the likes to be flown down from Chesapeake Bay the next afternoon, and he and his crew had set out traps that would snare more blue crab than her crowd could ever consume at one sitting.

So it had gone—three days of unexpected emergencies that rose in crazy succession only to be met with a solution by someone. And often that someone turned out to be Burke.

With the guests off to their rooms to freshen up for juleps on the veranda Allison drew a deep contented sigh and gave silent thanks to the Bunkers, Peg and the boys, Doc McGinnis and the *Ulysses* crew... and Burke Ransome. And she would be forever grateful to the island people who had come in a continuing stream with wagonloads of vegetables and flowers and stayed to lend a hand wherever it was needed. How could she have brought Plantation House to this point without the warmhearted efforts and devotion of all these people?

Just where Burke Ransome fitted in the list was a mystery she had neither the wish nor the energy to pursue. She was only too glad they had put aside their differences for the time being, and in those past three days they had even occasionally found themselves working side by side.

In appreciation she and Peg had invited the marine biologist and Burke for cocktails and their opening-night dinner that evening. Allison was a bit surprised when they accepted, but she found herself looking forward to coming together with Burke for the first time in a purely social ambience.

The arrival of a small contingent of latecomers on the veranda brought her forward with a special cry of welcome for her friend Bob Birch—and a twinge of guilt as she realized she'd almost forgotten he was coming. As penance she lingered on, visiting with him a moment longer, leaving Peg and the boys to see the other five guests settled in.

Bob was a dear, she thought contritely—as solid as the Rock of Gibraltar. She genuinely liked him in spite of his arbitrary dismissal of the Plantation House venture as an exercise in foolishness. Nor had he offered any sympathy when he'd caught her by phone the afternoon of her blistering encounter with Ransome. She had been so shaken she'd foolishly confessed she'd just learned the island didn't completely belong to her.

"Best news I've heard all week!" was his exuberant reply. "Sell out your half to the cousin and come back to the real world." The recollection brought her an instant of pique.

"So this is the land of the lotus eaters," he said now with an indulgent chuckle. "What do you people do around here to remind you that you're alive?"

What had ever led her to imagine he was a dear, she thought crossly. She was saved from saying as much by the unexpected appearance of Burke Ransome, striding purposefully across the lawn toward the house.

Seeing her, he broke step for an instant, then came on up the broad veranda stairs. Allison struggled to regain her composure, momentarily lost at the sudden appearance of the tall, broad-shouldered figure. His strong, golden bronze face and sun-streaked hair made Bob Birch—a man of not unimpressive stature or appearance—seem somehow effete.

She met his eyes with a show of calm she was a long way from feeling as she undertook to introduce the two men. "This is Bob Birch, an old friend from New York who is one of our guests, and this is Burke Ransome, Bob."

They shook hands and eyed each other in easy appraisal.

"Ransome? Ah! You must be the cousin—half owner of Ransome's Cay, I understand," said Birch amiably. "I came down to wish Allison luck with her half."

"I'll just bet you did!" Allison couldn't resist saying with a trace of asperity. She regretted it at once as Birch reached out and laid a possessive hand on her arm.

"Right! I lied," he said with an unabashed smile. "The truth is, Ransome, I came down to persuade the lady to give up all this nonsense and marry me. How'd you like to buy the rest of the island?"

Allison felt the white heat of anger burn her face, but before she could find words for her fury Burke smoothly intervened. "Sorry, Birch, but Mrs. Hill and I have agreed to let her lawyer handle property discussions," he said in a voice that closed the subject. "As for the other...well, may I wish you the best of luck?"

For an instant Allison stared at the two men, until she realized with a strange sensation that she was standing before them with her mouth agape.

Burke's sardonic voice filled the growing silence. "You'll excuse me, I hope. I didn't realize I was interrupting a tête-à-tête." He directed his words to her, then gave a nod to the faded jeans and work-stained T-shirt he wore. "I came to borrow the jeep. McGinnis took my transportation, and if I'm to get to the lagoon to clean up and be back here in time for dinner, I'll need wheels."

Finding her voice at last, Allison said weakly, "By all means take the jeep. I'm sure Hoddy left the keys in it."

With a feeling of helplessness she watched him go. She was at a loss to correct the false impression he took with him and troubled to find how much the misunderstanding disturbed her.

He left with a light-footed grace, easy yet at the

same time suggesting a lithe sinewy power at the moment only subtly revealed. Down the steps he went to vault over the side of the jeep, which sat where Hoddy had left it when he unloaded the guests' baggage earlier.

A second later the engine growled to life, and in a moment Burke headed off in the jeep, up the oystershell path toward the lagoon.

AS FAR AS THE MECHANICS of the affair were concerned, the opening-night festivities were progressing as planned, Allison tried to reassure herself.

The moment had come for her to leave the dinner table and lead the guests to the drawing room for coffee before the party adjourned to the veranda for dancing and an impromptu show by the Ransome's Cay jazz band. But she lingered a moment, trying to pinpoint exactly what was wrong.

Certainly not the food. The glazed, clove-studded ham, home-cured in Bunker's smokehouse and elegantly presented on a Sheffield platter by Effie, who had spent three days applying her own brand of culinary magic to it, had been consumed with gusto and compliments to the chef. Likewise Effie's corn fritters and pecan pie. The juleps, prepared by the admirable Bunker for the cocktail hour, had elicited paeans of praise. Yet pleasing as they were in their frost-coated silver tumblers, sprouting bouquets of fresh mint, they hadn't prevented the guests from standing around in isolated little clots. It was almost as if the people conspired to resist her efforts to get them to mingle.

"Looks like a pretty mixed bag you have here," Burke's ironic voice came to her quietly from behind as she rose and moved into the dining room. She glanced up over her shoulder to meet the gray green eyes, which looked even more deeply iridescent than she'd remembered.

"I wouldn't say that," Allison replied stiffly. His words upset her partly because he voiced her own growing concern that this very "mixed bag" would spell the downfall of the house-party ambience she'd hoped to create. But she felt even more disturbed because she knew intuitively that he derived some mysterious satisfaction from the way things stood at the moment.

In the drawing room she looked around her with a feeling of dismay at the twenty-six people assembled there and accepted the fact that for the most part they were strangers who stubbornly intended to keep it that way.

If the couple in the far corner of the room, owners of a chain of jazz-exercise salons, had anything in common with the neurosurgeon and his wife, none of them wanted to find out about it. The same held true for the electronics executive, the bank officer, the city manager, the owner of the auto agency and their respective spouses. Once they had exhausted their meager stores of small talk these people had nothing they cared to share.

Not so! she told herself in sudden inspiration. They all had one thing in common: they'd chosen to come to Ransome's Cay.

"Oh, Burke," she spoke out suddenly above the lagging conversation. She moved across the room toward Burke, who stood talking to the parents of the blond teenager with the round blue eyes.

The lightly brocaded sea-foam silk of her cocktail dress moved softly as she walked, sending out provocative hints of the curves it concealed. Allison was not unaware of the effect. Deliberately she created the unexpected diversion on the stagnating scene. Burke's eyes met hers in surprise, taking on a certain wariness as she came. She made sure her words could be heard by all.

"I've been meaning to ask you about the marvelous story I've been told of how your family happened to acquire Ransome's Cay," she said. "I've been afraid the story is much too good to be true." She knew she'd won the attention of everyone in the room. There was no longer any need to raise her voice.

Astonishment was mirrored in Burke's face, but she saw it quickly change to a look of amused understanding.

"Indeed it is true," he assured her. "The winning hand is preserved in the family archives. Remind me to show it to you sometime," he added, turning back to his conversation as if that ended the matter.

"Tell them about it, Burke," prompted McGinnis

from across the room where he'd been talking with Peg.

"Come on, Ransome. Tell us," one of the guests pushed. "You can't leave us up in the air after a teaser like that."

Burke responded with a smile and a modest shake of his head, but his listeners were hooked. When they persisted, he stilled the clamor with a brisk witty account of how the first Ransome won the cay on a poker hand.

It was as easy as that, marveled Allison at the unexpected teamwork between them. She felt a new and thrilling headiness in this suddenly discovered rapport and was at the same time a trifle bemused at the careless elegance of the man beside her in the flawlessly tailored raw-silk suit and pongee shirt.

There was a new congenial spirit in the room. Strangers, united in their eagerness to hear more, lost their diffidence with one another in the shared pleasure of island lore narrated in an amiable baritone with grace and skill.

How could she ever have thought this vital articulate man might look on Ransome's Cay as a plaything to be tossed aside, Allison mused. How arrogant of her to imagine she was the only one who really loved the place. To hear him speak of his childhood home was to understand he loved every knob of sand big enough to hold a few clumps of palmettos—not just Ransome's Cay but all the other islands off the coast of South Carolina and Georgia that made up the historic Golden Isles.

Allison listened in fascination as he captured his listeners and carried them along on the tide of his words, rolling the names of islands off his tongue like a litany: Rockedundy, Ossabaw, Hog Hammock, Wahoo, Hush-Your-Mouth, Little Egg. . . .

He loved the sound and feel of every one of them, she thought, caught in the music of Burke's voice as he explained how the islands were strung like jewels on a chain along the Intracoastal Waterway. Some were still primitive and untouched, their virgin subtropical forests populated mainly by deer and wild turkeys and razorback boars, their ponds and marshes the dominion of alligators; others, like Sea Island and Hilton Head, had been developed into settings of fabulous opulence; still others, once the private playlands of the very rich, had been turned into public parks to be enjoyed by everyone.

"One of Georgia's finest state parks, one of the few connected to the mainland by bridge, making it easily accessible, is Jekyll Island," he said. "In the twenties it was one of the most exclusive clubs in America. Membership was limited to a hundred families, among them the Rockefellers, Astors, Morgans and Vanderbilts. A fifth of the world's total wealth was said to be in the hands of the Jekyll Island crowd in those days before the crash."

Unexpectedly from a window-seat alcove where the twins had been indulging in sibling rivalry for the attention of the precocious blond girl, Hoddy Crewes spoke up.

"Hey, Burke, what about the pirates?" he asked eagerly, abandoning the girl to his brother and leaving the window seat to come closer to Ransome. "Some of the island folks say old Blackbeard used to duck in and out of our coves when things got too hot for him in the West Indies."

"Who knows for sure after two hundred years?" replied Burke. For the benefit of the guests he went on. "Blackbeard was one of the most notorious and colorful of the prerevolutionary privateers. An Englishman whose real name was Edward Teach, he claimed to be the devil's brother. According to legend he braided his beard in pigtails tied with red ribbons and wore a hatband lined with hemp matches. He'd light them whenever he wanted to appear in a cloud of smoke to convince a disbeliever. He's supposed to have buried a cask of treasures on Blackbeard Island to the north of here."

"You mean nobody's ever found it?" It was Max Crewes who spoke this time. With a sudden show of interest he left the young temptress at the window seat to join his brother and the rest of the party gathered around Ransome.

"The island was turned into a wildlife sanctuary in the twenties, so the old rascal's secret, if there is one, has been protected for the past fifty years," Burke told him. The twins exchanged looks of disappointment and were about to race each other back to the window seat and the girl when his next words held them back.

"Take heart, men," he advised. "Ransome's Cay is said to have some of the booty hidden here. There's a treasure map of the island hanging on the library wall that's supposed to be the original, if someone ever wants to decipher it."

"Hey! How about that!" Hoddy burst out excitedly.

"Every now and then Bunker runs across mainlanders here looking for treasure. He lets them have their fun as long as they don't make pests of themselves."

"You mean it's okay for us to look for it?" asked Max.

"Why not," said Burke. "I used to search for it myself. Anyone who wants to go treasure hunting, be my guest."

With that sentence he destroyed the warm sense of partnership that had sustained Allison from the moment he'd picked up on her cue with his reassuring grin.

"Be my guest," indeed! With the proprietary "my" Ransome had skillfully, purposefully, dealt her out, and it left her feeling unexpectedly let down and hurt.

From the veranda came the first strains of the jazz band, led by Jimmer Bunker in a lively disco number. Hoddy and Max, competitors once more, broke away from the circle of listeners and jostled each other back to the full-bosomed, pouty-mouthed girl who still perched on the window seat.

In the general exodus toward the music Allison found herself once more in the company of Bob Birch. She remembered she still hadn't set him straight on how she felt about him and his gratuitous interference in her affairs at Plantation House.

"What do you mean asking Burke Ransome if he'd like to buy my share of Ransome's Cay?" she'd said indignantly that afternoon after Ransome was gone. But she had got no further. Effie had come panting to find her with a minor emergency that required her immediate attention; on her heels had come Peg, to take over and show Birch to his room. Allison hadn't had a moment until just then to think of it. In the interim her annoyance had cooled.

Birch approached her at that second with an apologetic smile. "If I was out of line this afternoon, it wasn't because I was trying to interfere in something that's none of my business," he said.

"It doesn't matter," she replied without rancor. "I have no intention of selling in any case."

Birch eyed her curiously for a moment. At the far end of the broad veranda the band continued with the disco beat, interpreted by the dancers with fervor and varying degrees of skill.

"Look, Ally, is there someplace we can talk?"

Allison was suddenly very tired. It had taken a bit of doing, but the evening was a success. It could go on without her while she gave an old friend a few minutes of undivided attention. It was time to get things cleared up with Bob before he made any more embarrassing assumptions.

With a nod she led the way, walking quietly from the teeming veranda to a small, wicker-furnished screen porch off the morning room. There she took a seat on the sofa and slipped out of the thin-strapped, high-heeled sandals she wore. With a sigh she raised her unshod feet to rest on the cocktail table as Birch sat down next to her.

"It's been a day!" she said wearily.

Birch seized his advantage. "Well, my dear," he said, "don't forget it's only the first of many if you expect to go on with this place." He looked at her intently. "I wasn't kidding when I told Ransome I came down here to ask you to marry me. I did, believe me. It's not an impetuous thing. I've been thinking about it for some time."

Allison reached over and took his hand as if to soften what she was about to say. "You've been a wonderful friend, Bob, and I hope you will continue to be after I say I can't marry you. I can't, you know. I don't believe in marriage without love any more than I believe in loveless sex, and we've already been through that."

"That's for sure," groaned Birch, "every time I've tried to make love to you! I thought you were holding out for a wedding band."

"Hardly," she said wryly. "I'm terribly fond of you, Bob, but that's not enough. I've never pretended I love you, and it wouldn't be fair to let you think

I might fall in love with you in time. I was madly in love once when I was very young. It's not likely to happen again.''

Birch looked at her bleakly. "Excuse me if this sounds blunt, but I think I have a right to know," he said. "Is it the late Mr. Hill who stands in your way?"

It was on the tip of her tongue to make a flat denial when she realized for the first time that what he'd said was true, though not in the sense she'd first taken it.

Tyler had indeed left her wary of marriage. Young, naive, blind to what lay under the handsome captivating facade, she'd trusted him and been betrayed.

Was it because of Ty's betrayal that she tended to hold every attractive man at bay?

Had she let Tyler brand her with a distrust that could so profoundly affect her life?

"Oh, Bob, I'm sorry... you're right, of course," she told him, her sadness clearly reflected in her voice.

Birch rose to his feet and reached down to take her two hands. He pulled her up from the sofa until she stood before him. "I may as well go," he said regretfully. He bent and kissed her lightly on the forehead. "Maybe you'll look me up if you ever come back to Manhattan. If you'll excuse me now, I think I'll take a walk before I go to bed."

As he stepped quickly off into the darkness, Allison knew he would not stay after this night. She was sorry. Dear Bob! He had earned her eternal gratitude for pointing out the way Tyler had warped her viewpoint toward men—particularly attractive men.

Well, no more. She was not going to let the late Tyler Hill distort her relationships with men for the rest of her life.

With a sigh she leaned down and picked up the gray kid sandals. She was debating whether to desert the party and take her depressing thoughts to bed when a tall figure appeared silhouetted in the doorway of the dimly lighted morning room and stepped forward to detain her.

It was Burke Ransome. Though she could not see him clearly in the faint light of the open door, she would know his voice anywhere even in pitch-dark.

"I listened to your conversation with Birch," he said, his tone as aloof and formal as if they had never met.

"You...*what*?" gasped Allison.

"I listened," he repeated flatly. "I was looking for you to dance. I heard him ask you to marry him. I wanted to hear what you would say."

"You heard?"

"Every word." His voice was strained.

She attacked with fury. "And now that you've heard you have the unmitigated gall to come in and tell me you're sorry."

"Not at all. I can hardly say I'm sorry," Ransome said distantly. "I found out what I wanted to know. If you'll excuse me, I'll say good-night."

"Wait, Burke!" she cried out to detain him. "What's that supposed to mean?"

But he walked out the screen door of the porch as Birch had done a moment earlier and vanished in the darkness. A minute later she heard his noisy departure in the jeep.

A feeling of sickness rose in her. Everything had been going so well between them. There had been those few brief moments of closeness at the cocktail party—and all the help he'd volunteered during the past week. She'd let herself begin to think they might after all share the island in peace.

And now to have it all blow up in her face!

She felt bewildered and let down. After such hard-won harmony she couldn't imagine what Burke had read into her conversation with Bob Birch that would turn him back into the remote stranger she'd known in the beginning.

CHAPTER EIGHT

WHEN ALLISON LOOKED OUT next morning the jeep had been returned to the back door. Even Effie, who came to work each day with the morning dove, hadn't arrived yet. The vehicle's almost surreptitious return struck Allison as an ominous sign that Burke Ransome had washed his hands of the whole operation.

As morning waned and he failed to appear a new uneasiness beset her. What about the shellfish for the evening's Fourth of July supper—the most ambitious undertaking of the weekend and the one on which Plantation House's opening would succeed or fail? Suppose, in light of whatever he'd taken the overheard conversation to mean Burke had decided to renege on his promise to supply the fish?

"If Mr. Burke said he'd be here with that shellfish, honey, all you got to worry about is getting the cooking pit ready and making sure it's steaming on time," Effie scoffed, refusing to entertain such a thought. The other woman's unblinking trust caused Allison to regret she had given voice to her fears.

By the time people from the island began drifting

onto the beachfront in the late afternoon she still hadn't heard from Burke. Nor had she seen any sign of the shellfish that was to feed the crowd.

What on earth would they give all these people to eat, she fretted silently as she welcomed each new-coming group with the warmth of an old friend and a smile that masked her inner distress.

They came from all directions of the cay, these island folk; the entire population numbered perhaps seventy-five in all, from the newest-born baby, a boy of six weeks, to 102-year-old Miz Dade Pike, who spoke only the Gullah dialect she'd learned as a child. It was Miz Dade's grandmother who had saved the Ransome family sterling by burying it under her cabin floor during the Civil War.

Some families had lived on the island for more than two hundred years. They were descendants of early Timucuaan Indians, Anglo-Saxons, Gallics, Latins and African Blacks who had lived on Ransome's Cay rent free since the boll weevil had put an end to the island's cotton fields and a now long-dead Ransome had given up the struggle to support Plantation House on its own grounds and started a milling operation on the mainland.

This day marked the return of the last of their young to the island from factory jobs up north. The jubila-tion that spilled over as the community was reunited brought a lump to Allison's throat. In spite of her worry of the moment she felt a warmth of gratitude to Burke, who had given the island back to its young.

Before she knew what was happening, the Bunkers had organized everyone into task forces to take over presupper chores. While children frolicked at the water's edge, the adults began setting up long picnic tables on the lawn where it met the sand. Others broke ground for a pit they lined with seaweed gathered by the older children. When the pit was dug, they poured in tinder-dry chunks of hardwood and fired it to create a bed of heat that would later be covered with more seaweed when the shellfish was ready to steam. Meanwhile careful hands went over wheelbarrow loads of freshly picked corn, looking for spoilers, removing silks and recovering each ear with the peeled-back husks.

The beach was suddenly alive with their voices and laughter and the rhythm of island songs they sang as they worked, songs they'd sung together for five generations in their homes and in the island's one-room schoolhouse, which also served as their church.

The auto salesman and his wife left their croquet game and started down the gentle slope from house to beach. They were followed shortly by other Plantation House guests in twos and threes and fours, drawn as if by a magnet to the heart of the festivities. Guests were quickly and for the most part willingly pressed into service.

The doctor and the man from the exercise salon manned a keg of beer and took turns making certain no thirst went unslaked. The banker's wife helped ready the tables. The auto salesman and the banker began to set up chairs.

As the shadows lengthened and the sun became no more than a filtered brightness through the trees, Allison's eyes moved anxiously up the broad expanse of lawn to the great pillared house, where the flag rode high above the rooftop in the late-afternoon breeze. Soon it would be time for Bunker to perform his sundown ritual of lowering the flag.

And still no Burke!

She decided grimly that it was time to give some thought to a backup menu to forestall the impending crisis, and her eyes searched the crowd for Effie and Peg. The sound of a motor caught her ears above the cheerful pandemonium around her, and she raised her head.

A moment later a small pickup truck manned by Burke, with Doc beside him, nosed out of the woods to the north and rambled down the oyster-shell road to the gathering on the beach. Allison ran to meet them, her worry turning to relief then anger as she gauged with her eyes where they would stop. She was waiting for Burke when he stepped down.

"Well, you took your time about getting here, I must say!" she said, her voice low, to reach only his ears.

"Sorry. You should have told me you wanted it early," he said blandly. "I was thinking of the island folks. They'd rather have their shellfish fresh than early."

For a moment the sea-colored eyes dared her to argue the point. He walked around her and joined Doc at the rear of the pickup, where a dozen eager hands waited to help unload the huge containers of oysters and clams brought in by plane to the lagoon from Chesapeake Bay less than twenty minutes earlier.

Allison stood by uncomfortably, waiting for an opportunity to apologize for her hasty words. She watched Burke hand down the last heavy container and stepped toward him, her pulse unexpectedly fast. But before she could form the words the moment was lost.

A broad grin on his face, Burke raised his hands to the crowd and held up a gaudy gilt medal shaped like an oyster shell and hung on a flag-striped ribbon.

"Ladies and gentlemen," he called out when he had their attention, "I have here in my hand a genuine imitation-gold, oyster-shell medal. On it are engraved the woods *Champion Shucker*. This beautiful bauble is to go to the lucky person who can shuck the most oysters in the time it takes McGinnis and me to bring a load of shrimp and crab from the lagoon."

In the uproar his words created Burke and McGinnis were off in a spray of sand.

The ancient, nimble-fingered Miz Dade was the contest winner when the truck returned. She cackled with delight as Burke gave her a resounding kiss on each leathery cheek and pinned the award to her bright cotton dress. The crowd applauded with enthusiasm.

True to his word, Burke had brought shellfish in an abundance unlike anything Allison had ever seen. The generosity of the supply added an even deeper dimension to her shame.

There were washtubs of blue crab, shrimp and mussels, as well as lobsters flown in live that morning from Maine. In the seaweed-lined sand pit they were cooked with the corn to delicate succulent perfection, then served with Effie's special coleslaw and corn-bread, dripping with island-churned butter. All this was washed down with an ample supply of white wine and beer. The meal was topped off with fresh strawberry shortcake, made southern-style and served with clotted cream.

While the guests gave full attention to the table, Doc's men anchored the fireworks barge in full view of Plantation House. By the time the fireflies began to flicker in the early darkness the supper mess had been cleared away and the overstuffed guests had struggled up the gentle slope from the beach and found seats on the springy turf to watch the fire-works.

Doc's show opened with a teeth-rattling boom from offshore that filled the sky with a spectacular fountain of colored fire. It closed forty-five minutes later with a grand finale that included a recogniz-able facsimile of Plantation House in sparkling light against the darkness and a backdrop of shooting stars.

The show over, tree lights flickered on around the

lawn. In the next moment the first strains of a calypso beat came down from the veranda in a clear invitation from the island band for the crowd to move up to the house. Many of the island people stayed to dance. Others gathered up their children and said their goodbyes. In no time the scene of the festivities was deserted as the last stragglers strolled up to join the dancing already in full swing.

Allison was one of the last to go, her eyes searching for Burke among the few who still remained at the dimly lighted scene. She was discouraged to think how little she'd profited from the moment of self-revelation in her last conversation with Bob Birch. Hadn't Burke done what he'd promised to do? He'd never told her to expect an hourly progress report. Yet she seemed almost to jump at the chance to mistrust him when she heard nothing from him all day.

She had an almost obsessive need to clear the air with an apology and felt doubly frustrated she'd missed him. Giving up, she started up the slope toward the house barefoot, her sandals in one hand. Her tired feet took comfort from the coolness of the grass, but her malaise was more of the spirit than the body.

Spotlighted under each tree as she passed, she moved moodily toward the lights and sounds of the house, wondering how she could right matters with Burke...wondering even more why it mattered so much to her that she should.

But it did matter. And the problem was it was

growing daily to matter more and more. Her whole conception of Ransome had changed since that first night she'd confronted him at the foot of the Plantation House stairs. It seemed aeons ago. It was hard to believe this man she admired, respected—*yes, admit it, Allison*—to whom she was attracted deeply in every way, was that same Burke Ransome.

The climate between them had changed drastically the day he'd volunteered to wait until she could talk to Herb Canby to settle their differences about the island. They awakened to each other in a new manner when they put their Ransome's Cay quarrel on hold.

It became clear to her then that he could no more set out to seize something he didn't think was rightfully his than she could herself. She understood then that he was under some horrendous misapprehension about the island that only Herb Canby could set straight.

The understanding was followed immediately by a sudden fear of what it might do to the delicate balance of their relationship when Burke learned the truth. Would he turn away from her completely once he knew, seeing in her nothing but a bitter reminder of what he'd been obliged to give up?

She keened for the loss of something she couldn't name. Nothing she could pin down...more like the promise of something.

Burke, a voice within her cried out in desperation. *Oh, Burke, what's to become of us?*

Within a few yards of the lighted house she turned

aside and drifted into the near shadows to a storm-damaged live-oak tree with a low limb tortured into a natural seat. There she could watch the dancers on the veranda unobserved.

A small breeze from off the ocean flirted with her white cotton skirt as she hoisted herself up the trunk. She sat letting her bare feet and legs swing freely in the caressing breeze, savoring its kiss on her arms, neck and shoulders, left bare by the low-cut sleeveless white cotton shirt she wore.

She rested there, watching for Burke among the dancers on the lighted veranda across the lawn. There was Doc McGinnis, dancing with Peg, and the twins, competing for the attentions of the lissome blonde. But there was no sign of Ransome. He had gone, it appeared, without even bothering to say goodbye.

She leaned her head against the rough bark of the tree and closed her eyes, giving in to a feeling of defeat.

What could she have said if she'd found him, she asked herself hopelessly. As clearly as if she'd told him in so many words, she'd demonstrated one more time how much she mistrusted him. It was a hard thing to forgive.

"What the devil..." she heard a voice mutter tentatively from out of the near darkness. Her eyes flew open to see Burke coming through the shadows toward her.

"What are you doing up there?" the man asked

curiously. "You look like a great moon moth clinging to that tree."

Allison slid down from her perch and stood before him, bracing herself to offer the apology she knew was his due. "I looked for you," she said. "I was afraid you'd gone back to the lagoon."

"Just seeing an old girl friend home," Burke said, and she was dismayed at the quick stab of pain his words brought her—and the immediate relief she felt at his next remark.

"Miz Dade's a bit old to be out in the woods afoot this time of night," he continued. "I took one of the electric carts and chauffeured her home." Though he grinned, there was no real brightness in his face. "You were looking for me?"

"Yes," she said. "I want to thank you for what you've done for us here at Plantation House this weekend and to apologize for what I said to you when you brought all that beautiful shellfish." She spoke quickly, to ensure she would say all she wanted to before her nerve failed her. "I don't know what we would have done without you and Doc. What I said was inexcusable, and I'm sorry. You see I...."

She hesitated, not sure how to go on, then decided finally that she must talk to him candidly about Tyler. So far she had confided in no one but Peg.

She wanted suddenly to tell Burke that since Ty had made such a practice of disappointing people, maybe she'd grown to expect it.

After a moment she continued. "I was in a kind of

panic that you had let us down. You see, Tyler—"

An abrupt explosion of bitterness from Burke cut her off. "Don't tell me what my cousin said about me! You don't expect me to listen to the calumnies he's heaped on my head, I hope. I won't hear them, least of all from the lips of the woman who makes a monument to his depravity by taking anything the bastard said as gospel truth!"

"Now you wait just a minute!" Allison broke in, her heart pounding from anger at the injustice of his words.

But Burke was not to be stopped. "How can you imagine yourself still in love with Tyler Hill and keep any self-respect?" he demanded. "This posthumous devotion to someone who never did a thing in his lifetime that was anything but self-serving and irresponsible is sick. He was a liar and a cheat. You know that! You fell in love with an unprincipled scoundrel. Deny that, Allison Hill! The fact that he's now dead doesn't change the truth."

She stared at him in stunned disbelief. Was he trying to force her to say she'd never been in love with Ty? She'd been young and lacking in judgment, but to say she hadn't been in love with him once would be an out-and-out lie.

A sudden sickening chill shot through her. Suppose she admitted her real feelings about his cousin to him. Would he then say that since she hadn't loved Tyler from early on in their marriage she should in decency turn down any inheritance he'd left her?

It was in fact what she might actually have done, if Ty hadn't squandered so much of the money her parents had left her. For a moment she had a fleeting notion to tell Burke exactly why she found it so hard to trust a Ransome. Then she drew back. To admit how badly she'd let herself be gulled by Tyler was a humiliation she was not at the moment prepared to acknowledge to this man.

She was suddenly furious at Burke for trying to put her through this third degree.

"I can't see how I feel about Tyler now—or how I felt about him at any time—is any concern of yours," she said in a controlled voice, determined to bring an end to a conversation that grew ever more painful. She turned away, but his hand shot out and grabbed her.

"Wait!" he said, his hands lightly encasing her upper arms.

She might have pulled away but for a new troubled, almost desperate note she heard in his voice. She let his hands guide her back so they faced each other again.

"I have to know," he persisted doggedly. "How can you still love a man after what he did to you with that will?"

So it's the will, thought Allison dully. *It's still a case of who gets what. That's all he really cares about.*

"All right, so he exaggerated—only half the island was his!" she shot back defiantly. "But what he owned he left to me in a perfectly legal witnessed will.''

''That's where you're wrong again, my fair lady,'' Burke said scathingly, letting his full bitterness and frustration burst through. ''Tyler didn't own one pebble on a Ransome's Cay beach at the time of his death.''

''And you have the nerve to call Tyler a liar and a cheat!'' she retorted angrily.

The grip on her arms tightened as if in reflex, and for a moment Allison had a wild notion he was about to shake her.

''It so happens Tyler sold out to me years ago.''

For a moment Allison felt as if she'd been struck. It couldn't be. . . it mustn't be true. ''I don't believe you,'' she cried, her tongue catching on the words.

''Oh, God,'' groaned Burke. In the quick step she took away from him she stumbled. Reaching out involuntarily to steady her, he enfolded her in his arms and drew her to him. He buried his face in her hair. ''Forgive me. I saw red. That's the last thing I intended to say.''

She made no effort to pull away, but stayed quiescent against him. So staggered was she by the shock of his words she feared he could feel the trembling in the stillness of her body. Yet she had no will to free herself from his hold.

It was true what he said, of course. Even as she had burst out in denial the overwhelming truth of it had seeped through. Ty had sold his half of the island to Burke when she left him and cut off his funds.

Why hadn't she thought of it when Burke had first challenged her claim? It was so like Ty. It was the only thing that made sense.

Stunned by the suddenness of her loss, she hardly noticed when Burke stepped back and rested his length against the huge old oak, carrying her with him. Unresponsive, she lay against him, her head upon his chest, her arms hanging listless at her sides, while his loosely encircled her.

She'd lost everything that really mattered. What was she to do, she wondered dully. And because she couldn't bear to face her loss she shied away. She'd think about it tomorrow. No, not even tomorrow. Let Herb Canby do the thinking. Let Herb discover the truth when he came back the following week and opened the will to probate. He could explain the mess he'd got her into. It would serve him right.

A new thought burst suddenly on her distraight mind—one she'd completely overlooked in her state of shock. She'd called Burke a liar and a cheat. Every caustic word, every accusation she'd ever flung at him, came rolling back across her mind to destroy the rich feeling of relief that had engulfed her when she first realized he had never lied to her at any time.

Dear God! she cried inwardly. "Burke..." she said aloud out of her torment.

"Don't say it," he stopped her, clearly thinking

she was about to continue her attack on him, interrupted a moment ago. "We made a deal not to discuss ownership of the island and I broke it. How can I make you believe I'd give practically anything to take back what I said...to restore the harmony between us?"

The words seemed wrenched from him. She heard in them a sound of pain to match her own. In his loose embrace she slipped her arms up from her sides and around his waist, hugging her body to his, fiercely comforting him. His arms tightened in response, and in the silence she heard the fast hard rhythm of his heart next to her ear, felt the quick whisper of his breath stir her hair. In the poignancy of the moment tears welled in her eyes and rolled down her cheeks unchecked.

Supported by the ancient live-oak, they clung together almost sorrowfully, resting in separate private pain.

From where her head lay in the open vee of his shirt Allison grew gradually conscious of the heat of his body through the thin layers of clothing that separated them, and her forgetful flesh quickened. The matting of bronzed hair that sprang from his chest teased her cheek. She breathed deeply, filling herself with his heady male scent.

She was suddenly vitally aware of the slight play of muscles across the hard surface of his chest and abdomen. They sent a delicious shiver racing through her that erased all thought for anything but the sweetly exquisite, hungerlike pain deep inside that made her forget the pain of loss.

She felt the weight of his head lift from hers and raised her own in response. In the eerie half-light she saw that he was gazing down into her face. He reached to trace the line of her cheek with a forefinger, then stopped when he felt the moisture of tears clinging there. In a gesture as moving as it was awkward, he dabbed clumsily at the wetness, then drew his finger to press lightly up on the tip of her chin until her eyes were in line with his.

"Don't cry," he said brusquely. "There's no need for tears. You'll come out all right on this island thing, I promise you. I intend to see you get back everything you put into the old house and are reimbursed insofar as possible for whatever Tyler cost you in material terms."

She wished desperately to tell him her tears were for reasons far more complex than the loss of an island, but before she could find the words to begin, a groan of frustration came from the man.

"But what good are my promises? You don't believe a damn thing I've said!"

Her throat was so filled with sorrow for the injustice she had done him she could find no words of comfort and regret to express what overflowed from her heart.

At the same time the tactile surfaces of her hands against his hard muscular chest were suddenly attuned to the strong driving force of his body. As if by a will of their own her hands ventured down across the flat plane of his stomach, her fingertips tingling to the feel of the muscled firmness under his shirt.

With the first movement of her hands an involuntary shudder passed through the man's body and brought a suppressed cry from his throat. "Oh, lady," he said as if the words had been wrung from deep within, "I thought I could stay away, but there's no way. I'm obsessed with you."

In a gesture almost of comfort her hands ceased their wandering and lifted to pull his head down to hers. The strong sensuous mouth took control, almost unwillingly it seemed. His lips covered hers with a sudden eagerness that sent waves of yearning rushing through her body's secret coves. Whatever resistance lay harbored there was washed away, and with it all rational thought.

Against her lips he whispered words of half-coherent foolishness: "Moon moth...sea sprite... loveliest creature." She tasted their sound.

A tremor shot through her as the wide beautiful mouth covered hers in a seeking, seemingly endless communion with her own hungry mouth. Then a firm hand found its way inside her low-cut blouse and fumbled impatiently until it gained entry beneath the bounds of her scanty lace bra. Her breasts grew taut against the pleasant roughness, and a small cry of rapture escaped her as his fingers reached their goal and gently teased the small firm erection eagerly awaiting his touch. Her own hands played restlessly across his back, seeking access to the sinewy body denied her by the shirt tucked snugly into his belt.

The sound of voices and laughter breaking away from the veranda brought them reluctantly back to reality. There was no privacy in the spot where they stood.

"Come," Burke murmured hoarsely, knowing exactly where he was about to lead her. Wanting him with an intensity she had never felt before, Allison yielded to the strong arm that circled her waist. Moving as one, they slipped into the woods, where moss-hung trees and a screen of verdant undergrowth hid them from prying eyes. There a small fairy ring of ankle-high blue grass and sweet-smelling mint awaited them.

A thick melon slice of a moon directly overhead bathed the sylvan chamber in a pale golden light that let them see each other yet lent an air of magic to the scene.

In the circle of enchantment he began to undress her. The two beings who made up the person of Allison Hill locked for one last time in an agonizing struggle for control. The rational, clear-eyed Allison who had taken over after the debacle of her marriage to Ty warned her to pull away, but she waited a moment too long to obey.

The subtle seduction of her undressing moved on, and as Burke discarded first her shirt and bra, pausing to pay homage to each breast and bury his face in the valley between, good judgment went down to defeat.

In a single swift movement of his hands he slid the full white-cotton skirt and her lacy pants down over the swell of her hips; his mouth found and his tongue explored the convoluted dimple in the flat plane of her stomach.

A quick gasp of rapture escaped her lips. She was lost. Her own hands reached to encircle him and tug impatiently at his shirt until they found a way under. With the first touch of her fingers upon the hard sinewy satin of his naked torso an electric charge raced through her. She fumbled helplessly at his belt until he came to her aid. In the next moment they stood undressed before each other in the center of the magic circle.

Allison drew in her breath, so hypnotized by the beauty of the splendid body she could not tear her eyes away until Burke took her into his arms and carried her down with him to lie on the bed of blue grass at their feet.

"Allison, enchantress of Buttonhook Cove!" he exclaimed softly. "You're even more bewitching than I imagined that first day."

His naked body half resting on hers, he lowered his slightly rough-textured face down to be smothered between the soft firm mounds of her breasts.

Breathing heavily, he raised his face for a moment. "I can't get enough of you, woman," he said hoarsely. His words were broken off as he shaped his mouth around the curve of her breast, the hard edge of his teeth encompassing it lightly.

Unknowing, Allison held her breath, as if to breathe might break the spell, and gave herself to the seductive play of tongue on flesh that sent sparkling shafts of pleasure through her until she gasped aloud from delight. At the same time she became subtly aware of his work-roughened hands moving with a velvet touch down across her stomach to where the silken triangle peaked.

She waited, her whole being inwardly aquiver as his fingers moved on and found the touchstone within. With a rhythm that matched her beating heart he caressed her gently at first, then more firmly, until a deep cry of rapture escaped her throat. Suddenly the exquisite anticipation became more than she could bear. With a new urgency she reached out and encompassed the male hardness that mirrored her own desire, guiding him to her, murmuring soft expressions of rapture at his first tentative thrusts. When he plunged to the very core of her being, she heard herself cry his name aloud.

Lost to everything but the sweep of their passion, they lay together afterward, panting softly. Their urgency for the moment spent, their bodies loosely entwined, they shared a dreamlike contentment.

There was time now to explore the whole realm of kissing, time to titillate, to cosset, to tease, to caress each other intimately with their eyes.

In the pale light of the melon moon Burke's body appeared almost golden, as it had on that first morning when the early sun at his back reflected on his

tawny flesh. Allison's fingers traced the patterns of
his muscles absently, playing in the soft splash of hair
across his torso.

This is madness, she thought fleetingly, then
turned her attention to new raptures as his hands
found a secret sensitive zone of her own body.

More slowly this time, they carried each other over
untried paths toward the same goal. In that last instant as he plunged inside her she heard herself cry
his name once again. Later they lay enclasped, mind-
ful only—but with a new quietness—of the touch of
flesh against flesh.

Through the trees they watched the lights of Plantation House go out one by one but took no notice.
Nor were they aware of the silence when it closed in
around them, leaving them with no sound but the
sounds of the night. The only light came from the
fireflies and the melon moon that watched them
through the trees.

Still they lay pressed together, as if they feared the
bond would be forever severed if either moved. Allison's leg tingled under his weight and she felt the
ache of tomorrow on her. Breathing in the fragrance
of mint, she knew the smell of it would carry her
back to this night as long as she lived.

From the magnolia tree near the corner of the
house a mockingbird sang to the moon.

Let tomorrow take care of tomorrow, she thought.
This night was theirs.

As if she had somehow communicated the thought

to him, she felt the stir of his reawakening passion within her and met his ardor with joyous fire.

Slowly, wordlessly, at last they drew apart. Burke gathered up her clothing from where he had laid it. Kneeling before him, she let him dress her, watched him lift her breasts like gems, embracing them with his eyes before he covered them. With a sudden sense of impending loneliness she watched as he put his own clothes on.

Still without words they rose together and left their sylvan haven in a shared sadness. They moved slowly across the moonlit slope to the house, her head against his shoulder, her sandals dangling indifferently from one hand.

At the front door he kissed her. Then, before he let her go, his hands moved to cup and mold the curve of her breasts, as if to fix them in his memory for all time.

And even in her state of satiety Allison's body sprang to renewed life.

CHAPTER NINE

TOMORROW WHEN IT CAME was as bad as Allison had feared. To begin with it started far too early.

She'd heard the antique clock in the library strike twelve as she climbed the stairs the previous night. Moments later she was asleep; a deep dreamless sleep, as if she wanted to escape the unwelcome thoughts that had stormed at the gateway of her mind as she hurried absently through her preparations for the night.

Deep and dreamless it was, but short. Less than three hours later she was staring wide-eyed through the darkness at the ceiling, trying to accept the truth of her folly—for hers it was. She couldn't blame Burke. He hadn't wanted it in the beginning any more than she had. She'd been perfectly aware of his resistance, had known she had only to lay her hands against his chest and push to be set free. She had known it and intended to do it . . . and hadn't.

And so it happened. In spite of herself her whole body quickened when the memory of last night's enraptured interlude rose unbidden to her mind.

The irony was that after all the years she'd spent

keeping her own sensuous nature in hand, keeping clear of men as wickedly appealing as Burke, not letting relationships grow into anything meaningful, it had to be Burke Ransome—and only moments after he'd declared his contempt for her!

Where was her self-respect, she asked herself as she lay alone in the accusing darkness.

And what about Burke? With all his self-righteousness hadn't he made love to a woman he openly despised? How did that square with his self-respect?

Through the remaining early hours of morning, until daybreak gave her an excuse to get up, Allison rolled and tossed and pummeled her pillow, as if somehow to punish herself. Her rational mind told her repeatedly that except for one thing nothing between her and Burke had changed. She'd let herself become vulnerable, just as her witless emotions had made her vulnerable once previously. Except this time she couldn't be excused as a naive child, and this Ransome was more dangerous, an even more devious member of the line, perhaps, than the late Tyler Hill.

In spite of their moonlit tryst in the magic woodland bower of mint, nothing had changed.

Lately she'd mistakenly felt a promise of something developing between them, something deeper and more important than joint ownership of Ransome's Cay. Now even that false tie had vanished—a figment of her romantic imagination.

A week after Herb Canby brought it all to an end

there'd be nothing left to build on. She would go back to her job in Manhattan. Quite possibly she might never set eyes on Burke Ransome again.

Even as she reminded herself that he wanted her off the island and out of his life she was tormented with longing to stop this painful self-examination and relive the night's fulfillment in waking dreams.

She had still come to no peace with herself when dawn winked into her window. At that point she gave up whatever thought she'd had of sleep. Dressed in a yellow T-shirt and white jeans that had seen many washings, she wandered disconsolately downstairs to gather neglected bills and receipts from the pantry desk and spread them out on the kitchen table. Perhaps by turning her mind to this different sort of reality she could pretend to fill her terrible inner emptiness.

It was there Effie found her two hours later, working doggedly on Plantation House accounts, the faintest circles under the amber-flecked eyes attesting to a night of little sleep.

That morning was just the start of a week of discontent throughout the house.

It heralded the day for a turnover of guests. Weekend visitors there only for the Independence Day opening were seen on their way. They were replaced by newcomers, most of whom were booked for the remainder of the week.

Then, partway through the morning a couple who had come for the opening festivities with reservations for a full ten days appeared apologetically at the registration desk to check out. They'd had a "divine time," they said, but something had come up.

It seemed reasonable enough. Yet, they'd left Allison with an uncomfortable feeling as they'd dashed off to catch the morning launch back to the mainland, leaving Plantation House with its first vacancy.

The parents of the sulky blue-eyed teenager arrived at the desk a short time later, daughter in tow, for the same purpose and with the same half-apologetic air.

"May I ask if it's something to do with Plantation House that's causing you to leave?" Allison queried with genuine concern. "Please don't think I'm trying to influence you to stay. You see, we're very new at this business. If there's anything we can correct to make our guests' stay more pleasant, we'd really appreciate knowing about it."

The couple exchanged embarrassed glances, clearly of no mind to offend, but their daughter was under no such constraint.

"Don't look at me—I'm not the problem," she said in a snippy voice, turning a resentful eye on her parents. "It's them. They're bored. Not enough going on. I want to stay."

I bet you do, thought Allison. Where else could the girl find two more attractive lads willing to destroy a perfectly amicable sibling relationship for one of her silly smiles?

"Well...uh, you know. The weekend with the

fireworks and all—that was fine,'' the girl's mother
hastened to explain, shooting her daughter an accusing look. "It's just that when that was over...
well.... There's no place to go! No shopping, no
golf. Not even a movie. What in the world are we to
do with ourselves for the next ten days?"

Their departure left three immediate unexpected
vacancies—a costly percentage of their overall accommodations and vacancies not likely to be filled
on the spot, thanks to the sea-locked isolation of
Plantation House.

Surprisingly the incoming boat that was to carry
the departing guests away brought an occupant for
one of the vacant rooms—one Orrin Travis. He was
in investments, he said, and his Los Angeles address
prompted Allison to ask curiously how he happened
to hear of Ransome's Cay as far away as the Pacific
Coast, as well as what had decided him to favor their
new untried resort with a visit.

Travis was noncommittal. "I got a lot of contacts.
I get around," he said with something of a swagger.
"I like to look over places—that's all."

He declined lunch and expressed immediate eagerness to take a tour of the island. Allison showed him
to his room, then sent him off in an electric cart with
a precautionary word to stay on the oyster paths
unless he didn't mind getting lost.

It was early afternoon—lunch was over and the
other guests were off to the stable or beach—before
Allison and Peg had time to sit down and talk.

Though she knew she must soon tell her friend the truth about her tenuous hold on the island, Allison gladly postponed it for the moment to listen to Peg's personal problems.

"It's that darn marine biologist, Ally," Peg said with a worried frown. "He's going to drown my sons."

"Don't be silly," Allison told her, too tired from lack of sleep and beset by her own worries to play along with her friend's neuroses. "He's not anything of the sort. He wants to teach them to scuba dive and they want to learn. They're both powerful swimmers. You'd see for yourself if you'd just screw up enough courage to watch them in the water sometime."

"You know how it worries me to have them out in that ocean," Peg said plaintively. "Trouble is, Doc McGinnis is too blasted persuasive. He says Burke will let them work on the barge once they learn to dive. Now that the big jobs are finished here at the house they do need something to keep them busy. I know that, and they could use extra money that doesn't come out of your till. Still, I just can't bring myself to say yes."

TRAVIS LUNCHED at Plantation House the following day. After finishing his second piece of Effie's brown-sugar pie, he left his place at the table and walked out of the dining room right behind Allison. "I'd like a few words with you, Mrs. Hill," he said smoothly.

Surprised, Allison nodded and led the way to the morning room.

"I've been from one end of Ransome's Cay to the other," he said, two steps behind her. "It's just what I'm looking for. I can make a bundle of money for the both of us, Mrs. Hill."

Allison stopped in her tracks and turned to look at him curiously, wondering if she understood where the words were leading.

"I'm not sure I know what you mean," she said.

"I can offer you a price for this little island that sounds like a winner in the Irish Sweepstakes," he said. "In cash or a share in the development or both. You name it. I'm talking about condos from two hundred thou up, shopping center, tennis courts, Olympic-sized swimming pool, an eighteen-hole golf course—all built around the old house here to keep it authentic, see."

"Mr. Travis, wait," Allison said, stepping away from the morning room to discourage further talk. "I thought you were in investments."

"Sure I'm in investments," he blustered. "I invest in real estate. Invest and develop, that's me."

"I may as well tell you, you're wasting your time here," Allison said. She hesitated. Somehow she couldn't bring herself to articulate what Burke had told her the previous night. With no belief in the truth of what she was about to say she continued. "I only inherited half the island, and the estate hasn't been probated yet. There might even be some litigation. It could be tied up in the courts for some time.''

"I got time to wait for the probate,'' said Travis. "Who owns the other half?''

"My late-husband's cousin, Burke Ransome.''

"When he hears what I've got to offer, maybe the three of us can get together and make a deal that could save you a hassle in court,'' said Travis. "I can save you both the costs of high-priced litigation by selling the whole enchilada to me. Now where can I find this guy, Ransome? I'd better look him up, then get back to you.''

Again Allison hesitated. It was hardly her place to answer for Burke. With a feeling that there might be some more effective way to handle the situation, one she couldn't think of at the moment, she directed him toward the lagoon.

In less than an hour Travis was back. From the morning room Allison saw the electric cart arrive outside bearing an unmistakably angry man who charged up the front stairs of the veranda and into the house. Allison was there to meet him in the reception hall.

"What the hell's the idea of leading me on,'' Travis demanded roughly. "You don't own any more of this island than I do.''

"There does seem to be some question...'' she faltered weakly.

"The hell there is!''. he shrilled. "Not as far as Ransome's concerned. He owns the whole damn place and everything on it, and I think you knew it when you sent me up there on that wild-goose chase.'' He glared at her. ''He isn't about to sell. Nothing short of a charge of dynamite is going to get that buzzard off Ransome's Cay.''

He let out his breath in an explosion and started up the broad stairs, then turned back. ''When's the next boat out of here? I'm checking out.''

''There's not another coming over until morning,'' Allison told him politely. ''I'm sure I can find someone to take you to the mainland for a reasonable fee, Mr. Travis.''

''See that it's waiting for me when I come down!'' The order was something short of a snarl.

The confrontation once again filled her mind with Burke, and after she had waylaid Hoddy and asked him to take their obnoxious guest to the mainland in the Plantation House motorboat she sat down at the pantry desk and buried her face in her hands.

The irony of it, she thought mournfully, was that for a while there, before Burke listened to Bob Birch propose to her on the morning-room porch and something turned him against her again, something she did not understand, she and Burke had somehow *fitted*.

In the week before the opening they'd managed small miracles of accomplishment together. There'd been no need to talk anything over. They'd simply done whatever there was to be done and laughed together doing it. It was as if there were a tacit understanding between them.

It was in their lovemaking, too. No need for words. It was as though she could look into her own heart and read his—and reading it know without doubt that his need for her consumed him and the desolation of his loss matched hers.

They could have made something stable and enduring out of the island working together, she at Plantation House, Burke with his project up at the lagoon. The people would have benefited from a duo-economy that would open to them more than one source of income. Given time and the opportunity to be together under amicable conditions, she and Burke might even have made of their own relationship something enduring and stable—something *fine*.

"Allison!" Peg's voice from the drawing-room entrance freed Allison from the futile meandering of her thoughts.

"What did that carpetbagger have to say?" Peg asked anxiously as she saw her friend's face. "Are you all right?"

"All right? Of course," Allison answered shakily. "Travis is checking out. Could you get rid of him, please?" In her own ears her voice sounded almost pleading. "Hoddy will have the motorboat down at the landing for him."

Words failed her. Leaving Peg without explanation, she hurried up the stairs to her room.

Even the twins had their discontentments and were not their usual ebullient selves that week. Rivalry over the girl, which might well have been forgotten in

scuba lessons had their mother given in, was trans-
ferred to hunting the island for the missing pirate
treasure.

Where normally they would have put their heads
together to solve the mystery of Blackbeard's map,
they now made separate surreptitious pilgrimages to
the library to study the rude sketch, each making
notes and maps of his own, then sneaking away from
the house without the other. Each took elaborate
pains to make sure the other did not see which way he
had gone.

Separately they disappeared for long hours on
these forays. By midweek their mother, who liked to
imagine she knew where they were a reasonable
amount of the time, confessed to Allison that she was
of half a mind to appeal to McGinnis for help. She'd
grown used to expecting Hoddy and Max to look out
for each other. To have them poking around without
the other's protection through wilderness areas of the
island known to be the habitat of rattlers and alligators and wild boars was driving her frantic. Maybe
it would be better if Doc taught them to dive after all,
she said. At least they'd be in it together.

As for Allison, the golden aura that had for so
long hung over Plantation House was lost to her.
Along with the terrible emptiness that came from the
impending loss of the island and the absence of
Burke, who had not been back since the night they'd
made love, there were problems with the guests.

People who came looking for golf and tennis were

disappointed. Some left before their bookings were up. Others complained when they found there was no regular transportation back and forth to the mainland so they could go tooting off to be where the action was whenever the mood struck them. The twins reported numerous overheard complaints that there were no movies, no place to shop.

Paradoxically, knowing it was only a matter of time before she was obliged to close the resort and leave, Allison was determined to find solutions to the problems before they were forced to depart. To leave behind a failing business was something her pride refused to allow.

"We've got to rethink things, Peg," she said, knowing even as she said this that what she really should be talking to her friend about was the fact that they were on the brink of being dispossessed. "This house-party idea of mine just isn't working out."

Peg grinned ruefully. "Don't I know it," she said. "Most of these people wouldn't be caught dead with each other under any other conditions. The only thing they have in common is they think Ransome's Cay is dullsville. We can't expect them to buddy up just because it's Plantation House."

Peg must be told, Allison thought guiltily. She had a right to know. Yet was there any real harm in waiting another day or two for the news to come officially from Herb? He was bound to phone soon, and though Allison dreaded the finality of his call, at the same time she looked forward to it with a sense of relief.

She said to Peg, "The trouble is, they all want the glamour and luxury of Sea Island's Cloister at Plantation House prices."

Peg nodded thoughtfully. "There's nothing basically wrong with your house-party idea. The place is too small for anything else to work. The country is full of nice people who want a vacation away from it all in exactly this kind of spot but don't know where to find it."

"Then we've got to figure out a way to find them— and pretty darn quick," Allison said grimly. "How about this? 'Looking for an historical, southern-sea-island haven for the enjoyment of nature, the sun, the sea amid contemplative luxurious surroundings? Vacation at Plantation House—riding, boating, miles of unspoiled hiking paths. American plan.'"

"That about says it," Peg replied. "We could run an ad in some of the leading scholastic journals and the *New York Times*."

She looked at her friend encouragingly, and her next words made Allison's heart sink. "Don't worry, Ally," she said. "Things can only get better. And remember, we're in this together."

CHAPTER TEN

IT WAS LATE FRIDAY MORNING. Armed with a container of rug cleaner, Peg was on an emergency call to one of the upstairs rooms where a bottle of cola had been spilled on an old and valuable Aubusson rug then left to dry by a now departed guest.

Allison was once again at the kitchen table going over another week's bills and receipts, momentarily distracted by news of the damaged rug. If only guests would tell them when things happened. They might have saved the carpet from permanent damage. It was sure to leave a stain now that it had dried.

From the pantry off the cooking end of the kitchen the phone rang. Before Allison could get up to answer it, Effie closed the oven door on the cake she was testing and went to get it. "It's for you, honey," Effie said. "It's New York. I didn't catch the name. Cranny? Canning? Something like that."

So the phone call had come at last. *Herb Canby.* For a moment panic almost suffocated Allison. *Not now! Just a few more days,* something in her cried out.

"Tell him—"

"What's the matter, honey?" Effie asked anxiously. "You look like you seen a ghost."

The housekeeper's voice brought her around to her senses.

"It's all right, Effie," Allison replied, wondering if the trembling inside her could be heard in her voice. She was appalled that she had been about to have Effie tell Canby she wasn't there.

She stood up and took a deep breath to steady herself.

"I'll take the call."

Followed by Effie's concerned eyes, she lifted her chin and walked into the pantry. Pushing the desk chair aside, she picked up the phone and prepared to take what Herb Canby had to tell her standing up. "This is Allison," she said.

"Allison, hello! You sound great. Herb Canby here." The voice on the line spoke heartily, all in a rush, as if eager to get everything over and done with. "I just got back a couple of days ago. I see you've been trying to get me."

"You're right about that, Herb."

"Uh...listen, Allison. I've been checking out that will of Ty's and...well, I hate to tell you this, but there's been a kind of mixup."

"Tell me about it, Herb," she said, rallying to the point of sarcasm. "Tyler never owned more than half of Ransome's Cay at any time in his life. I've heard it twice already, Herb. Isn't it about time I heard it from you?"

"Honest to God, Allison, Ty didn't tell me. He just said, 'Give the damned island to Allison.' It never occurred to me...." He let the words drift off into nothing.

Steadying herself, Allison cleared her throat and asked the big question. "Out with it, Herb! He didn't own even half the island at the time of his death. Not even one blasted rock."

There was a long loaded silence before Herb cleared his throat and croaked, "Well, about that, Allison...I've been checking the records since I got back and...well, it does look like Ty didn't have any share in the island to leave you." There was a pause, then Herb continued miserably, "Seems he sold his half to Burke four years ago. It must have been right after the two of you split."

Right after he lost his meal ticket, Allison thought wryly. Swamped with emotion, she could find nothing to say.

"Sue me, Allison," begged Herb. "Why don't you sue me?"

Why not, she asked herself dully.

"I've got coverage," he said.

In spite of herself she let a half-hysterical giggle escape. "Oh, Herb, don't be such a twit! If I thought it would come out of your pocket or really make you squirm I'd almost do it. It might help make a better lawyer of you."

She hung up then. Letting herself sink into the desk chair, she cradled her head in her arms, dry-eyed, too overwhelmed by her loss for tears. If she had lost only the island maybe she could cry, she thought dully. But the emptiness that threatened her was beyond the solace of tears.

"I gotta find Allison, Effie, but don't tell mom."

Max Crewes's voice in the next room brought Allison's head up in sudden alert. She'd been hardly aware of the sound of his running steps or the slam of the back screen door as he reached the kitchen, but the panic in his voice got through to her. Wrenched from her own tormented thoughts, she jumped to her feet and hurried into the kitchen before Effie had time to reply.

"What is it, Max?" she asked in alarm, seeing distress clearly written on the young man's face.

"It's Hoddy. The cave fell in on him. It's all my fault," Max told her in a sick voice, his words piling up on one another in his haste.

Allison had trouble making out what he was saying. "Slow down, sweetie," she said, laying a calming hand on his arm. "What cave? Where?"

"Buttonhook Cove," Max went on breathlessly. "I knew he was on to something, so I followed him this morning and sure enough he'd found a cave back behind the waterfall. Only when I tried to sneak up on him I guess I knocked something loose, so that everything fell down and closed the hole."

"Oh, my God," cried Allison softly. "Is he...is Hoddy...."

"He's okay," Max replied, but there was reservation in his voice. "He was when I left, but I'm scared the earth will shift again and the blockage will get worse," he continued, his voice stricken. "There's a crack between the rocks so you can talk to him now. He's not hurt and so far he's got air, but it'll take a lot more than me to get him out."

"What are we waiting for?" Allison broke in, heading for the back door before Max stopped her.

"It'll take a lot more than just me and you, Allison," he rushed on. "There's maybe half a ton of dirt and junk in front of that hole. You better go get Burke and Doc in the jeep and anybody else that can help. I'll go back and tell Hoddy help's coming."

As they started off, Max turned back to Effie, "Don't tell mom. Please, Effie. You know how she is. Not till we get him out."

Effie looked at Allison uncertainly. Allison hesitated before giving a nod of agreement. Peg was rock solid on every other front, but when the welfare of her boys was concerned, she was inclined to fly apart. Why alarm her when there was no way in the world she could help?

"Find Bunker and send him along, please, Effie?" Allison said as she followed Max out. "If Peg comes down, keep her busy until we get Hoddy back." She set out running toward the carriage house to get the jeep.

Only once, as she neared the lagoon, did she consider that this would be her first meeting with Ransome since the night they had made love. It was something not to be thought about—certainly not now...maybe not ever again. It was too poignant. Too much had changed since then.

Her overriding thought as she went to him now was for the trapped young man. Yet even that deep concern didn't forestall a quickening of her pulse as she came upon Ransome walking across the sand toward the edge of the lagoon where a dinghy lay anchored.

Bare to the waist, his faded blue jeans molded to the lean muscular thighs, he looked like a bronzed Apollo in the morning sun. The sound of the jeep brought his head around, and he stopped and turned as she skidded to a halt and came flying across the sand to meet him.

"Allison!" he called out in astonishment, coming toward her. "What in the world...?"

"Hoddy's trapped somehow up at Buttonhook Cove and we need your help," she said. "Get Doc and Jimmer and anyone else you can." She gave a hasty account of the problem as told to her by Max.

Ransome wasted no time with questions. "Doc's working out on the barge," he said. "I'll radio him to bring Jimmer and come by boat." Emerging a moment later from the mobile lab, he loaded a crowbar, a pick and several shovels into the back end of the pickup.

"Don't take the road," he advised as she was about to get back behind the wheel. "We can make time if we hit the beach."

She hesitated uncertainly. "I've never driven on sand," she said. "I'm afraid I'll get us bogged down."

"Not a chance," he assured her. "This buggy's fixed for it."

She was still doubtful, but there was no time to waste. She headed in the direction of the water, and soon they were bouncing over the sandy beach.

On their way Ransome quizzed her for details, but Allison had little she could add. "Max says he was looking for the Blackbeard booty," she told him quickly, then directed her attention once again to keeping the jeep from getting stuck.

It was a wild ride to Buttonhook Cove—far faster than Allison would have thought possible. There they found Bunker and young Max already struggling to roll aside a heavy rock behind the veil of the falls.

"You okay, Hod?" Ransome called out when Max showed him the crevasse that was now the only opening to the cave. From somewhere back in the earth came the muffled voice of the other twin, affirming that indeed he was.

"We've got enough crew out here to dig the Panama Canal," Burke called out again in a jocular tone. "Here come Doc and Jimmer and one of the guys from the barge."

Surprised, Allison glanced around to see the three men landing on the shore of the cove—just as Burke had advised the captive with such reassurance. At least there was no lack of manpower, she thought, taking some measure of comfort from the numbers. She turned her attention back to wonder again at what had happened to this spot that had always been special to her.

The last time Allison had been here she had stood in a crystal-clear pool where the brooklet cascaded over a moss-covered embankment heavy with vines. Now the pool was a cauldron of muddy water. The side of the bank had collapsed, dumping a great mound of rocks and brush and sandy soil into the moss-lined grotto hidden behind the falls.

As the men shoveled off the debris, Allison began to see for the first time that the waterfall, whether through intention of its builder or otherwise, might have been used for another purpose besides a sylvan shower, for the rotting wooden framework of a small subterranean cellar had begun to take shape. Camouflaged by a heavy blanket of moss overgrown with vines and curtained by the waterfall, it could have been a hiding place for anything—even a pirate's cave.

When they had reached a certain point in their excavations, Burke called a halt and examined the underlying timbers with concern. "They're pretty rotten," he said. "We'd better move with caution from now on. We don't want the whole blasted thing to collapse."

As if he sensed a moment of transition, Hoddy called out from within, "How're you guys doing out there?" The voice was not as breezy as it had been earlier. It sounded a new note of concern. "You're not running into any trouble, I hope."

"Keep your shirt on, old man," Burke called back. "We'll get you out. The big job's done, but we've got to take it a little easy from here on out. How big's the cave?"

There was a moment of silence. Hoddy was either measuring or thinking it out. "About the size of the pantry at Plantation House, maybe, only not so high by a couple of feet," came the answer. "Hey, Burke," the muffled voice continued, the natural ebullience regained for a moment, "there's an awful lot of rum in here."

"Rum?" Max, who had worked in dogged silence throughout the digging, suddenly came to life. "Hey, Hod, what do you mean, rum?"

"Ten wooden boxes of bottles full of the stuff," came the voice from inside. "Get me out of here, Maxie, and you and me'll get drunk on rum."

"Good!" called out Ransome. "Hold off a bit and we'll all join you." His voice was suddenly very serious. "Listen to me now, Hod. Listen closely. I'm going to start breaking in. I want you at the back of the cave. Make a shelter for yourself out of those boxes but move them carefully. You understand? Call out when you're ready for me to begin."

There was no response from inside. Then Hoddy's voice sounded, tight with fear. "You think it's gonna cave in again, Burke?"

"Just a precaution," Burke replied. "I don't think

it'll collapse, but I want you out of there as quickly as we can get you just in case it should.''

As they waited, frozen in motion outside the cave, listening for the signal from within, the tension mounted until Allison could almost hear it. *Thank God, Peg's not here,* she thought, and paid a silent tribute to young Max, who'd had the judgment to sense this was an ordeal his mother might better be spared.

After what seemed an endless wait, Hoddy's far-away call came to proceed.

Allison's eyes never left Burke as he worked at one of the rotted planks that blocked the opening. He worked alone, operating with the same caution a man would use if he were handling explosives. The very way he moved and the fact that he'd ordered everyone else back told her how dangerous he considered the situation to be. She could hardly bear to watch, but she could bear to turn away even less. At last he gained an opening large enough for his lean muscular body to slip inside.

Watching, waiting, Allison forgot to breathe.

A shout of relief arose from the attentive rescuers as Hoddy's sandy head and square face appeared in the opening, wearing a silly grin. A moment later he and Max were pounding each other and yelling joyfully.

"Hey, how about that, man! It wasn't old Blackbeard's cave at all. It was a rumrunner's from Prohibition.''

"Boy, Maxie ole twin, for a while there I thought I was gettin' me a case of claustrophobia."

"Whatdy'a mean, man, hoggin' all the fun stuff for yourself? Next time I go, too."

"Yeah...next time."

All eyes were on the twins. All, that is, but Allison's. Hers hadn't left the escape slot since Burke had disappeared inside. Then to her vast relief the lean strong face appeared in the narrow opening, looking tense but satisfied. His head with its thatch of tawny hair emerged first, then his body, inching its way to freedom.

Then time stopped for Allison. She was aware only of the man and the paralyzing fear that came upon her as she realized the escape space had narrowed in the moments since Hoddy had crawled out. She recognized in it a warning of another impending structural collapse and saw the same awareness in Burke's eyes as he struggled, less cautiously now, to free himself from the slit that had a scissors-like grip on his body.

"Stay back, Allison," he warned as she started toward him without a notion of what she could do to help but driven to his side.

Disregarding his precautionary command, she kept on. In a wave of panic she saw that the same earth slippage narrowing Burke's escape hole had dislodged a large boulder from above. Rolling down the embankment, it moved directly in line with the head of the trapped man.

Without a second thought, Allison threw herself forward to deflect the rock. It glanced off her shoulder, its flying force pitching her into the pool of muddy water. The clear stream from above cascaded down upon her.

Behind her she heard the crash of the cave's collapse, and her own physical pain was lost in an agony of fear for Burke. Then she blacked out.

As CONSCIOUSNESS RETURNED she heard the voices around her but shut her mind to them. Whatever they said, it had no meaning for her now. She couldn't bring herself to find out what the collapse of the cave had done to Burke. She wasn't ready. First she must rally her strength.

She'd seen him pinned there half in, half out, and heard the terrible rumble of collapsing earth seconds later. No one could be buried under a ton of dirt and debris and survive. If by some miracle he was still alive, the damage to his body would be insupportable. That splendidly vital man...she couldn't bear to think of that possibility.

She was fully conscious by this time, yet couldn't summon the will to open her eyes and come back to the world. Then she heard her name spoken, and her eyelids parted wide.

"Allison, wake up." The voice she heard was Burke's, and the face so near to her where she lay on the ground was his. He knelt beside her and behind him the rescue crew looked down. Oblivious to all but Burke, not daring to believe her eyes, she extended a hand to touch his face tentatively. The gesture sent a wave of pain through her, but she scarcely noticed.

"You got out," she marveled, the taste of mud in her mouth.

"And you darn near got yourself killed. Whatever made you do a fool thing like that?" he asked, his voice gentler than his words.

Her mind was still fuzzy from the impact of her head against what had felt like a stone slab, and it took her a moment to pull her thoughts together. Then it all came back to her. She began to tremble suddenly in delayed shock.

"I had to," she said through chattering teeth. "You would have been killed. It was coming right for your head and you couldn't duck it."

Her eyes fell upon the grid of angry red stripes across the bronzed skin of his bare chest and shoulder where the flesh had been scraped raw as he'd pried himself out of the cave. She reached up to lay her fingers on it but drew back.

"You're hurt," she cried. She struggled to get up, but Ransome held her down with a firm hand.

"Just skinned a little," he assured her. "You're the one who's hurt. You took the full force of that rock on your shoulder, and I suspect you've got a slight concussion. The lump on your head where you landed knocked you out. It's the size of a golf ball."

Unexpectedly Allison began to cry. Soft uncontrollable sobs of relief and joy came pouring out because he was alive, unscathed, when she'd been so sure he was either dead or destroyed.

"Go ahead," Burke said uneasily. "Cry if it makes you feel better. It was a nasty blow. Your shoulder must hurt like hell."

As if by common agreement, the other men moved away and left Ransome, who had rashly sanctioned the tears, to deal with them. He took one of her hands and stroked it gently.

Allison quickly swallowed her unwonted tears, in control of herself again. For the first time she noticed that her clothes and hair were soaked with dirty water. She tried again to get up. "Let me up, Burke," she insisted. "I'm a mess. I've got to get under the waterfall and get rid of some of this muck."

"Stay where you are. You may have a concussion. Besides, the waterfall is gone."

Her eyes followed his, and she was horrified to see that where the lovely little waterfall had been there was nothing but rubble out of which water eddied and spilled down the slope. In the terrifying rumble she heard behind her as she blacked out the walls of the man-made cave had crashed in, bringing down the ledge over which the stream had poured to create the falls. With no ledge to direct it, water had rushed in to fill every crevasse of the ruins, eventually flooding over and breaking up into rivulets. These swift fingers of water were spreading out over the vine-covered hillock, feeling their way through the greenery in search of a new course for the stream.

Allison looked at the disaster area for a moment before she turned her head away with a shudder. What if Burke lay trapped beneath that cauldron of muddy water, she thought sickly.

A dry chuckle from the man himself diverted her. "The Crewes twins are inconsolable," he informed her. "Ten cases of smuggled rum lost to them forever!"

Not until Allison lay in the back of the jeep on a small rubber raft Doc had brought from the boat and inflated to serve as a stretcher did physical pain take over, and then it was with such intensity it blocked everything else from her mind. In contrast to their mad dash to rescue Hoddy, Burke drove slowly, holding the jeep steady along the narrow oyster-shell road back to Plantation House. Still, even the slightest bounce brought a new stab of pain to her shoulder and intensified the dull throb that had taken possession of her.

After what seemed a nearly endless ride Burke brought the jeep to a stop at the kitchen door at the rear of the house. Doc stepped down from the tailgate, where he had ridden to steady the raft, and the twins pulled up behind them in one of the electric carts.

The four lifted the raft with Allison on it from the jeep and carried her into Effie's kitchen. There they set her carefully down on the big walnut table at the far end of the room.

Peg, who had seen their arrival from upstairs, came flying in and was promptly waylaid by Doc and her sons. Allison was relieved when they hustled her away. Normally she found Peg's observations diverting, but today she wasn't up to dealing with her friend's recriminations on discovering that a son of hers had been seriously endangered and she hadn't been told. Nor could she tolerate Peg's clucking over her in her own determined way. Peg was so prone to take charge she might cause Burke to think she was in competent hands and he was no longer needed.

Burke's hands were already exploring the back of her head, his strong fingers slipping up the nape of her neck and into her hair, sending a sensuous shiver through her that overrode the pain. He probed cautiously along her injured shoulder. In spite of herself Allison winced. Tears of pain oozed from under her tightly closed eyelids.

"This won't do," Burke said quietly. "I can't see what I'm doing. I'm hurting you. Effie, suppose you find me a pair of scissors."

Effie, who had been standing quietly beside the table watching, her eyes liquid with sympathy, hurried off and was back in a moment with a pair of sewing shears.

To Allison's astonishment, Burke took them and made a bold cut down the center of the yellow T-shirt, dividing it neatly in half. Two more slashes on either side from the neck to where the sleeves ended and the shirt fell away, leaving her upper body uncovered except for a scanty lace bra.

"It's a good thing I didn't wear my designer T-shirt," Allison said to cover her unexpected embarrassment at being exposed to him thus in the presence of a third person.

But neither of them was listening to her. Both were bent over her shoulder, examining it closely. She heard a quick intake of breath from Effie. To her relief, Burke didn't make any further effort to probe the spot.

Cautiously she turned her head and was shocked to see that the hurt shoulder jutted out at an alarming angle. The flesh around it was already swollen and turning dark. She moved her arm gingerly and couldn't hold back a cry of anguish. She turned worried eyes to Burke, questioning, then forgot everything for a moment when he leaned over and kissed her gently on the mouth.

"It looks strange, but I'm reasonably certain there's nothing broken. It's all out of shape because the shoulder's been dislocated, I think." Turning to Effie, he said, "I suppose there's nothing stronger than aspirin in the house?"

"No, but I can get that. It'll help some."

"I'm going to take you in to Atlanta," Burke told Allison as the housekeeper hurried off.

A moan of dismay escaped Allison. "Oh, Burke! Couldn't I just go to Savannah? Atlanta's such a long trip."

"Less than an hour by plane. I have a friend in Atlanta I'd like to have tend to this. He's a specialist in one of the big hospitals there."

Before she could rally the spirit to protest further Effie was on the scene with the aspirin bottle and a glass of water, putting an end to discussion by popping two of the tablets into her mouth.

Burke said to Effie, "Could you put an ice pack on her shoulder while I call Air Ambulance. Have Peg pack a few things for her in case the hospital wants her to stay over night."

And then he was gone, leaving Allison wondering in a dazed sort of way what had prompted Burke to suddenly become her self-appointed guardian.

HOURS LATER, before the medication she'd been given to relieve her pain and put her to sleep took effect, Allison lay in her Atlanta hospital room, looking back on the day with a feeling of bewilderment.

Would she ever understand this man who had seen to her care with such authority and tenderness these past hours? Had there ever been such a person as the man who had confronted her with hostility in the early days of their meeting? Except for occasional unsettling flare-ups after he'd overheard her conversation with Bob Birch, he seemed almost a different person.

From the moment he'd rescued her from the muddy torrent pouring over the spot where she'd been knocked unconscious he'd scarcely left her side—comforting, ordering, organizing, until at last he put her in the hands of his friend, Jack Frazier, chief orthopedic surgeon at the hospital in Atlanta.

Dr. Frazier had called in two consultants to make sure her head injury was minor, repositioned her shoulder after X rays revealed no broken bones and, because she'd shown some evidence of shock, ordered her into the hospital overnight.

Incredible as it now seemed, Burke was waiting for her in the doctor's office and walked beside the gurney on which she was wheeled to her room. There he folded his long body into a chair designed for a lesser frame, pulled a small book from his pocket entitled *Mollusks and Crustaceans* and settled himself to read.

There was a dreamlike quality to the scene, Allison thought, and it was not due to the pain medication she'd been given. There sat her golden centaur, watching over her like some great guardian angel, not letting her talk, not talking himself because, he informed her gruffly, "Frazier wants you to rest."

She'd gone along with it. The truth was, she didn't feel like talking, at least not to Burke, not until she was able to stand on her feet and admit to him she knew what he had known all along—that no part of the island belonged to her. Whether there would be anything more for them to say to each other after that she dared not guess.

Meanwhile there he sat in her room reading about shellfish while she dozed. She wakened to find him still there. He stayed until a nurse came to give her medication and turn out the light. There was infinite tenderness in the kiss he laid on her lips as he said good-night.

In the last moments before the sleeping pill took over the petrifying sight of the small boulder catapulting down the embankment directly in line with his head came suddenly into her mind. She felt again the sense of impending disaster that had sent her flying heedlessly into its path. She shuddered, thinking what her condition might be had the rock smashed into her head.

In that moment had her past life flashed before her as it was supposed to do, she wondered fuzzily. And in spite of the progressing effect of the sleeping pill she knew it hadn't. It wasn't the past she had seen. It was the future—a gray, meaningless future unless she stopped the oncoming projectile from destroying Burke.

CHAPTER ELEVEN

THE GOLDEN RIDER leaped from the stallion's back and strode purposefully across the short distance to where she stood naked under the falls. Her body was suddenly alive with the excitement of his approach. Avidly she watched his hands as they moved to the top of his jeans. She stood breathless at the sudden deep throb within as he peeled them down over his lean thighs and left them behind him on the ground.

He was with her then under the cascading water. His hands played across the rise of her breasts and the flatness of her belly. Their mouths joined and moved hungrily, tasting, as if they supped nectars from wild exotic fruits. Their bodies molded together. She was ready for him. . .ready. . .ready.

"Time to wake up, honey."

The dream was lost. Breathing heavily, Allison began a reluctant return to reality. "Go away," she moaned.

But the morning nurse who was there to get her ready for the day was as intractable as a drill sergeant. "Come on, now. That's a good girl. We must get you washed and breakfasted before doctor makes his rounds.''

Allison half lifted one eyelid to peer at the broad stolid face that hovered over her. She closed it again. If she opened both eyes it would be an admission that the day she dreaded had begun. Once she was awake the morning would move irrevocably on to the moment when she must tell Burke she knew Ransome's Cay belonged entirely to him.

At least she would do it with dignity and no whining about the way she'd been taken in by Tyler—no defensive explanations, no recriminations, no whimpering about her squandered estate. Ty was gone. A sense of decency would not let her use the wrongs done her by her late husband to prove to Burke she was not the neurotic fool he took her to be.

Allison gave in to the morning and opened her eyes as the nurse snapped open the slatted blinds of the window. The sun streamed across her bed. She faked a cheery smile when the square-rigged woman came back to her side.

For all her officiousness the nurse had a gentle touch as she gave Allison a brisk tub bath and shampoo to remove the last traces of mud she'd carried away from the cave-in. Efforts by Peg and later an aid at the hospital the previous day had failed to sponge it all off, and Allison was relieved to see the last of the ugly reminder float down the drain.

''You're doing so well I'm going to release you to Burke's care,'' Dr. Frazier told her when he'd checked the strapping that held her shoulder in place. "You may as well get dressed. Burke's getting a couple of prescriptions for you. One for pain and—because you'll no doubt need it—one for sleep. You may still have some discomfort from that shoulder tonight."

To her surprise, when she opened her suitcase she found a soft mauve silk dress neatly folded on top of her other clothes. For all its simple line it was definitely a "dressy" outfit, one she had no need for under the circumstances. Nor did she need the selection of other things Peg had packed—enough to see her through a weekend at least. Peg must have been still rattled over Hoddy's narrow escape, Allison guessed.

From the suitcase she lifted a wraparound dress of knit cotton with cap sleeves that was reasonably easy to put on over her solidly strapped shoulder with the help of the nurse's skilled hands. At least Peg had used her head on that one, thought Allison. Besides the fact that the dress was easy to get into, she was glad, in the light of Burke's expected coming, for the lively red-on-white sea-gull print. It gave her a deceptive air of verve.

In the pain and confusion of the previous day she hadn't thought about how she was to get back home. As she sat waiting, knowing that at any moment Burke would come to get her, she churned inwardly with a turbulence of ambivalent emotions.

Rising out of the trauma of the past twenty-four

hours was the clear unequivocal understanding that
she loved Burke Ransome with a depth and surety she
hadn't known was possible for her. There was also
the painful certainty that she must soon banish herself from his presence and take leave of Ransome's
Cay.

Her love had little to do with the inescapable sensual yearning that had swelled between them from
the first idyllic moment he had come upon her at the
waterfall. It had to do with the quality and substance
of the man himself—his personality, his character,
his mind—qualities she had closed her eyes to until
only the past few days.

Still, the sensual attraction and the love for the
whole man were inseparable. The one, for all its
overwhelming power, was shallow, transitory and
meaningless without the other.

It was small comfort to have recognized from the
first that Burke's physical desire was as strong as her
own. It meant nothing. That much was obvious from
his bitter outburst moments before they'd both been
caught up in a tide of passion the night they'd made
love under the trees. His acrimony had said clearly
that he didn't care for her in the same deep important
way she cared for him. The sweet new hope that
trembled in her later that night when they'd kissed
and parted had stilled and was lost as one day and
then another had come and gone, bringing no sign of
Burke. By the middle of the week she'd understood
with growing emptiness that she would not see him

again until the call came from Herb Canby and she would be obliged to seek him out and surrender the island to him.

Even now, in spite of the gentle concern he'd shown for her since the accident, she wondered if he would have continued to stay away if she hadn't had to go to him for help when the cave collapsed on Hoddy.

This morning she felt a driving need to get everything out in the open with Burke. She would thank him first for seeing her properly cared for after the accident. Then she would apologize for calling him a liar and confess that she had known his words were the truth a moment after he'd said them but had not had the courage to admit it.

Dressed and ready to go, she waited impatiently for him to arrive, forcing herself to think ahead to what she must do after she made her confession to Burke.

She would have to tell Peg at once, of course. Peg who looked on Plantation House as her haven, her career, her livelihood in that soon-to-be future when her sons would fly the nest and she would be left alone.

Allison did not look forward to her own return to Manhattan, either, though she knew returning was the reasonable thing to do. Thanks to Bob Birch, who had spread the word among friends in the city that in his opinion Plantation House would not last out the summer, she knew she'd have a job to go back to. During the week her former employer, Mr. Barron, had called her and with great tact let her know there was a spot for her in the firm if ever she should decide to return.

A firm knock on the door brought her back to the present with a panicky start, which she quickly controlled. In a reflex from years of living in a Manhattan apartment she called out, "Who is it?" Then, not waiting for an answer, knowing it was Burke, she called out again over the sudden rush of her pulse, "Come in."

Even in her anxiety over the unpleasantness that could no longer be postponed she felt a quickening pleasure at the sight of the lean strong face, the dark gold brows arched quizzically over iridescent eyes that revealed nothing of what lay behind them.

How could she read a man whose eyes were as open as the sky one minute and veiled and mysterious like the sea, the next, she wondered helplessly.

As he came through the door and across the room to where she stood at the window, an unexpected shyness kept her from crossing the distance to meet him. For a moment he seemed a stranger.

Wearing a well-cut suit of heavy, nubby brown silk with a dusty pink shirt and buff-colored tie, he looked every inch the corporate executive. She found it hard to reconcile this cool-looking businessman with the man of the sea and the island she had come to know and love. She had too often seen that hard-muscled torso bared to the sun or casually sporting a faded work shirt tucked into a pair of jeans.

He covered the few steps that lay between them, and the veil lifted. He embraced her with his eyes. His mouth curved in that sweetly sardonic smile she'd seen previously. They were in tune again. If she reached out and slipped her hands inside the well-tailored coat she would feel the play of muscles in the marvelously constructed body beneath the pale cotton shirt.

Half tempted, she wondered what he would do. She closed out the provocative thought, reminding herself that playfulness was inappropriate at a time when she was about to say the words that would bring whatever there was between them to an end.

"For a person who tried to play catch with a small boulder, I must say you are looking fit, though a little pallid," Burke greeted her lightly. He took her face in his hands and tipped it up to look at her closely. His own expression took on a sudden seriousness.

"I can't tell you how beautiful you are," he went on. Bending his head to hers, he took her lips in a poignant lingering kiss that brought tears welling behind closed eyelids and stirred in her a fear it was a kiss of farewell.

He let her go then, and to hide her tears she leaned down and picked up her closed suitcase beside the night stand as if to leave. Burke took the suitcase from her, but she escaped to the adjoining bathroom on the excuse of checking to make sure she'd left nothing behind. There she dabbed at her eyes with a tissue, then emerged in a moment to join Burke. She had to submit to being transported in a wheelchair to Burke's car by a hospital attendant.

"Jack Frazier wants to see that shoulder again tomorrow," Burke told her on the way down in the elevator. "If everything is okay then, he'll relieve you of the strapping and put you in a sling arrangement you can pop in and out of. He says it will keep the shoulder in place until the danger of its slipping out again has passed."

Allison looked up at him in alarm. "Burke, I can't let you fly me back here again tomorrow."

"Why not? You wouldn't be here if you hadn't taken that rock that was coming for me." His voice had become quite serious. "I might not be here, either. I find that hard to forget."

There was silence for a moment, then he went on. "Actually, I wasn't intending to take you back to the cay until tomorrow. I have some business here in Atlanta and I'd like to stay over. It will save us both another trip. I've made hotel arrangements. You may spend the day in bed if you don't feel like shopping or seeing the sights."

This was an unforeseen and troubling development, but Allison said no more until the attendant left them at Burke's car. Then, as Burke was about to turn on the ignition, she laid a detaining hand on his arm. "Wait, Burke," she said. "Before we go there's something I've got to tell you."

He looked at her expectantly.

Allison felt herself sinking into the sea-deep pools of his eyes. "When Max came running for help yesterday, I'd just finished talking to Herb Canby. Since then things have been so hectic. . . ." Her voice all of a sudden faltered.

"So you know," he said. She saw no sign of satisfaction in his eyes.

"I already knew," she said miserably. "That night, a moment after you said that Ty had sold his part to you. I knew it was true, but I couldn't bear to face it. Oh, Burke, I called you a liar. . .a cheat! I can't expect you to forgive me. The lie was mine when I said I didn't believe you."

Burke laid a hand over hers, his eyes dark and unfathomable again, his face taut with anger. "This isn't the first time I've wished my cousin Ty had never been born into this family, and it's probably not the last."

Allison pulled her hand free. "Please, Burke, don't blame Tyler. When he wrote the will he actually did own half of the island. He had every right to sell it to you if he wanted to."

"He had a right to sell it without telling you?" Burke asked scathingly. "You knew, didn't you, that he'd made a will leaving the island to you?"

Allison hesitated uncomfortably, tempted to tell Burke exactly what she'd thought about the will, that she'd come to see it as Tyler's device to persuade her to put her own property in joint tenancy so he could dip into her assets freely, which he certainly had done. But even as she hesitated, she knew it was something she couldn't do. It would sound self-serving, accusing, as if she held Burke responsible for what his cousin had done, as if she expected Burke to reimburse her for what Ty had squandered of hers.

"Yes," she said at last, quietly. "He told me that when we got married."

"Then he had an obligation to let you know it was gone!" Ransome exploded with contempt. "He didn't even have the guts to tell Canby!"

"Actually, Ty never talked with me much about whatever business he had," she confessed truthfully. Again she hesitated. "Once it was sold I guess it just slipped his mind to tell Herb."

She hated the lie. Having withheld the rest, she could hardly tell Burke that far from slipping Tyler's mind, for some last perverse antic notion known only to him, Ty had actually led Herb to believe he owned the island and wanted the old will to remain in effect.

The eyes Burke turned on her were bleak. "Excuses—always excuses," he said, his voice grown cool. "You won't let yourself admit Tyler was rotten to the core. Why try to make a hero out of him? Face it, Allison, he was no damn good."

"Not a hero," said Allison stubbornly, "and besides, that's not the point. I can't blame Ty about the island. There's no one to blame but myself. If I had waited until I knew exactly where I stood, I would never have got into this mess. Something kept telling me right from the first it was all a dream, but do you think I'd listen?'' She managed a rueful grin.

Burke's face softened. He reached across the space between them to lift a strand of hair back from her forehead and look directly into her face.

"It's not your fault,'' he said. "The bottom line is Herb Candy. He should have been tending to business.''

"No, don't even blame Herb,'' Allison insisted. "The bottom line is me. It's up to me to do what I can to straighten things out. Peg is my first concern. I brought her here under false premises.''

Burke's forefinger gently stroked her cheek. "Don't worry about Peg. Things will work out all right, I promise you. Forget about the island for now. We'll talk about it when we get back tomorrow.''

"That's another thing—I've really got to get back today, Burke,'' she said firmly. "If you can't take me I'll get there some other way. We've got to start closing up the business without delay. We owe it to the people who have advance reservations to let them know we're closing so they can make other vacation arrangements.''

"Why the blasted hurry?'' he asked almost crossly. "Nobody's going to run you off.''

"Since when?'' she couldn't resist asking with a wry smile.

There was a flicker of humor in his eyes as he replied, "Since the morning after we rode double on Cherokee if you're asking for an exact day.''

There was a long moment of silence between them before Allison said, "Well, thanks for not pushing."

"Then it's settled. You'll stay here like a sensible person until the doctor dismisses you tomorrow?"

Allison gave a resigned sigh. "Oh, I suppose it's the only thing to do. Peg could start notifying people with reservations that we're closing, but I hate to break this to her over the phone."

"Then don't," advised Burke. "There's no rush, I told you." Then, as if on a sudden welcome thought, he said, "Why not keep the place open until the current reservations run out?"

Allison looked at him in surprise. "You mean it? You realize it would mean some delay. We're booked ahead solid for the next two weeks, and it would take at least another week or so to get out after that."

"Is that all?" There was a strange note almost of regret in his voice. Unexpectedly he turned his attention to starting the car, then pulled out of the hospital driveway, saying nothing more. They rode the full distance to the hotel in silence.

From her seat beside him Allison watched the strong handsome profile surreptitiously and puzzled over the closed mask that had come down over his face. What inner turmoil had their conversation stirred in him, she wondered. The subject contained no surprises for him, including the fact that she soon intended to turn Plantation House back to him.

The golden brows were pulled low; the sensuous mouth had firmed into an ironic, self-deprecating line. He drove with eyes straight ahead. Then, at an intersection where he brought the car to a full stop for a red light, he turned to look at her with restless eyes. She met his gaze questioningly and saw a haunting uncertainty on his face.

Almost angrily his hand left the wheel and reached out to take hers, as if he were afraid she would leave. So intent was he on some strange inner conflict that he ignored the changing of the light and lifted her hand to lay a soft kiss in her palm, until a cacophony of horns behind them brought his attention back to the wheel.

Oh, Burke! the silent voice cried out within her as she understood that whatever battle the man was fighting had to do with her. As if holding a fragile treasure, she curled her fingers over the hand he had kissed and withdrew into herself.

Conversation between them remained minimal until a bellhop showed them to the room Burke had secured for her in the hotel where he was staying.

"I've got to call Peg, Burke," Allison said when they were alone. "She really must be told not to take any more reservations beginning today."

"I thought it was clear there's no need to rush into this moving," he insisted, an edge to his voice.

"You did, and I appreciate your offer to let us stay on until the reservations run out," Allison replied wearily. A dull ache in her head reminded her of the bump that lay under her hair. "You must understand, though, that every new reservation we take can mean another day before we can get out. If we don't start cutting off at once we could be here all summer.''

''What's wrong with that?''

''Everything!'' exclaimed Allison, a note of desperation in her voice. ''Can't you see? Peg and I have got to get on with our lives!''

For an instant she saw his face darkly masked again, and even after it cleared a shadow of stress remained. ''Supposing we could work something out?'' he said.

Allison's skepticism could be heard in her voice. ''In what way?'' she asked.

There was a long moment of silence. Then, as if he had come to a decision, Burke said abruptly, ''I hadn't intended to get into this, but it looks as if we already are.''

Listening closely, Allison scarcely breathed for fear even so discreet an action might deflect him from whatever mysterious course he was about to pursue. She sensed a reluctance in him that seemed to give in to what he had to say as he continued.

''It's an idea I've had for a long time,'' he began. ''I hope to set up an experimental research and study center for sea farming on Ransome's Cay. One of the foundations interested in the world food supply had already agreed to underwrite it with grants to qualified scientists and technicians, and we have other potential funding.''

''It sounds like a worthwhile undertaking, Burke,

but I can't see what it has to do with me," Allison said in a puzzled voice.

"I haven't told you about the Plantation House end of it," he said. Quickly he outlined the plan as he and McGinnis had discussed it several days earlier.

As Allison listened the concept began to come alive for her, and by the time he had finished her mind was already racing on to consider how much more smoothly the house could be run under the arrangement Burke proposed.

The problems that plagued them in the opening days of Plantation House as a commercial venture would, by the very nature of the project, no longer exist. Scientists and technicians and their families would be birds of a feather. No more trying to make a congenial mix of bluejays and owls and peacocks. With a handpicked guaranteed guest list there'd be no scrambling to keep a full house, no more worries at the end of the week that there wouldn't be enough money in the coffers to meet the bills.

Beyond all this she saw another plus that she refused to let her mind even consider: such an arrangement would call for regular—perhaps even daily—meetings with Burke.

Attractive as the proposition appeared, she couldn't agree to it until she knew exactly what had impelled him to make such an offer. If she had correctly read the silence between them on the ride over from the hospital, he hadn't reached the decision to do it easily.

Did he feel a family indebtedness to her because of his relationship to Tyler? Or a personal sense of obligation because she'd been hurt by the catapulting rock and he had escaped? In either case she could not accept the offer, however much she longed to.

Ransome seemed almost to read her mind. "This research center is one of the great dreams of my life," he said, "but it will have to be shelved unless we can work out something together along these lines. If I shelve it now, someone else will get the green light from the foundation."

After a moment he went on. "If you really want to leave the cay, I will pay you in full, of course, for all the money and time you and the Crewes family have invested in the restoration of Plantation House to bring it up to modern standards. To be perfectly honest, without jeopardizing the oyster project at the lagoon, I don't have the money at hand to get the center rolling unless you're willing to continue to operate Plantation House as your own business, with participants from the center as guests. That way perhaps we could write off my indebtedness to you as rental over the long term."

She made no effort to hide the tears of joy that welled up in her eyes. "It's a deal," she sniffed with a shamefaced grin. "I'm sure Peg will be glad to agree."

She was in his arms then, and he was kissing her salty eyelids and cheeks until a faulty move brought a stab of pain from the damaged shoulder and a cry of anguish from her lips.

With a groan of contrition he let her go. Gazing down on her, he muttered hoarsely, "Oh, God, Allison, I don't know if this is going to work."

Before she had time to wonder about it he turned away. But at the door he looked back, and in a constrained voice he said, "Rest. I have an appointment. I'll be back around eleven and we'll work out plans for the rest of the day."

CHAPTER TWELVE

THE SUDDEN UNEXPECTED CHANGE in her fortunes buoyed Allison's spirits into such a euphoric state she felt the ever-present pain of her shoulder only on the fringes of her consciousness. Even Burke's strange parting mood stirred in her no more than a passing uncertainty.

As for his order to rest until he came for her, it seemed a bit high-minded in retrospect and best ignored. There were better things to do with the next two hours than lie in bed.

She took a quick glance in the mirror and saw that pleasure had put a glow of color in the face Burke had said was pale. She ran a comb through her hair and added a touch of lip gloss. Slipping the long strap to her white linen handbag over her uninjured shoulder, she left the luxurious room Burke had secured for her. A minute later she was dropping fifty floors to the hotel's breathtaking atrium lobby. From there she stepped out into the summer warmth of Peachtree Street.

It was an ideal day for window-shopping, and Peachtree Street, one of the South's most fashionable thoroughfares, was exactly the place to do it. Allison dawdled from one eye-catching shop window to another, at the same time taking genuine aesthetic pleasure in the beauty and chic of many of her fellow strollers.

She might have walked the full length of downtown Atlanta had not an inadvertent bump by a hurrying pedestrian set her shoulder suddenly on fire. A glance at her watch reminded her then that she had no time to waste moaning over her hurt if she were to be back in her hotel room before Burke arrived at eleven.

Her shoulder throbbed with pain by the time she reached her room. Yet she decided against taking one of the capsules the doctor had ordered for her. She looked forward to having lunch with Burke too much to put herself at a disadvantage by fogging her wits with a painkiller. This might even mark the beginning of a significant change in their relationship that could take them . . . well, who knew where it might take them, she thought with a stir of excitement. The point was, she intended to give it her best shot.

A knock at the door and Burke's answering voice to her obligatory "Who is it?" sent her heart pulsing faster. A moment later he was in the room, surveying her face critically.

"It doesn't look as if your rest did you much good," he observed with concern. "You're even paler than you were at the hospital this morning. Are you sure you're all right?"

"I was fine until somebody accidentally bumped into me down on the street and started this blasted arm throbbing again," she told him honestly. "It's a good thing it's tied down tight, or I suppose it might have slipped out."

Burke gave a disapproving grunt. "What were you doing down on the street?"

"Window-shopping," she replied. "Walking. No...floating, really...floating on air. My feet never touched the sidewalk." Her voice reflected some of her earlier buoyancy. "Oh, Burke, you don't know what a relief it is to be able to stay on at Plantation House. I couldn't spend the morning in bed!"

Ransome gave a reluctant grin and shook his head. "You really care for the old place, don't you?" he said wonderingly.

She hesitated, finding it strange he had to ask. "Of course I care! Why else do you think I'd put myself and everything I own on the line for it? All the wise heads advised me to sell out. 'Take the money and run,' they said. But I couldn't."

Her mind went back to those first days of his hostility, and she felt a stir of resentment that he could have misjudged her so.

"I've loved Plantation House from the moment I saw it years ago. I've thought of it as home almost from the first," she added quietly. "Surely you must have known."

"The possibility never occurred to me," he admitted regretfully. "I've been the only one who cared anything about the place for so long I guess I took it for granted I had a monopoly on caring.''

His arms reached to take her, but her body stiffened. She refused to allow the embrace. What he had just said wasn't enough. His former accusations butted their way rudely into her mind. What had he *really* thought? That she'd been motivated by avarice all along?

"No, Burke, not until we've finished this," she said evenly. "Exactly what did you think my motives were?"

She could see by his face it was a line he wasn't eager to pursue, though he let his hands fall to his sides and made no attempt to distract her by pressing the interrupted embrace.

"I was wrong, and I'm sorry," he said. "Does it really matter now what I thought?"

Something told her it was a mistake to push this, but it was too late. She had already replied stubbornly, "Of course it matters!"

Burke flashed her a wicked look. "Before I unburden myself perhaps I'd better remind you I wasn't the only one to harbor misconceptions in this case," he said. "How about bringing yours out in full view and we'll compare them, Allison. We may find we have a matched set."

She drew in her breath quickly. Under his steady gaze she felt her face grow hot. "Avaricious," "conniving," "dishonorable"—a whole glossary of abuses she'd heaped on him came flashing across her mind. For a moment she was stricken with remorse, disconcerted she hadn't seen the parallel until he'd been obliged to point it out.

As she fumbled for words to express her chagrin, the situation began to seem increasingly ludicrous to her. She caught a truant glint in his eyes and an effort to hide an unexpected quirk of humor with a clumsily faked cough. She tried to hold back her own madcap giggle rolling up from within, and the next moment they were leaning into one another, laughing hilariously. When their laughter was spent, she rested against him weakly, her head pillowed on his collarbone. She breathed in his clean male smell with secret pleasure as he held her loosely, taking care to avoid undue pressure to the injured side.

He moved his head, his lips whispering teasingly across her temple. The tip of his tongue played at the lobe of her ear until pain was lost in a well of sensual enjoyment. He rubbed his cheek along hers, and she felt the tantalizing roughness of the new beard pushing up beneath the recently shaved skin.

Then, to her frustration, the kiss he gave promised nothing more. "About lunch," he said abruptly.

She blinked at him owlishly and swallowed her dismay at the sudden end to a scene that had shown such promise. Robbed of the lovely distraction, she felt her pain come back intensified, seizing her attention with such stridency she wondered helplessly how she could make it through lunch without giving in to one of the doctor's pills.

"You hardly look ready to go down on the street again," Burke observed. "Maybe we'd better cancel at the restaurant and order from room service. The food here is very good."

"I suppose you're right," she said resignedly, "although I'm not all that crazy about lunching in my bedroom—even one that's a symphony of muted apricot, blues and buff with Dufy racing prints on the walls."

"Who said anything about lunching in your bedroom? We'll eat outdoors overlooking one of the best views in Atlanta."

Walking to the door on the far wall of her room, he flipped the one-way lock and threw back the door. The matching door behind it had already been opened, presumably by Burke, from the other side. A wide connecting passageway, at the opposite end of which was another door leading into what appeared to be a second bedroom, was furnished with a built-in wet bar of walnut-and-stainless steel. To the left of this she glimpsed a small section of a pale gold and gray living room.

"Have you taken any of those pills Frazier gave you for pain?" Burke asked. "You look as if you could use one, lady."

Allison managed a ghost of a grin. "I'm saving them for when it really hurts."

"You get no points for martyrdom," replied Burke. "Take two and lie down for a while. I'll call room service and cancel at the restaurant. When your lunch is on the table I'll come for you.''

She watched him until he closed the door to the room behind him. The pain was so demanding she gave only a passing thought to the fact that Burke had settled her into a suite she was obviously sharing with him. Under the throbbing ache she was incapable of carrying the provocative thought beyond the moment.

Hurrying into the alabaster bathroom, she shook two pain capsules from the plastic prescription bottle and washed them down with a glass of water. Back in the bedroom she slipped off her sandals. Pulling back the quilted bedspread and covers, she lay down on the matching pillow and closed her eyes to wait for the capsules to take effect.

Gradually her pain subsided. When Burke came from the adjoining room to get her some thirty minutes later, she smiled up at him muzzily and held out her good arm for their hands to meet. He pulled her gently to her feet. She was acutely aware of his hand resting lightly on her waist as they walked into the suite's comfortable living room.

They lunched on chilled cucumber soup and curried chicken salad, piquant with seedless white grapes. The meal was served on a shaded balcony a step down from the living room beyond massive French doors.

The spectacular view of the city promised by Burke was lost on Allison. Under the effects of the capsules she grew lethargic, and the simple act of carrying a forkful of food to her mouth required most of her energy. She felt lazy and witless and hadn't the will to care. Burke appeared as comfortable in the long silences as she was and made no effort to engage her in conversation during the meal.

"No coffee for you, dear one," he informed her as he poured a cup for himself when the meal was over. "It won't do to take the edge off that drowsiness. It'll carry you away once I get out of here."

The small endearment bemused her. "I don't really want any coffee anyhow," she murmured agreeably.

"Good," he said. "I've got a full schedule of conferences for the afternoon until six. We'll see how you feel then. If you're up to it after a good long sleep, we'll see if we can find someplace rather special for dinner tonight."

She would have been quite content to spend the afternoon there on the balcony in the healing comfort of his presence, she thought dreamily as he rose and came around to move the small, linen-covered table so she was free to stand and walk away from it without moving her chair. She allowed herself to be ushered inside and back to her bedroom, where she fell asleep almost before Ransome was out the door.

She slept away the afternoon and was awakened shortly before six by a phone call from Burke, asking if she felt up to leaving the hotel for dinner. She assured him she was fine and would be dressed and waiting when he arrived.

When she took stock of herself she realized she actually did feel fine. The afternoon of immobility had done wonders for her. As long as she kept her arm still she felt no more than a mild discomfort.

But the simple act of getting out of the rumpled clothing she had slept in and ready for the evening proved to be a challenge. The soft silk dress she now had reason to thank Peg for packing was designed with flowing sleeves and closed with a dozen pearl buttons from neckband to hem, making it easy to step into without disturbing the injury. Yet it soon had her ready to swear from frustration.

The doctor had cautioned her not to use her left hand for a day or so. She quickly discovered, to her dismay, that buttons on women's garments were on the wrong side for easy buttoning by the right hand without some backing from the left. And the fact that these buttons were small didn't make the process any easier.

She was still only halfway up from the bottom when a rap on her bedroom door told her Burke had come and was ready to depart.

But for the buttons Allison was ready, too. Before she stepped into the dress she'd run a comb through her hair and touched eyelids and lips with the bit of makeup she normally used. She'd also added a touch of color to her cheeks to forestall Burke's saying she looked pale. She slipped her feet into the thin-heeled, taffy-colored sandals and went back to her frantic fumbling with buttons.

Punctuality was a matter of principle with Allison. It bothered her greatly to be late.

"I'll be with you in a minute," she called out, hoping to keep the sound of frustration from her voice as one of the pearl buttons slipped away again from a buttonhole.

"Do you have a problem?" Burke called back through the closed door, his voice reflecting concern.

"It's these blasted buttons," Allison replied with exasperation. "Have you ever tried to do up a button with your right hand? I've been at these for the past half hour."

There was a momentary silence. Then Burke's puzzled voice came from beyond the door. "I never thought of it before, but I find the right hand's the only one to use."

"Then come in here," she said with a sigh of defeat. "Either you finish buttoning me or I'm going to have to get back into the dress I slept in all afternoon. The only other thing I have with me is a cotton skirt and a blouse that has buttons on it, too."

"No wonder. This dress buttons the wrong way," Burke observed as he took over the half-finished task.

"That's the way women's clothes button. Don't ask me why!" Allison retorted, a hint of asperity in her voice.

Burke grinned. "The real problem is that you weren't foresighted enough to knock out the right shoulder."

Relenting, Allison matched his grin. "You've got a point," she said in return.

She felt a sudden uneasiness as his eyes moved up the line of her dress opening to where the lacy camisole top of her slip and the beginning rise of her breasts above it were exposed. Did he take the fact that she'd called him in there to be an invitation to make love to her, she wondered with growing embarrassment, furious with herself for having let frustration provoke her into asking him to come in.

"Burke..." she began as his hands came up to slip her dress down over the injured shoulder. A dark, blue black discoloration radiated out from around the firm strapping that held it in place. She heard him draw in his breath sharply.

After a moment he leaned down and touched his lips to her bare neck near the edge of the tape. "Sweet...lovely...gallant lady to take such a risk," he murmured. "You should have let that boulder hit me. I can promise you, it wouldn't have made a dent in this oak-hard head."

She was relieved then that he lifted the dress back to cover her shoulder and gravely finished the buttons to the top. And yet didn't she really want to have it both ways? Even in the face of the humiliating possibility that he might believe her purpose in asking him in was to make love Allison had known a sudden breathless anticipation as he'd slipped her dress down from her shoulder. Her relief at the reassurance was dulled by a shadow of regret.

They dined at a beautifully restored 18th-century plantation house. The white-haired owner and master of the kitchen, Jean-Paul Le Seur, left his lair and came to their table to greet Burke personally and suggest they dispense with the menu and leave their selections to him.

"Do I get the impression you are rather special to Monsieur Le Seur?" Allison asked when the Frenchman had left them.

"Mostly it's a tribute to my father," Burke told her. "Jean-Paul came to Atlanta as a young man after serving a long apprenticeship under a four-star chef in Lyon. My dad loaned him the money to start his first restaurant and sent friends there. It was a good investment for dad, as it turned out, but Jean Paul doesn't forget."

From the lobster quenelles, cloud light with a delicate white wine sauce, through the herbed crown roast of lamb—which Allison was obliged to let Burke cut for her—the salad mimosa and the soufflé grand Marnier it was a meal of exquisite perfection. Jean-Paul presided over the serving of each course with such intensity Allison hardly dared decline a glass of the French wine he brought with his compliments, fearing to offend the proud little man. She was glad to have Burke come to her rescue.

"Mrs. Hill suffered a severe injury to her shoulder yesterday and is taking strong medication for pain," Burke explained. "The doctor advises no alcohol while she's on it."

Monsieur Le Seur's eyes were so clearly sympathetic that Allison hastened to say, "I'm sure a taste wouldn't hurt, Burke. A small glass? It's been hours since I took the capsules."

The restaurateur's face lighted up with pleasure. Burke nodded agreement, and he filled the glass at Allison's place.

The single glass of wine gave her an unexpected glow. Across the candlelit table she watched Burke dreamily as he talked, and gradually she became aware of a wonderful sense of well-being that had nothing to do with the improved condition of her shoulder, which, for that matter, had begun to hurt again.

She was mildly surprised that she was content to let Burke decide whether she should have wine. Secure in her own independent spirit and a belief in herself as a person, Allison sensed a growing understanding between them of each other's worth. She felt no need to defend herself as a woman with this man. Nor did she object to letting him take charge of things for a time. The ordeal of pain on top of the uncertainty of the past weeks had drained her. There was something wonderfully restorative in Burke's light undemanding talk after the hostilities and passion that had flared between them from the moment of their first meeting.

Across the table their eyes met unexpectedly and held in a long poignant renewal. Deep within, a delicious core of pleasure trembled into sudden life.

Burke reached across the table and laid a hand upon her unhampered one. "Come," he said. "It's time to go."

As she stepped from the curb into the waiting taxi, a slight misstep caused her to bump against the door frame of the car and jar the injured shoulder. The discomfort she'd managed to ignore all evening exploded at last into a throbbing ache. She turned her head away to hide the sudden tears that were brought to her eyes, but Burke was not to be fooled.

"You could have done without that," he said with concern, and settled her protectively against his shoulder when he was beside her in the cab. There she rested and let the tears stay damp on her cheeks until he dabbed them away with his own linen handkerchief.

As they crossed the lobby a few minutes later on the way to the elevator, Allison was aware of a vaguely familiar figure approaching them. It was a somewhat porcine man with longish hair too painstakingly styled. He was wearing a plaid polyester suit in a color Allison thought of as seasick green. Around his neck was draped a heavy gold chain from which hung a medallion the size of a demitasse saucer. Her mind dulled with pain, she made no special effort to recall where she had seen the man previously until she sensed a tension in the strong arm that supported her lightly.

From a corner of her eye she saw the man hasten his steps with the obvious intention of waylaying them before the elevator could swallow them up. He caught them at the closed door and extended a hand, which Burke managed to overlook. At that moment Allison remembered where she'd seen him. It was the Los Angeles land developer, Travis, who'd had his eye on Ransome's Cay.

"Well, if it isn't Ransome!" Travis cried out in phony surprise. "I didn't expect to get a chance to talk to you again before I left Georgia for LA."

Remembering the imp of malice that had impelled her to send the man down to the lagoon to make his pitch, Allison had the grace to dart a sheepish glance at Burke. She was taken aback at the dark look she saw on his face.

"You were quite right—I said all I had to say to you the other day at the lagoon," Burke answered him coldly as the elevator doors parted. "Now if you'll excuse me. . . ."

He ushered Allison into the elevator, leaving the sentence dangling. He stepped in beside her and pushed the button for their floor. To her surprise Travis followed them in. The door closed on the three of them. There was a grim set to Burke's jaw. He ignored the intruder's presence.

"Well, well! And if it isn't Mrs. Hill," Travis exclaimed, as if seeing for the first time that she was there, too. "I sure didn't expect to find you here with Ransome."

The leer on his face matched the tone of his voice. She noticed a muscle begin to twitch ominously in

Burke's cheek, and she slipped a hand quietly into his to give it what she hoped was a restraining squeeze. The last thing she felt up to at the moment was an elevator donnybrook, and she had no measure of how far Burke could be pushed.

She underestimated Ransome's restraint.

"What's your floor, Travis?" Burke said with frosty disdain. "I'll push the button for you."

"Same as yours," Travis replied. "Don't look so surprised. I figured if we talk a little more about that island, I might make you see things my way."

The elevator came to a stop and the door opened. Ransome moved a step to prevent it from closing again and motioned Allison out. Travis made a move to follow, but Ransome barred his way. Travis hesitated no more than an instant before he moved back a step.

"You're going back down, and if I see your miserable face again during my stay at this hotel, I'll have the house detective on you for harassment," Ransome said, his voice icy and controlled. "Before I let you go you're going to tell me where you got my room number and how you managed a room for yourself on the same floor. And don't tell me it's a coincidence."

Intimidated though he'd been for a moment, Travis's brashness again showed through. "It's an old trick," he explained smugly. "I called that outfit of yours on the island, and they said I could reach you at Ransome Mills in Atlanta. Your office there gave me the hotel. I told them at the desk that we were old business buddies, so could they give me a room next to yours. The clerk looks at his cart and says 5108 and 5110 are taken. It's not hard to figure the one in between is 5109. Once I knew where I could find you I told him to give me one directly across the hall.''

"You went to a lot of trouble," Ransome said contemptuously. "Just what do you expect to gain?''

"I thought I'd pay you a little visit—thought you might be interested in what I had to say. It might have made you change your mind about turning down my offer on Ransome's Cay. But that don't matter now. That was before I found out you had this lady staying with you. That changes the picture some." There was a note of gloating in the developer's voice and a self-satisfied smirk on his face.

Ransome reached and grabbed his lapels in both hands, pulling him forward until he was less than a foot away. Watching, Allison held her breath. Travis, who was nearly as tall as Burke and outweighed him by a number of pounds, struggled vainly to get away.

After a moment Ransome gave a disgusted grunt and let Travis go so abruptly he reeled backward, steadying himself against the elevator wall.

"You are a bastard, Travis," Ransome said scornfully. "Now get the hell out of here and don't let me hear of you again." He stepped out of the elevator, and the doors slowly began to close, leaving Travis alone inside.

In those moments before the doors came together

and the elevator began its descent Travis had the last word. "You'll hear from me again, Ransome, I'm telling you!" he shrilled. "I'll get that island of yours. Wait and see."

"He must be crazy!" Allison exclaimed as Burke took her arm and hurried down the broad corridor in the direction of their suite.

"I wish I thought so," he said grimly. "He's working some kind of a scam to get Ransome's Cay, but I'll be damned if I know what it is."

Allison came to a full stop. "You mean he's trying to swindle you out of the island?"

Ransome urged her along. "Let's get in before he reaches the bottom and comes back up," he said. Moving again, he answered, "Not a swindle. More like extortion...blackmail. He seems to think he's got some kind of secret leverage that will force me to sell to him, but for the life of me I don't know what it is. I'd go after him if I did."

"It couldn't be much, Burke," Allison said soothingly. "It's got to be something cooked up in a hurry. He thought the island belonged to me when he came to Plantation House, so he must have cooked up his ploy on the way down to the lagoon that day. I'm not surprised he came back in such a hurry if he went down there with a threat."

"He didn't threaten me then," Ransome said. "I had no interest in selling. Besides, he struck me as a pretty sleazy operator. I told him to get out."

"Then how did you know...?"

"The threat came later. He called me a couple of days ago to say in effect that if I didn't change my mind I'd be sorry. He was aggressive as hell, as if now he were calling the shots."

"He actually threatened you?"

"No question about it. Had the gall to tell me it would be in my best interests to drop everything and fly into Atlanta to talk to him about it. I hung up."

Ransome quickly closed the door of the suite behind them and stopped in the entryway to take a close look at Allison.

"I'm sorry," he said quietly. "You look a little shaken. Take a couple of those capsules and go tuck yourself in. What you need is a good night's sleep."

The peremptory dismissal sparked a flash of anger in Allison, but she gave him a level look, then turned on her heel to march into her bedroom and close the door. She leaned against it and let the waves of pain radiating down her arm, which she'd tried to ignore, feed her fury.

Who did he think he was, telling her what she needed was a good night's sleep. How did he know what she needed? What she really needed was the good-night kiss he hadn't given her. She wasn't asking him to make love to her. Just a kiss. Was that such a lot to expect?

"You want me to unbutton you?" Ransome called cheerfully from the other side.

"No thanks."

Kicking off her sandals, Allison went to the bathroom to take the pain capsules and a sleeping pill before beginning the slow task of undressing herself with only one hand. By the time she'd washed her face and brushed her teeth and was in a pair of tailored silk pajamas, ready for bed, the combined medications had begun to work. Her crossness disappeared in direct ratio to her pain, until she was willing to concede Burke had been right to send her off to bed. Still, he might at least have kissed her good-night.

She slid her feet out of her slippers and was about to tuck in when a knock on the connecting door stopped her. Burke's voice came softly from the other side. "Is it all right if I come in?"

Caught off guard, Allison called back, "Please do." Detecting a note of eagerness in her own voice, she wondered with a kind of dreamy, drug-dulled detachment if it was perhaps inappropriate.

The door opened, and at the sight of the man paused for a moment in the doorway she decided she didn't care. This new beginning would be built on candor and trust. She wanted him there. Why should she hide it? Simply because she was a woman and he was a man?

In the minutes since they'd parted he had been able to dismiss the unpleasantness in the elevator that had set his sensuous face in a hard line. He smiled now, his eyes embracing her with a tenderness that at the same time was questioning.

"You left in a hurry," he said. "I wasn't sure I would be welcome," he said.

"I'm sorry, the shoulder was giving me fits," she apologized truthfully. "It did things to my disposition. I wanted to be cosseted, I guess."

With a wry laugh Burke crossed the room to where she stood. "You had every right to be angry. I was still carrying on the battle of the elevator."

He took her gently in his arms. His hands slipped under her soft silk pajama coat, the long strong fingers finding their way beneath the band at the waist, fanning out to move down in a sensuous path to clasp her satiny body to his own. She lifted her face to meet his. Their lips clung.

She felt herself drifting into a strange fantasyland of sensual acceptance where she simply took, incapable in her dreamlike state of giving anything in return. She luxuriated like a pampered kitten under the stroke of his hands as they relaxed their hold and moved up the curves of her waist. His fingertips found the rising surface of her breasts, sending a delicious shiver through her.

"That's lovely," she murmured thickly, her syllables fuzzy.

A hand encountered the taping that held her shoulder in place. Even in her euphoric state she knew he was about to leave her. A part of her wanted him to go, to leave her alone to dream out the fulfillment reality was about to rob her of.

But another part of her wanted to hold him there. When he lifted his mouth from hers she sensed in him a reluctance as great as her own. Even so, the most she could do to detain him was to let her head drift lazily to his breast. He held there for a moment, his cheek grazing the surface of her hair.

She heard a sigh. Then gently, firmly, as if performing an act of sterling self-discipline, he pushed her away from him. "Enough cosseting for one night," he said in a strained voice. With a light goodnight kiss to her lips he was gone.

A night without wakening brought Allison to the new day clear-eyed and refreshed. The deep throbbing ache in her shoulder that had plagued her the previous day had slacked off, leaving her with nothing more than a tolerable discomfort. Except for a coated tongue and a tendency to dawdle, the aftereffect of the double medication the previous night, she felt almost herself again.

She bathed clumsily but managed to keep the strapping dry. When Burke rapped on her door for breakfast she submitted to having him button the melon pink blouse she had put on with the dark, cotton-print skirt.

He greeted her with a warm smile, but his light kiss was directed to her cheek and he performed the required ritual impersonally. She was troubled by a certain reserve she sensed in him. It was no stranger to her, certainly, but it hadn't been there the previous night.

Together they walked from breakfast to Jack Frazier's office. Burke left Allison there while he went to take care of some final business at the mill.

The doctor removed her strapping and exchanged it for a sling, which he told her to wear for support a few days longer.

Later, as they were checking out at the hotel's reception desk, ready to fly back to Ransome's Cay in the company plane, Allison was surprised to hear Burke inquire about the man who had given them trouble the previous night.

"Orrin Travis?" The clerk looked through his files and turned back to Burke, a puzzled expression on his face. "It looks like he came and went. It seems a little strange, though. According to this he checked out last night shortly after he checked in."

Burke thanked the clerk, and when he turned back to Allison she was once more surprised at the dark look on his face.

"Let's hope he's gone back to LA," she said,

Burke shook his head. "I should have had you go on to bed and followed up on him last night," he said grimly. "I should have found out once and for all what his game is. It's too much to hope that I've seen the last of Orrin Travis."

CHAPTER THIRTEEN

THE TRIM FOUR-SEATER PLANE was out of the hangar, its engine already running when they arrived at the airport, but there was no pilot in sight. It was not until Burke settled her in one of the passenger seats and took the pilot's place that she realized there had been a change of plans and he intended to fly them back himself.

Before she could ask any questions Burke gave himself over to a preflight checklist with a single-mindedness that discouraged interruptions. It was yet another side of the man she hadn't seen previously. She watched with growing fascination, awed by the total concentration he bestowed on the instrument panel as he revved the engine and let it idle again, listening, observing, noting each gauge, before he exited from the plane to examine the tires and landing gear. There was a competence, an economy of motion about all he did, that she found exciting to watch. He was sure of himself; he knew what he was doing, whether riding a horse, checking out a plane, starting an oyster farm or...pleasing a woman?

Squinting against the sun, he looked up from the

ground at the window where she sat as if he read her thoughts. A light breeze ruffled the brown, sun-gilded hair, feathering it across his broad forehead.

His eyes found hers. He lifted his shoulders, as if in the movement freeing himself from...she could not imagine what. In the next instant the tightly locked face opened up in a wondrously sensuous smile that ravished her heart.

Yes, she thought half ruefully, pleasing a woman...of course. Yet in this he seemed somehow unaware of the power of his compelling charm, quite comfortable to let things happen, as if he didn't feel completely easy with his ability to take control.

From the ground where he looked up at her the momentary seduction turned into a disarming grin. He touched thumb and forefinger together to form a circle and gave her an A-okay salute. A moment later he was in the pilot's seat again, warming up, and they were off.

"I didn't know you were a pilot," Allison remarked when they'd cleared the city and were cruising high above the Georgia countryside.

Burke turned to her with a smile. "I made my first solo flight on my eighteenth birthday," he told her, his face showing his delight in the recollection. "I don't know how many hundreds of flying hours I've put in since, but it's been a few."

"That preflight routine you went through?" she asked. "Do you go through all that checking every time you take off?"

"There's an old saying: 'There are old pilots and there are careless pilots—there are no old careless pilots,' " he said lightly. "When I was a kid I got in the bad habit of letting other people check out the plane. Then someone slipped up one day, and I cracked up a company plane. I was lucky. I walked away from it. But my dad grounded me for six months."

"You mean he blamed you for someone else's carelessness?"

"He didn't ground me for totaling the plane," Burke explained with a grin. "He grounded me for not running the checklist myself. He always contended that the guy who stays on the ground doesn't have the same interest in making sure the plane's ready for flight as the guy who's going to fly it."

Their flight plan that morning took them east and south from Atlanta to the coast, where they turned due south to follow the long lacework of the famed Sea Islands.

"This may seem a long way for us to fly home, but it's time you saw this remarkable string of islands from the air," he explained. "You can't get the full flavor until you do. A lot of them have belonged to four different countries in the past three hundred years, not counting the American Indians, who were here first."

Nearing Ransome's Cay, Burke once more directed Allison's attention below, this time with a trace of nostalgia in his voice.

"See that little triangle of land?" he said. "That's Razorback. But I called it Treasure Island—after my favorite book when I was a kid. I liked to take a bedroll and some food and row up there. There wasn't another soul on it then. Sometimes I'd hang out there a couple of days."

Allison looked at him in surprise.

"Didn't your mother worry?"

There was a moment's pause. "That was after she died," he said. "Dad wasn't paying much attention at the time."

For a moment she saw on his face the shadow of a motherless boy forgotten by a grief-stricken father. She had a compelling urge to reach out and comfort the boy he had been in a loneliness twenty years past.

"It's strange," she said. "Sometimes I feel I know all about you, and then something like this comes up and I realize I don't know much about you at all. I wish I did."

He didn't answer. After a moment he turned to look at her, and she was surprised at the change that had come over him. It was as if he had walled himself off from her. His face was no longer open. The gray green eyes had grown dark.

"Burke, I'm sorry," she said, not even sure what she apologized for. "I happen to believe that the more two people know about each other, the more open they are, the better their relationship."

Ransome's eyes were wintry. "There are exceptions," he said.

Then before she could respond, he ordered, "Check your belt—we're going down. That's Ransome's Cay ahead."

For the next few minutes he devoted his full attention to bringing the plane smoothly to rest on a broad strip of sand that faced the east side of the lagoon.

His words prickled in Allison's mind. She scarcely noted the grace of the landing, so impatient was she to throw the words back at Burke.

"About those exceptions," she said as he reached to unbuckle his seat belt when they were on the ground.

His hand stopped. "Exceptions?"

In his face she read his reluctance to go back to the subject again.

"Exceptions to what we should know about each other," she prompted.

Again his eyes surveyed her bleakly. "For starters, I'd just as soon not know about your...ah...devotion to my late cousin," he said, his voice bitter.

"I'm sorry," she said. "Whatever you know you didn't hear from me, Burke, nor will you. For whatever it's worth, I was very young and fell blindly in love as only the young can do. Forget it. It has nothing to do with you."

"It has everything to do with me," he disagreed coldly. There was a note of despair in his voice. He reached across the space between them and took her face in his hands.

"You know he was a swine, Allison!" he burst out with a terrible intensity. "Say it. Say it!"

Looking into his tormented eyes, Allison was tempted—not to say the actual word, for it was not her word or one she would think to use to describe Ty. She would say, "He gave me a bad time, Burke, but when he killed any love I had for him he lost all power to hurt me. All I've felt since then is a kind of sorrow for the man who made a mess of whatever he touched."

But hers was a self-serving indictment against someone who'd lost his last chance for human dignity. To utter it would be like stripping the shroud from the dead. She couldn't say it any more than she could say he was a swine.

"He's dead," she said instead. "Isn't that enough?"

With a short harsh laugh he let her face slip from his hands. "I was actually sorry he was killed when he crashed his car," he said. "Somehow I'd managed to forget . . . and then you came to remind me."

"That doesn't change anything. He's gone, Burke. What does it take to make you forget?"

There was a long silence. With a note of self-contempt Burke said at last, "Maybe I need to hear you say you hate him."

"I can't say it," she answered him dully. *Not after all the time it took me to learn not to hate,* she thought. "It would be a lie."

Unexpectedly he reached for her face again and

gave her lips a hard quick kiss. "It's all right, Allison," he said, his voice suddenly at peace. "I guess I wouldn't even want you to."

WELL, SKIPPER, YOU REALLY BLEW IT! Burke berated himself bleakly a few minutes later as he stood by the plane and watched the jeep with Hoddy Crewes at the wheel and Allison beside him speed away down the beach in a wake of swirling sand.

There'd been no time to say more. On hearing the plane, Hoddy had come roaring up to carry her back to Plantation House, and the moment was gone. Maybe it was gone anyhow. Maybe there was nothing more to be said. Still, it left him unsatisfied.

Moodily he plodded through the sand toward the lab a short distance down the shore to look for Doc McGinnis, though he doubted he'd find him there. Doc would have been out to meet the plane if he'd been ashore.

He found the lab empty and put in a call to the barge and then to the *Ulysses*, moored in the lagoon, only to be told the biologist was underwater but would come ashore as soon as he surfaced.

Leaving the lab, Ransome stretched out in the shade of a clump of palmettos nearby to wait for Doc. He closed his eyes. Before he took off for Atlanta again he wanted to hear how things had gone with the oyster frames during his absence. He also wanted to tell McGinnis about the new arrangements at Plantation House in case he didn't get back from the mainland again for a day or two. At least that news should please Doc.

If Burke had held any hope the proposal he'd made to Allison would work for him, the flight from Atlanta had erased it. His whole reason for taking the plane himself had been to provide for a long uninterrupted talk with Allison. As it turned out, he'd blathered on about the Sea Islands most of the trip, all the time wondering how to ask her the one thing he wanted cleared up. When the opening had arisen it had been disastrous.

She hadn't said it in so many words, but she had added substance to Effie's appraisal of her continued devotion to Ty.

Under the circumstances how could they work together as closely as this new order would require? How could he maintain an impersonal business relationship with her day to day when every time he was alone with her he fought a losing battle against taking her in his arms? To make it worse, he saw in her eyes a desire that matched his own.

Whatever her feelings for Ty, the two of them were drawn together like magnet to steel. The previous day and night, when even in pain she'd welcomed him with her eyes, he'd gone through a kind of hell he could never learn to live with. He'd suffered an even greater hell the night they'd given themselves to each other. He had lain awake most of the night wondering if she'd been pretending all the time he was Ty.

What irony, he thought bitterly. First Margo, now

Allison. The two women in his life, both commandeered by his prodigal relative.

In the long run, though, it hadn't really mattered
with Margo. She'd never been worth the youthful
passion and agony he'd squandered on her. He'd had
to grow up and become his own man before he'd
known this to be true.

But am I really my own man, he asked himself, or
was his cousin still calling shots from beyond the
grave?

Rejecting the premise, Burke sat up in sudden restlessness and squinted across the lagoon, where he
could see a figure getting ready to debark in the
dinghy from the *Ulysses.* The small boat was too far
away for him to discern exactly who was in it, but he
knew by the old-fashioned, wide-brimmed Panama
hat it must be Doc.

Burke dropped his head on his knees and waited,
his thought focused on Allison. Allison...Alli-
son...lovely, decent, bright, courageous, passionate.... There was no end to his glossary of praise.
Here was a woman worth any agony one had to en-
dure to win her love, he thought. What did it matter
if she was still carrying a torch for Ty? She was not a
neurotic casualty clinging morbidly to widowhood,
as he had wanted to think. She was a high-spirited,
healthy-minded young woman secure in a strong
belief in herself.

Was anything else really important, after all?

For the first time he probed deeply into his reactions to the ugly scene he'd walked in on that long-ago night at Plantation House, searching now for undiscovered meanings.

Almost from the beginning there'd been little worth saving between him and Margo. Early in their marriage he'd lost his illusions and knew her for what she was. The real shock that sent him into two years of bitter retreat was not that he'd found her with another man—in a way he'd hardly been surprised—but that the man was his cousin, Ty. If it had been anyone else, he understood suddenly, he would have felt little more than disgust and a profound relief to have their travesty of a marriage come to an end.

The fact was, he'd been rocked to his very foundations at being betrayed in such a fashion by a wastrel of his own blood—the drone he had rescued in the name of family honor from more scrapes than he cared to count.

He realized he'd been in mortal danger then—the only time in his life—of letting Tyler destroy him.

As for Margo, he'd left her to Ty. And how like his cousin to mail him a picture of Margo, clipped from a Reno newspaper, who was presumably there for a quick divorce. She was clinging to the arm of a Nevada gambling-casino czar and wearing a black mink coat and diamond earrings she hadn't owned when he'd seen her last.

Ty had hoped to rub a little salt in the old wound, he guessed, never imagining that it no longer mattered to Burke.

"He's gone, Burke. What does it take to make you forget?" Allison's words came rushing back to him with a jolt.

For you to forget, he answered her in his mind, and in the next instant found the true answer in his heart.

It was all up to him!

The answer exorcised the old ghost of his cousin at last, and for the first time in years Burke Ransome was free.

What difference did it make how she remembered Tyler Hill? Ty wasn't important. He'd been only as important as Burke had let him become in his own mind.

The important thing was to win Allison's love.

With Doc pulling in to shore and no one to hear him Burke said softly aloud, "Look out, Allison Hill! You're in for the damndest wooing it's in me to devise."

Suddenly alive, he jumped to his feet and sprinted across the sand to greet McGinnis, who had cut his motor and was floating into the shallows on the tide. At the edge of the water Burke leaned forward to grasp the prow of the boat and pull it up on the sand as Doc jumped out. "Sorry to bring you up from the deep, Doc, but I need to talk to you before I head back to Atlanta," Ransome said when the two of them had the boat beached.

After bringing each other up to date on Allison's recovery and the oyster frames, Ransome came to the subject that had lain dormant between them since he'd cut it off short some days earlier.

"About the research and study center, McGinnis," he began. "You might like to know I've talked to Allison about your suggestion, and she's willing to go along with it." He quickly explained his conversation with her the previous morning after they'd left the hospital.

McGinnis eyed him quizzically as he talked. "I thought the subject was closed," he said bluntly when his friend paused. "What miracle caused you to change your mind?"

Burke's grin was an apology. "I saw some merits I hadn't seen at first," he hedged. "I plan to stop at Sapelo on my way back from Atlanta to see a couple of men at the marine institute and get the show on the road."

"You just got back from Atlanta. What's all the hurry to go again?"

"I'm going back to see if I can get a line on this Orrin Travis," said Ransome. He told McGinnis about the encounter in the elevator the previous night.

"He checked out only a short time after he checked in, so I guess we can assume he was there to nail me," Ransome said. "I've got to find out where he's gone and what his racket is. It may take a few days."

"What makes you so sure it's a racket?"

"That phone call he made here last week. It

smacked of blackmail or extortion. I didn't give it much thought until the business in the elevator.''

"Blackmail? Extortion? Based on what—or do you have any idea?''

"Only that it's got something to do with my late cousin," Ransome said. "I sure as hell can't think of anything in my own past for which I'd be willing to sell Ransome's Cay to keep the lid on, so it must be Ty. There's no one else.''

McGinnis grunted. "Your cousin is beyond the need of protection," he pointed out wryly.

"Well, it's not me, so it must be Ty," Burke repeated stubbornly. "It wouldn't be the first time I've paid for his misdeeds to protect the family honor.''

He puzzled over the enigma a moment longer. Suddenly he began to laugh. "Only this time it's different," he said with a wicked grin. "What Travis doesn't know is that I've quit settling up for my cousin. Let him do what he likes with his information. I'll find a better way to preserve the Ransome honor than to pay for it with Ransome's Cay.''

Doc let him have his moment of satisfaction. Then he said, "It couldn't have anything to do with Allison, could it?''

A wave of shock rushed through Burke.

"My God, that's what it is," he said aghast. "I don't know what he's up to, but he's got it in his mind to involve Allison somehow. You could almost see the light turn on in his head last night when he saw her with me in the elevator. I thought there was something salacious going on in that rotten little mind. If she hadn't been there I would have gone after him on the spot. It never occurred to me that he'd thought of a way to use her to get Ransome's Cay. He may even think he can get at me through her.''

McGinnis gave him a long level look. "Well, can he?'' he asked.

There was a second's pause before Burke said soberly, "Yes, I suppose he can.'' He put his hand on his friend's shoulder. "Look, Doc, I've got to run him down and put a stop to whatever he's up to. When you see Allison don't mention Travis. Tell her I've gone to Sapelo about the center.''

A short time later Ransome was airborne, heading inland on a direct course back to Atlanta.

ON THE PORCH off the morning room Allison and Peg had settled down with a pitcher of iced tea to discuss what had transpired since that fateful morning two days earlier. Just then the sound of the plane's take-off brought Allison's words to a halt. She paused to listen. She hadn't thought about Burke's having to turn around and return the plane to Atlanta right away. Bemused, she supposed the company pilot would bring him back to the island again. She wondered why the pilot hadn't brought them over in the first place and saved Burke the extra round trip.

"You were saying...?'' prompted Peg, watching her friend curiously.

Blinking, Allison brought her attention back to the moment. "Excuse me, I...." She looked at Peg blankly. "I'm sorry. I don't know. I haven't the faintest idea what I was saying," she confessed with an abashed chuckle.

The other woman's face was flushed with exasperation. "What's the matter with you, Allison? First you tell me Burke actually does own the island and everything on it, just like he said, and then right in the middle of it you forget what you're talking about as if you couldn't care less. You're not doped up on painkillers or something are you?"

Allison grinned and shook her head. "Heavens, no," she said. "I haven't had any medication since last night. It still hurts enough that I haven't forgotten, but not enough for pills."

"Then I'm really worried about you. I feel like going up there and punching that lawyer out. Don't you understand what this means, Ally? You've got to sue him. You should get punitive damages if nothing else." The round face flamed with near-apoplectic fury.

"Calm down, Peg," soothed Allison. "It's not nearly as bad as it sounds." She went on to describe Burke's plan to turn Plantation House into a center for research and study in farming the sea.

Her friend listened closely and the flush on her face gradually subsided, but her eyes remained negative. It was not until Allison explained that she and Peg would be operating Plantation House for the center's guests with money from already promised grants that Peg's face began to show approval.

"It's what every innkeeper dreams of...no scrambling for money or guests...nothing to concern us but the three c's of hostelry—comfort, cleanliness and cuisine." Peg rattled on excitedly.

Then she came to an abrupt stop. "I'm sorry, Allison," she said contritely. "I forgot for a moment this is costing you Plantation House. I wasn't thinking of anybody but me. I'd still like to get my hands on that rotten lawyer. It's a darned shame you had to lose the island a little bit at a time."

"Don't worry about it, Peg," Allison reassured her. "The island's in good hands. Burke's been planning for Ransome's Cay since long before I ever heard of the place. His oyster farm at the lagoon is bringing the young people back home. The center will give them jobs and a market for all the produce the island farms can raise. He's making it possible for the island to support its own, and that's as it should be."

Peg sighed. "I still think it's a shame you didn't get Plantation House to make up for all the money Tyler wasted of yours. What's Burke going to do about that?"

"Nothing. He doesn't even know about it. And I'm not about to tell him. It's not his problem."

"Take my advice and tell him. He might even feel it's his responsibility as the last remaining head of the Ransome clan to make it good."

"He just might at that—and that's why I've no intention of letting him find out about it," Allison said evenly, daring her friend to say more.

Accepting the challenge after a moment's pause, Peg muttered, "I think you're making a mistake."

"You know, we're lucky at that," Allison said, changing the subject abruptly to let her friend know the issue was not negotiable. "If Plantation House were mine, we'd be sitting here right now worrying about how we were going to keep the bills paid and the place full."

"Don't I know it," agreed Peg. "When you're as short of working capital as we've been, every cancellation or vacancy hurts."

So intent were the women on their conversation that they didn't hear the arrival of the pickup from the lagoon. To their surprise Doc McGinnis appeared in the door of the morning room, looking for Peg. Under his arm he carried a small package.

"I'm going to give Hoddy and Max their first diving lesson pretty soon," he said after he'd observed the usual amenities and inquired about Allison's shoulder.

Allison darted a quick curious glance at her friend.

Peg gave a sheepish shrug. "Among the three of them they talked me into it," she admitted with a sigh of resignation. "After all the trouble my sons managed to get into at Buttonhook Cove I decided they'd be better off under Doc's eye doing something they really want to do."

McGinnis turned to Peg. "I want you to come down to the lagoon and see what we'll be doing. You'll feel easier about it if you do. Do you have a bathing suit?"

Peg shook her head.

"I thought not." He handed Peg the package he carried. "It hasn't got much style, I suppose, but it's all they had at the anchorage store over on the mainland. I had to guess at the size. Go see if it fits."

Peg pulled an amply proportioned maillot in an electric shade of blue out of the package. "What on earth for? I don't need a bathing suit to watch, for heaven's sake!"

"When I get through with the twins I'm going to start teaching you to swim."

Peg looked at him in horror. "Doc, I've told you. I'm scared to death of the water."

"I know," the marine biologist said gently. "It's a shame. I promise you it's something we'll overcome."

Peg hesitated a moment, then with a shaky smile at Doc, which turned silly when she met Allison's approving eye, she went off to change into the suit. It was then that Doc gave Allison Burke's message. Burke had gone to Sapelo to see about getting the center started, he told her. He wasn't sure when he'd be back.

"So that's where he went," she said. "I heard the plane take off again after I got to the house. I wonder why he didn't mention it." Her tone was amiable, but she felt chagrined that he hadn't bothered to tell her. After all, the center involved her, too.

Peg emerged a moment later, the bathing suit, which she pronounced a "pretty good fit," discreetly hidden under a blue-and-green-print muumuu.

Allison couldn't stifle a small feeling of envy as the pair rode off companionably in the pickup, talking and laughing together like two old friends.

CHAPTER FOURTEEN

WHEN THE NEXT DAY PASSED and Burke didn't return, Allison began listening for his plane. Hardly aware she was doing it, she would pause in mid-action and cock her head at the distant drone of an aircraft until it was near enough to identify as commercial or navy or some smaller plane bound for destination other than Ransome's Cay.

Guests came and went. Though Allison went through the motions hospitality required, she was hardly conscious of the visitors as individuals, so preoccupied was she with her own efforts to understand her changing relationship with Burke. While she knew her own heart and head, she couldn't guess from his behavior toward her what went on in his. At one level, she and Burke were so easy together. They had no need for words. In their understanding they often read each other's thoughts in their eyes. And then there was the intoxicating sensual response that lay always so near the surface between them, teasing forever to be let loose.

Yet for all that there was another dark level to Burke's nature from which he closed her out. It had something to do with her marriage to his cousin—of that she had no doubt.

But there was something more. She sensed in him a bitterness toward Tyler she couldn't explain. She tied it somehow to the time two years before Burke had bought the *Ulysses* and taken off on his round-the-world junket to learn how to farm the sea. During that time she had been on her honeymoon at Plantation House.

She remembered asking Effie if the absent cousin ever came to visit the island, and Effie had given her a guarded look and said he hadn't set foot there in more than a year. Thinking Ransome's Cay belonged to Tyler, who never mentioned Burke except to revile him, Allison hadn't found his absence surprising and asked no more.

There had been a reason she hadn't been told why Burke had almost literally abandoned Ransome's Cay for a time. Whatever it was, at the bottom must lie Burke's enduring animosity toward Ty.

Her attempt to draw Effie out on the subject met with no success. The housekeeper's reticence encouraged belief in her own theory, but she had too much affection for the kindly woman and respect for her loyalty to the Ransome family to question her aggressively.

In spite of Allison's inner distraction, affairs moved on according to program at Plantation House. Hoddy and Max took parties of guests on tours of the island, giving special emphasis to the ruins at Buttonhook Cove. The twins had renamed it Smuggler's Cove in sorry recollection of the rum that lay buried under tons of rock and dirt at the cave-in site.

Their mother managed to nail them for occasional small maintenance chores that cropped up. Otherwise the pair spent much of their time on the oyster barge with McGinnis, who managed to slip some of the elements of marine biology into the daily diving lessons. Surprisingly Peg gave them little static, even arranging for one of the island's young men to keep the acre of velvet-green bluegrass cut and clipped to give them more time at the lagoon. They showed a real curiosity about undersea life, and Doc told her they had a genuine aptitude for science.

"It's the first time they've shown an interest in college or careers," their mother confided to Allison with wonder. "Their idea of a career was to become an itinerant handyman team. Now they're talking about which universities have the best marine-science school and signing on with Jacques Cousteau!"

Peg herself had an early-evening swimming lesson at the lagoon each day, from which all spectators including Allison were barred.

"She may never swim the English Channel or even across the lagoon, but she's getting over her fear, and if she falls out of a boat in quiet water she'll be able to get herself ashore," Doc told Allison. "And might I add, when she takes off that tent she insists on hiding under she looks just fine in a bathing suit."

So went the week, with Allison growing ever more impatient for Burke's return.

"He might at least have taken time before he went off again to work out a solid arrangement for Plantation House with me," she complained to Peg the morning of his fifth day of absence. "Why go flying away to recruit for the center until he's sure our end of it won't fall through?"

"That's not likely, Ally, and you know it," said Peg. "Besides, there's nothing we can do for the center until we've finished with the people who've already made reservations. Just because his cousin gave you a bad time.... Look, Allison, don't you think it's time you started trusting Burke? Doc says he's absolutely reliable—one of the most honorable and decent men he's ever dealt with."

"It's not that!" Allison replied indignantly. "I *do* trust him completely. It's just that—"

The sentence dropped off into nothing.

It's just what, she asked herself, and answered disconsolately, *I miss him!*

THE DAY was hot and sultry, with banks of thunderheads rolling up in the late afternoon to growl and threaten, then rumble on. Allison was busy all afternoon taking a supply inventory of the house and was hardly aware of the sullen state of the weather.

She had expected usables such as soaps and cleaning materials would be running low and ready to be restocked. What came as a shock was that towels and soap dishes had vanished, as well, in the short time they'd been open. Even blankets, stored in the top of closets for the summer, had been taken from one of the rooms.

Maybe the guests felt they were entitled to a little something extra to make up for no tennis courts, she thought with uncharacteristic cynicism. She knew the generalization was unfair. For the most part the guests had been pleasant agreeable people she would welcome into the house any day. The towel and ash-tray takers were simply careless or else were souvenir collectors who'd assumed these extras were accounted for in the price of the room. As for the blankets, a pair of complaining faces came at once to mind. Yet she knew she had no right to make such accusations—five different couples had occupied that room. This was precisely the kind of conclusion-jumping she was overly prone to, she chided herself, and it had caused her to be very wrong about Burke.

By late afternoon when the job was done she felt a sudden wild need to escape, as if she'd spent the day locked up in a dungeon. She had a driving urge to get out of the air-conditioned house and ride off on Godiva for a plunge in the sea. She put the notion reluctantly aside. This was the first day she'd gone without a sling to protect her shoulder. It would be foolish to push her luck. Riding the mare was more strain than she dared put on the nearly mended dislocation.

She thought then of Buttonhook Cove. According

to Hoddy and Max the recent catastrophe that had destroyed the pretty little man-made falls and sent the stream off to find a new outlet in the cove had left the small quiet inlet unharmed.

She was suddenly curious to see the cave-in, to see for herself if the cove was as lovely and undisturbed as it had been years earlier when she had swum alone there the summer of her ill-fated honeymoon. She could swim there again without putting undue strain on the damaged arm.

She went in search of Peg but couldn't find her.

"Tell Peg I've taken one of the carts and gone up to have a swim at Buttonhook Cove," she told Effie. "And don't worry about me for dinner. I'll forage in the fridge when I get back."

When she came down from her room with a towel and a bathing suit, Effie was waiting for her with a picnic basket.

"I fixed you some supper," she said, following Allison on the veranda. "Y'all better eat before you start back after that swim." Effie was a great believer in the efficacy of a full stomach.

Just then a low rumble of distant thunder sent the housekeeper down the steps. She turned her eyes upward, a worried frown on her face. "You reckon you oughta start off, Allison, with such a broody-looking sky?" she asked anxiously.

"Don't worry, if anything comes of it, I won't waste any time getting home," she assured Effie. "I'm not all that crazy about loud noises—thunderstorms in particular.'' In a sudden burst of pent-up energy, she took off at a fast jog for the carriage house to pick up a cart, the picnic basket bouncing cumbersomely at her side.

Scooting down the road toward the cove in the electric cart, Allison thought she heard the sound of an approaching plane. She stopped for a moment to listen, giving up with a dissatisfied sigh. Whatever she'd heard had been lost in the persistent roll of thunder far off to the west, where the sky looked dark and threatening.

She hesitated a bit longer, wondering if she should go back, then decided to go on. The atmosphere was heavy and oppressive with a damp, electric-charged heat, but the sky above was open and the storm a distance away. It could very well miss Ransome's Cay completely. In any case, it would be a while before it hit, if hit it did. She should have time for the swim she needed to untie the kinks and with luck eat Effie's picnic supper before she had to run for it. Summer storms were hard to gauge. Sometimes they rolled up without warning; other times they threatened and rumbled most of the day and then moved on. The important thing was not to forget to keep an eye on the sky.

When she reached the cove she parked the electric cart beside the magnolia tree from which the golden bronze horseman had plucked the blossom to toss at her feet. It seemed such a long time ago.

She stood for a while staring regretfully at the

caved-in rubble into which Buttonhook Creek now flowed, dividing the creek into a number of shallow rivulets that meandered across the slope to find the waters of the cove not in one small vital stream but in thin trickles that were all but lost in the sand before they reached it.

Again she saw the waterfall as it had been on that unforgettable morning. In her imagination she stood in the small basin where it had overflowed, the water spilling down over her naked body, and watched the man and horse rise out of the sea. A shiver of pleasure ran through her in recollection. Then she was staring again into the ruin, wondering restlessly when she would see him again.

Under the magnolia tree she changed into a butterscotch-colored bikini that all but disappeared on her lithe body so nearly did it match her tanned skin. Leaving her clothes on the cart, she ran across the thick stand of wild grass to the sandy beach that bordered the inlet and on into the gentle waves warmed by the Gulf Stream lapping in from the sea.

It was not cold, but even so it was some twenty-five degrees below her body temperature. She gasped at the sudden change but adjusted quickly as her feet lost touch with the sandy bottom and she went under. Surfacing, she swam toward the inlet's mouth and the open sea. Out of consideration for the tender shoulder she fell into a modified sidestroke that put all the work on the right arm. Her motions were slow and labored, though, and she quickly tired.

At the mouth of the cove she trod water for a moment before working her way to the beach on the far side. She lay on her stomach and rested there for a time. Restored, she arose and was about to plunge back into the water when a movement far up the ocean beach beyond the mouth of the cove caught her eye and held her to the spot. It was a man on a horse, pounding down the hard sandy beach at the water's edge. They were coming toward her, and the horse was galloping as if a pack of hounds were at his heels.

"Burke!" she cried aloud.

In the next instant she was swimming across the mouth of the cove in her usual swift freestyle to meet him, the injured shoulder forgotten. By the time she reached the opposite shore the horseman was only a short distance away. She left the water on feet that skimmed the ground. At the same moment the rider leaped from the moving animal and ran toward her.

They came together with abandon, his hard-muscled, sun-browned arms reaching to crush her to him, her own entwining his bare torso as they pressed against each other in a long yearning embrace. She buried her face in the springy hair of his chest and reveled in the feel of him, his smell, the taste of his skin as their bodies moved to find once more the exquisite pleasures of flesh upon flesh.

He lavished a storm of small kisses across her forehead, down her cheek, her neck; his tongue lightly touched the lobe and intricate chamber of her ear as a spasm of joy raced through her body.

Her mouth hungered for his kiss. She raised her face, her lips full and rosy to receive his, half parted in invitation. He took them, his lips covering hers; their mouths played softly upon each other at first and then with a growing urgency.

As they kissed she knew the unguarded tumescence of the man and felt a sudden swell of ripening within her. With a will of their own her hands traveled down the bronzed back to the top of his faded jeans. As her fingers slipped beneath the belt line and caressed the warm flesh she felt a surge of desire. Impatiently she fumbled with the top button of the fly.

Still swollen with passion his mouth slowly, gently, withdrew from hers. A soft sound, not quite a groan yet more than a sigh, escaped from his lips. Her hands paused in their self-appointed chore as she glanced up to find him looking down at her, the iridescent eyes glazed with desire.

As if to right himself, he shook his head and stepped back from her. When his eyes met hers again they were warm, even loving, but Burke Ransome was once more in control.

She stood stunned, her hands hanging loosely at her sides, and watched him reach for the button she'd been working at. With sure, swift movements he stripped off the jeans and left them in a heap on the sand. Underneath he wore a brief pair of blue swimming trunks.

He reached for her hand, but she held it back as her sense of indignation increased. He seized it nonetheless and began to run, forcing her also to race across the sand and into the water until the bottom dropped away beneath their splashing feet. Obliged to swim, he let go of her hand.

From the moment of their meeting they had not spoken a word to each other.

Released, Allison pulled away from him. Reverting to the limping sidestroke in answer to a warning twinge from her shoulder, she made her way ploddingly back across the cove's mouth. When she reached the shore she stretched out on a beached log left there by some past high sea, her head pillowed on her arms, her pulse beating rapidly as much from anger as from the swim.

Her fervor of welcome was spent, replaced by a cold bewildered fury. After a minute she lifted her head enough to peer out and see what had become of Burke. When she could see no sign of him in the water, she raised her head all the way, scanning the waters of the inlet and even looking out to sea.

He couldn't have just gone, she thought in shocked disbelief. Her sense of outrage brought her to her feet, half expecting to catch a glimpse of him galloping up the beach on Cherokee in retreat.

At last her eyes found him on the other side of the inlet; he was not on the beach, not actually running away, but was walking purposefully toward the big fawn-colored stallion grazing on wild grass not far from where his rider had jumped from his back. Watching from across the cove with a resurgence of anger and hurt, Allison saw the animal's head come up as if he were about to bolt. She fervently hoped he would and was disappointed when the horse stood still and let Burke come to him.

To her surprise, instead of mounting and tearing away as she'd waited to see him do, he led the stallion to a clump of small trees and tethered him there. When the animal was secured, he ran back down the beach and plunged into the water, cutting through choppy little waves with a strong clean stroke toward the spot where she stood.

Not wishing to be caught gazing, Allison stretched out on the log once more and cradled her head, listening for his approach. The deep sense that she'd been wronged stayed with her.

She did not raise her head when she heard him near, but from under the shelter of her arms she spoke aloud to him for the first time. "Why did you do that?" she asked evenly, striving to keep the injury from her voice.

"I didn't want to press my luck," he said.

Allison's head flew up, her eyes round with astonishment and dismay.

"When he has the halter on, he knows it means he's to stay," he went on conversationally. "It works particularly well when the other end of the halter's tied to a tree," he added with a grin.

Allison glared at him for an instant before she dropped her head back into her arms.

"I wasn't talking about the blasted horse," she

said, her muffled voice coming from underneath. "I think you know that."

Burke let himself down on the log beside her, lifting her head so he could look in her face.

"I know," he said, his own expression serious and intent. "I was playing for time. Forgive me."

When she deigned not to speak, he continued, "We got off to a bad start in the beginning. I can't let it happen again. There's too much at stake now."

She had expressed her love in the most perfect way she could, but to him it was "getting off to a bad start," she thought with a shrinking heart. Aloud she said curtly, "You needn't worry. It won't happen again."

"Speak for yourself," he said, a wry smile lifting a corner of his mouth for an instant. "Frankly, dear Allison, at this very moment it's all I can do to keep from removing those two delightful scraps of fabric you call a bathing suit and.... Look, Allison, from the first time we saw each other here at almost this very spot we were both aware of a tremendous attraction. I never see you without wanting to make love to you." He hesitated before he went on. "I've had some reason to think you're affected in much the same way."

Allison felt her face flush. "Regardless of what you make of it, I'm not all that much of a wanton, Burke," she said stiffly.

"You are a warmly sensitive, sensuous woman," he replied. "That's what I make of it. If you were less of either, perhaps I would find it mattered less that I keep my runaway passions on a tight rein.'' His eyes were focused intently on her. ''I'm looking ahead to a different relationship with you, Allison. While I was away you were constantly in my mind.''

He was quiet a moment, as if seeking the right words.

''Oh, Allison,'' he said then, ''I'm deeply afraid to let this physical force take over. It could eclipse everything else. There's something more to be developed between us and it's too important to jeopardize. If it fails, physical fulfillment alone won't have much meaning. Don't you see?''

Allison rested her head on her arms again, hiding her face. She hardly heard the new rumble of thunder coming up from the south.

If he was telling her he thought it was a bad idea for the boss to make love to the help, he was probably right, she thought with reluctance. But she somehow felt that what he said went far deeper. When he spoke about a ''different relationship'' and ''something more to be developed'' between them, was he talking about their business relationship involving Plantation House or was he referring to something as important as a personal relationship not directly tied to any arrangement for the center?

Whatever it might be, it offered a rationale for what he had just done, however depressing. She tipped her head up again and gave him a sporting smile.

"I can't say I agree wholeheartedly, but I suppose it makes a certain amount of sense," she said dryly. "If you think Plantation House will run better if we stick to the straight employer-employee line, far be it from me to play the temptress."

"Now wait a minute," Burke protested. "That's not what I said. It's not what I mean."

But in a sudden movement she slipped away from where she lay. She plunged back into the water. A split second later he dove in after her, catching her in a few swift powerful strokes.

Treading water, he held and kissed her lightly. She tasted the salt on his lips. Then like two sleek otters they dove and surfaced and dove and surfaced, again and again. When their bodies brushed against each other in the water it was with a new restraint that lent a certain piquancy to the touch.

Swimming on their backs, treading water in a single spot, sometimes going forward side by side in a lazy crawl, they eventually made their way back down the length of the cove and came out near the magnolia tree where Allison had left the cart. There they shared her towel, and she peered into the picnic hamper she'd stowed aboard.

"I'm starved," she told him. "It looks like Effie packed enough for two people. Care to join me?"

Looking into the basket over her shoulder from behind, he elaborated. "Enough for two people stranded on a desert island for two weeks. Considering the abundance, I accept."

Laying his hands on her shoulders, he turned her around and kissed her soundly, then held her away from him with a groan. "This isn't gonna be easy! Don't you have something you can put on that will take my mind off that enticing expanse of flesh? You look more naked than naked, I swear."

"Sorry!" Allison said agreeably. Reaching for the Plantation House T-shirt she'd started out with, she pulled it over her damp head, smoothing it over her wet hips to where it came to a stop just below her bikini.

"Better?" she asked with a grin. But before he could voice the negative answer she saw in his eyes, she had another question for him. "Incidentally, how come your bathing suit?" she asked curiously, thinking he gave a rather provocative display of body himself.

"Peg was up at the lagoon when the pilot dropped me off. She said she'd just missed you at the house and Effie told her you were down here for a swim. I decided to join you."

As they surfeited their appetites with Effie's fried chicken, deviled eggs and beaten biscuits stuffed with paper-thin slices of country-baked ham, their talk turned to the forthcoming Ransome's Cay Research and Study Center. To her surprise Allison discovered that the Marine Institute of the University of Georgia at Sapelo was only one of the places Burke had touched during the week of his absence. He spoke with satisfaction of the cooperation and encouragement the project had received wherever he went.

He'd talked to scientists, economists, leading practical authorities in the field of aquaculture in places as far apart as California and New York, she learned. Already many of them were working to compile a list of candidates eligible for invitations to the center as soon as it was set up, he told her.

"And here I thought you were just up the coast at Sapelo," she said. "I've been dying to start planning the Plantation House part of the center. Why didn't you tell me you were going? I was beginning to think you weren't ever coming back. Doc might have told us you were going so far."

"Actually, he didn't know," Burke replied. "I didn't know myself when I took off."

She felt a sudden affront as his eyes unexpectedly closed a door on her. He hesitated, and she imagined his mind editing what he was about to say.

"I had other business. . . it took me farther afield than I anticipated," he said, the words somewhat formal, almost aloof. "Since I found I had to be in Southern California and then in Manhattan, I took time to see a few people about the center, as well."

Pride would not let her question him further, even if his manner had been more encouraging.

"Tomorrow we'll sit down and work something out on this Plantation House arrangement," he continued, his eyes dropping their guard as he deftly changed the subject. "I'm sure you'll want Peg to sit in on it. You can have your lawyer go over it once we work out the initial stuff."

"You mean Herb Canby?" she asked with an astonished laugh, forgetting he'd offended her a moment earlier.

Burke grinned. Back on a companionable footing, they resumed talk of the center while they finished the last of the thermos of minted lemonade.

The storm broke as they nibbled the crumbs of a cheese pie split between them. A crash of thunder suddenly shook the earth around them and brought Allison's hands up to cover her ears until it passed. The sky overhead, she noticed as she glanced quickly up, was now rolling with dark ugly thunderheads.

"I'd forgotten about the weather," she admitted unhappily as she scrambled to her feet and hastily gathered together the remains of their picnic.

Ransome was more leisurely. "That was an attention-getter, all right," he agreed, "but it's not really close. You start hurrying when the lightning and thunder come right together. Thunder can't hurt you, and the lightning that hits you, you never see."

Allison darted him a grim look and continued to hurry. Ransome poked the empty thermos and other things within reach of where he sat into the hamper, humoring her. Still he made no move to get up, even though the background rumble that had been going on and off all afternoon had taken on a more ominous sound.

"I hate it, Burke," she said tensely. "Please, let's get going!"

A crack of lightning sent a jagged graph-line of light across the sky, followed seconds later by a nerve-shattering clap of thunder that brought the storm almost over their heads. Allison flinched and covered her ears as Burke jumped to his feet to pull her into his arms.

As the sound began to subside, they heard above the rumble of the sky the wild screaming whinny of a terrified horse.

"Oh, my God!" Burke exclaimed in horror. "I forgot Cherokee. I can't leave him tied up down there in a thunderstorm."

Allison pulled herself out of his arms. "Go, Burke," she cried. "I'm all right. Let the poor beast loose."

Again there came a flash of lightning, a blast of thunder. Allison flinched, but she kept her hands clenched at her sides. Burke hesitated, seemingly undecided about whether to leave her, until she pushed him urgently on his way. "Go!" she shouted above the storm.

Still he hesitated. "You'll be all right?"

"Of course!" she yelled back indignantly.

He took off running down the slope toward the clump of trees where he'd left Cherokee tied, the length of the inlet away. After he disappeared into the leafy jungle, Allison steeled herself to keep cool. She got busy stowing the basket aboard the cart.

When Burke returned she wanted to be ready for a speedy retreat.

A new flash of lightning hit somewhere nearby in the woods. There was no mistaking the sound of splintering tree, followed at once by thunder so loud it seemed to burst inside her head.

Burke! Could he have been near the tree? Wings of panic carried her down across the slope toward the beach. She was no longer aware of the thunder and lightning building up to a Wagnerian climax around her. Halfway there she saw Burke come loping out of the woods.

Running, they came to meet each other on the open slope, where Allison threw herself sobbing into his arms. In the same instant the lightning struck nearby again. With a swoop of his body he pushed her down. They lay in the wild grass panting furiously, as the thunder broke over their heads with such force it seemed it would drive them into the ground.

Still gasping for breath, Allison said in his ear, "Oh, Burke, I was afraid for you."

Holding her to him, he turned so he lay half over her, sheltering her from the storm with his body yet letting her bear no more than a small portion of his weight. With his hands pressed over her ears to shut out the thunder he kissed her fiercely.

When her lips were no longer captive, she said with a resignation that admitted she already knew the answer, "You think it's better for us to stay where we are?"

"It's the safest place for us now," he replied. "Our bodies looming up above ground level could attract lightning if we ran for it."

Giving in to the inevitable, she pressed a cheek against his bare chest and buried one ear in the curve of his shoulder. He laid a strong gentle hand over the other ear to muffle the sounds of the storm.

Once, in a momentary lull, she raised her head to ask, "Aren't you afraid?"

"Not now, but I sure as hell was out there trying to untie the horse," he admitted flatly. "That tree that got struck was too close for comfort, and the stallion was about to go ape. I wasn't sure which one was going to get me, the lightning or the horse. I was certain one of them would."

"What about Cherokee?"

"I turned him loose. He knows how to take care of himself."

"You're sure we're safe here on the ground?" she asked, using all her will to keep her voice steady.

"We're safe," he assured her, then added with a grin, "I have to confess I'm enjoying it. If you'll just forget about the thunder you might find it enjoyable, too."

But there was no forgetting. Directly over their heads a battle of the gods raged on and on. Still clad in no more than T-shirt and bikini, Allison lay pressed against Burke, her body trembling not from erotic excitement but from sheer primitive fear of the elements that no manner of sophistry could still. It seemed the storm would never end.

What a coward I am, she thought, continuing to burrow into the shelter of his body although there was a sudden break in the barrage.

After a minute of near silence the fat dark clouds above them opened suddenly and drenched them in a river of rain. Routed, the thunder grumbled off and left the water pouring down on them in torrents that washed them clean of ocean salt.

Allison turned her head on his shoulder to catch the water on her face, her mouth, her eyes. With the release of tension came laughter, deep and throaty until it was silenced by Burke's rain-washed mouth. She welcomed him ardently. Still, a certain perversity willed her to lay quiescent against him there on the sweet grass in the warm bath of falling rain. She raised no hindrance, nor did she help. The restrictions he had put on himself and by extension on her were of his making. Let him override them.

It was Burke, then, who lifted her and stripped the sodden T-shirt off over her dripping head, and it was his impatient awkward fingers that untied the stubborn wet knots of the bikini and in the last instant peeled down his own skin-fitting trunks.

He held himself in suspension over her for a long moment, his lean strong hands firmly planted on either side of her body. Lingering as if to memorize a vision he feared to lose, his eyes moved from her face to her neck and breasts, on down the firm plane of her abdomen to the dark guarding triangle, its secrets hidden by the two slender legs.

His long body made a canopy over her from which the rain streamed off on all sides. Rivers of sweet water rolled off his sun-streaked hair onto her face and neck, flowing down the valley between her breasts to divide into two small rivulets that emptied into the grass.

Gazing down the length of the beautiful gold bronze body above her, the mystic flame deep within Allison sparked to life. She lifted her arms and pulled his streaming body down to hers. Running her tongue up the sinewy cords of his neck, she savored the exciting male taste of his skin.

She continued to lick away the rain that still clung to his neck and face until he caught her tongue between his lips and covered her mouth with his own.

Allison's body tingled with growing excitement as his tongue teased the delicate inner surfaces of her mouth with soft stroking thrusts that left her breathless with anticipation. She wondered in some obscure questing chamber of her mind how she could ever have felt anything but love for Burke; he was everything she had ever looked for or wanted in a man.

Glossy and swollen with passion, their lips played on each other for a last moment. Reluctantly they pulled apart, whispering small wordless endearments. Then it was Burke who lowered his face to her neck, pressing moist kisses against her soft flesh, moving down across her breast until his lips caught and held the rosy bud that thrust up from the firm soft mound.

At the same time his hand found the satiny inner surface of her thigh and followed its curve upward until his palm covered the dark triangle of curls with an urgent possessive pressure. The mystical flame within her flared with a new hungry heat.

"Oh, lady, lady," he moaned softly as his fingers slipped between the folds to play upon the gem of eroticism hidden within. Allison's whole being throbbed with desire. She gave up all effort to hold back the small wordless cries of ecstasy that rolled up from deep in her throat.

When she could bear the exquisite torment no longer, she moved her arms to clasp his sinewy buttocks and pull his body down upon hers, lifting her thighs to meet his hard answering thrust. In the last instant before he plunged down the warm guarded passageway to the center of her being, he was the golden rider of the sea, carrying her with him on a golden tide that crested in that ultimate moment of joining in a golden spray.

Together, then, they were the tide. In wave upon wave of rapture they flowed and ebbed as one. A new torrent of rain pounded down on them, striking their bodies like power-driven water jets. But they were no more aware of them than was the sea itself.

Nor did they notice when the torrential rains eased up and at last stopped. Lost in fulfillment, they paid no attention to the physical world around them until at last a ray of sun pierced through the dispersing thunderheads. Finding them nested together in the sea grass, it stabbed them with a beam of glaring light that brought them rudely back to reality.

Spent, like the rain, they blinked into the brightness, both half confused for the moment. An instant later the sun dropped behind the trees to the west and left the slope bathed in a graying sulphurous light.

"It's stopped raining," Allison observed foolishly.

Languid, they lingered over small commemorative kisses, then slowly left each other and collected the bits of clothing around them.

"What a thing to have to put on," Allison remarked as she pulled the sodden T-shirt down over the wet bikini she'd tied herself back into.

Together they started back up the slope arm in arm, their wet bodies touching lightly, Burke trailing streams of water from the sodden jeans he'd tugged on over his trunks.

At the last moment before they climbed into the electric cart and started back toward Plantation House, Burke held her to him and looked into her face for a long time. He bowed his head at last and kissed her gravely. With a feeling of frustration she read a promise in the deep iridescent eyes. She had no idea what the promise implied, and it troubled her deeply.

IT WAS NEARLY DARK when Allison and Burke arrived back at Plantation House looking like a pair of shipwrecked refugees. They were met by the twins. The self-appointed advance team came roaring down the oyster-shell road toward Buttonhook Cove to meet them.

"Boy, you guys sure got 'em all scared up at the house," Max informed them. "Everybody figured you holed up someplace till the storm was over, but then when you didn't show they began to think one or both of you was hurt."

"No need to worry," Ransome said coolly. "As you can see we're both in one piece."

At Plantation House Allison let Burke do the talking. He obliged with a vivid account of the storm, the release of Cherokee, how he and Allison had flattened themselves in the sea grass and weathered it through. In the drama of his telling the elapsed time between the end of the storm and their belated appearance was overlooked.

Only Peg asked the question after Doc and Burke had driven away in the lagoon pickup, leaving the two women alone on the veranda. "What the dickens took you so long after the storm?" Peg asked bluntly. "We were really worried about you, Ally."

With a vague noncommittal shake of her head Allison said, "Oh, Peg, you know how I am about thunderstorms!"

As completely irrelevant as the answer was, it apparently satisfied her friend. Peg nodded, as if everything had been explained, and took off in an unexpected direction. "Remember that creep, Orrin

Travis, Allison?'' she asked. "You know...the one who wanted to buy Ransome's Cay.''

Relieved to be let off so easily, Allison replied, "Of course. What about him?''

"Burke didn't say anything up at Buttonhook Cove, did he?''

'About Travis? Why should he?'' she asked curiously.

Peg hesitated, then said half reluctantly, "I got the feeling I was kind of expected not to tell you this, but I don't see why—and Doc really didn't say I shouldn't.''

Allison was suddenly round eyed with curiosity. She waited, holding her breath, afraid that the slightest show of interest would scare Peg off whatever it was she was about to reveal.

"There's something fishy going on with this Travis,'' Peg confided. "Doc sort of let it slip. It wasn't center business that kept Burke away all week. It was Travis. Burke's been chasing all over, trying to get a line on the guy.''

Allison looked at her friend in confusion. "I can't imagine why,'' she said. "Surely Doc's mistaken. Burke's been working on a whole variety of things for the center, including a list of people who are to be considered for participation. He visited Scripps in San Diego and....'' Her voice trailed off uncertainly as she wondered for the first time what the "other business'' he'd mentioned was.

"You don't suppose he's decided to sell out to

Travis after all?" Peg asked anxiously. "You always used to say he was another rich dilettante who'd soon tire of Ransome's Cay. Suppose you were right."

"Well, I wasn't! I was wrong!" Allison said sharply. After apologizing quickly for snapping at Peg, she went on in a more normal tone. "Burke loves Ransome's Cay, Peg. If he really was looking for Travis, it was for something else—certainly not to sell." Briefly she told Peg about the encounter in the hotel elevator.

"Apparently Travis had some kind of blackmail or extortion plot in mind," she finished. "Burke couldn't imagine what it was about. He didn't seem very concerned about it in Atlanta."

Obviously Burke was considerably more concerned than he let on, Allison brooded later that night as she lay in her bed and tried to sleep.

What dark chapter in his life was so shameful that it sent him across the country and back trying to track down Travis, who threatened to expose it? Could Ransome's Cay and Plantation House be in jeopardy, and if they were, why hadn't Burke trusted her enough to tell her what was going on? She had cast her lot with Plantation House. She, too, had a right to know.

CHAPTER FIFTEEN

ALLISON WAS HAVING a second cup of coffee on the porch of the morning room early next day when Burke arrived on Cherokee, taking her by surprise. The sound of a horse's hooves crunching through the crushed shells of the narrow road brought her head up and a small gasp of pleasure to her throat. Would she ever see the splendid bronze figure of the man astride the huge stallion without an instant of déjà vu and the illusion of a centaur rising out of the sea?

This morning he was dressed in riding boots and faded jeans into which was tucked a white cotton shirt that had seen many washings. The open collar fell back from his throat, exposing the thatch of soft wiry hair where her cheek had found comfort the previous night.

In the first evocative moment after she looked up her eyes remained on him. It was a second or two before she saw that the mare, Godiva, was following close behind, pulled by a lead rope in Burke's hand. The mare and Cherokee were both saddled.

Held back by a sudden unaccountable shyness, Allison hesitated, half reluctant to put to test the

nebulous unvoiced commitment she'd sensed between them the previous evening, a commitment con-
ceived in the eye of the storm and born of a love
washed clear and pure by the rain. Peg's later dis-
closure that Burke had been off on a cross-country
hunt for Orrin Travis had triggered a restless night of
wondering what other secrets Burke withheld from
her. Had that unvoiced commitment been no more
than wishful thinking on her part—unspoken because for Burke it didn't exist?

What did he actually want of her? She'd been so
caught up in the realization she loved him as she'd
never loved anyone that she hadn't stopped to consider if his feelings for her were the same. She had
given herself to him in ways she'd never dreamed
possible for her to give to anyone. Had she only
imagined she'd read in his eyes, his face, his tenderness, a love that transcended the tacit physical attraction. . . a love to meet her own?

Held captive by her fears, Allison didn't at once
rush forth to meet him. She watched as he tied the
horses near the kitchen garden and hurried toward
the house in his long easy stride before she shook off
her reservations and ran down the steps to meet him.

His face made no secret of his delight in her
presence as he gave her an unexpected good-morning
kiss. Though he released her almost at once, the un-
mistakable fervor of his embrace caused Allison to
dart an embarrassed look back at the house to see if
they were being observed.

"The morning's as near perfect as a morning can be," he said, smiling down at her. "I brought Godiva just in case I can persuade you to take a ride with me before we settle down to the business of the day."

"Give me a minute to get into my boots," she said quickly, and disappeared into the house.

Their world sparkled that morning, cleansed by the storm. Leaves bejeweled with drops of rain caught the glint of the early sun.

A maze of bridle paths, cut through the woods by wild creatures for the most part, netted the island from one end to the other. Allison and Burke soon left the man-made paths, wending their way among moss-hung trees. Where the trail narrowed, they were forced to ride single file, but more often they traveled abreast through sun-dappled woods seldom visited by human beings.

There was an unspoken something, a secret sense of intimacy between them. They talked little, and on the surface their mutual silence was comfortable. But in spite of herself Allison felt the prickly knowledge that some dark secret known only to Orrin Travis lay between them. Then, too, there was the realization, admitted reluctantly, that each time they had made love Burke had at first held back. And with that came the plaguing recollection of the scene between them upon his arrival at Buttonhook Cove the previous night.

What did he mean: "different relationship... afraid to let this physical force take over....too im-

portant to jeopardize?'' Would he bring this up again
or simply let things take its course?

Her throat constricted in a sudden spasm of fear as
she realized that her love for Burke was irrevocably
entwined with her future at Plantation House. So
what was this ''different relationship,'' something in
her cried out. Was it to be based on deep mutual love
of the kind she felt for him, or did he have in mind
something more in the line of a congenial business
arrangement with some occasional lovemaking on
the side?

One thing she knew for certain: if what Burke
wanted was a Plantation House manager-cum-lover,
she would have to pass.

What do you want of me, Burke, she desperately
longed to cry out. But some deep inner fear that his
answer, when it came, might be one she couldn't bear
to hear stayed her tongue.

Godiva gave a sudden side-step as some small furry
creature scurried across the path under the mare's
feet. A moment later, up the path some fifty feet
ahead, a spotted fawn stepped out on shaky legs and
stopped cold in its tracks to look them over. Burke
came to a halt and reached across to lay a detaining
hand on Allison's reins.

''Do you suppose I could get near enough to pet it?
It seems so tame,'' Allison whispered, starting to dis-
mount, before he stopped her.

''Don't even try,'' he advised softly. ''Better
stay on your horse. The mother's near and fiercely

protective. Her sharp little hooves are deadly.''

The words were no more than out when a sleek doe crashed out of the brush and came to stand beside the fawn, lifting her head to glare at them, her nostrils flaring. When they made no move to advance she nuzzled her offspring a moment as if to make sure it hadn't been harmed and dabbed it with her tongue. But when the fawn tried to push its nose up under her flank to suckle the doe gave it a sharp nudge and the two took off, running down the trail a few yards until they veered off to one side and disappeared into the woods.

Allison and Burke came upon Buttonhook Creek some distance above the cave-in. They stopped to let the horses drink. Burke jockeyed the stallion around so the two animals stood shoulder to shoulder. As they began to drink, he leaned across the distance to touch his lips to hers in a playful sort of way. Lightly they brushed and lifted, then brushed again. Quite suddenly all playfulness was lost. They kissed with a wild sweet passion, each seeking the other's most sensitive tactile points as if to discover a longed-for but prohibited point of no return.

It was the stallion that separated them, backing away from the stream with a sudden impatient whinny to nip at the mare's flank. They were torn apart with such suddenness that Allison nearly lost her seat. Only a quick grab for a hold on Godiva's mane kept her from rolling off into the creek. Upright again, she looked around to find Burke had pulled

Cherokee up on a tight rein a few steps away, his face flushed with anger.

"Are you all right?" he asked at once. When she assured him she was, he said, "You could so easily have been hurt. Having free run of the island last night must have gone to the beast's head. He goes back in the pasture today with the rest of the animals." She could see his anger cool as he talked. "Actually he's gone soft since I got home. He was at the gate this morning waiting to be let in," he said with a grin.

Shaken more by the force of the kiss than her near spill, Allison said, "Maybe we'd better start back. Peg will be looking for us. She can hardly wait to get the arrangements for Plantation House worked out."

Allison shared her eagerness. Yet at the same time she wasn't ready. *What do you want of me, Burke?* The question beat again on her consciousness, distressing her, spoiling her pleasure in the morning. Twice she brought herself to the point where she was about to ask the question bluntly, aloud, and each time she drew back, afraid of what he might say in return.

Troubling her, too, was his pursuit of Orrin Travis and his failure to mention it to her the previous evening. Yet if Doc had been asked not to speak of it, Allison might cause embarrassment for him if she let on she knew. There was another, more important reason she chose not to make a point of the issue. Interrogating him about it seemed to imply a lack of trust in him at the very time old doubts between them had been resolved.

Did whatever Burke have hidden in his past really matter to her, she asked herself finally. She knew the answer was no. He was Burke, whom she loved completely, come what may. Nothing that had happened in his past could change that, however much it might hurt. Nor could it have anything to do with her.

She simply had to believe that whatever Travis's threat, Burke would not let it affect the future of Ransome's Cay.

Allison, Burke and Peg spent the rest of the morning in the library working out an agreement for the long-term operation of Plantation House as the headquarters and home of the Ransome's Cay Research and Study Center. Allison was to be its vice-president and head of the house and Peg would be manager.

The terms of the proposal Burke offered were so gracious and reasonable Allison would have signed at once had he let her. But he insisted she have her friend and former employer in New York City recommend a lawyer to represent her in the matter and make certain her every interest was protected. In the end she agreed to do this.

At the same time it was agreed that when the last of the people with current reservations had come and gone the following week, Plantation House would be closed to the public to make whatever changes would be needed for the opening of Ransome's Cay Center in September.

"This calls for a celebration," Burke declared when the last of the agreement had been worked out and he was about to leave. "McGinnis and I would be honored to have the two of you come to dinner on the *Ulysses* tonight, if you would. Our limousine will call for you at...oh, say eight o'clock? That should give you time to get the Plantation House guests fed and dispersed for the evening."

"Limousine? That sounds pretty flossy," Peg said after Burke had gone. "How do you think we should dress?"

Caught up for a moment in the vision of a full moon casting a pathway of light across the waters of the lagoon and she and Burke entwined on the deck of the boat, Allison looked at her friend, bemused.

"I don't know about you, but I'm going to wear the most smashing thing I have," she said dreamily, indulging herself a moment longer before forcing her attention back to Peg. "Just don't wear one of those darn muumuus," she advised when she saw her friend eyeing her curiously.

THE "LIMOUSINE" that arrived at Plantation House promptly at eight, turned out to be the Ransome Cay pickup. Behind its wheel sat Doc, wearing an ancient navy blazer with lapels at least a decade behind the times. He escorted the two women to the pickup with courtly aplomb—but not until he had cast a long appreciative eye over Peg, who appeared in a short apricot-colored dress Allison hadn't even known she owned. The dress followed her ample curves with flattering grace and lent veracity to Doc's confidential appraisal a few days earlier of Peg in a bathing suit.

Delighted with her friend, whose appearance, usually was just as well overlooked, Allison didn't mind in the least that her own gown didn't merit so much as a second glance from Doc.

From the shore they were transported across the lagoon to the *Ulysses*. There Doc handed them aboard to Burke, who was waiting at the rail for their arrival.

Whatever Doc lacked in sartorial perfection was made up for by Burke, who looked resplendent in white trousers and a navy blue yachting coat, a maroon scarf knotted loosely at the open collar of his white shirt.

Allison didn't conceal the pleasure that being near him gave her. She smothered the swarm of worries that had cast shadows throughout the day and stepped down on the deck beside him, surrendering her hand to be kissed in a continental greeting. It seemed so out of character she was about to make a flip comment, but it was never spoken. As he raised her hand he turned it over and pressed his lips into the cup of her palm, lingering there for a long moment, savoring it as one savors a vintage wine. A delicious warmth washed through her. Her throat was so choked with such sudden inexplicable happiness it was impossible to speak at all.

His eyes, quite green that night and mysterious as the sea, embraced her with a kind of formality. "I must send McGinnis out more often," he murmured for her ears alone. "I never expected he'd bring a siren up out of our own lagoon as lovely as the one I once saw at Buttonhook Falls."

She smiled, and her eyes expressed the pleasure and amusement his words brought her. She was delighted that the cool little sleeveless dress of leaf-green voile with its snug low-cut bodice and swingy skirt had evoked that particular memory for the man.

In the golden light between sunset and dusk they sat on the leeward deck and toasted the morning's agreement with champagne sipped from crystal tulips a cabin boy never let run dry.

As darkness fell, Burke seated them at a damask-clothed table, candle-lit and set with Ransome heirloom silver and a single magnolia blossom in a silver bowl.

Except for the chateaubriand steak, which Burke admitted probably derived from an animal raised in Kansas on Kansas corn, all the ingredients of the dinner had come from Ransome's Cay soil or the lagoon. There was pride in Burke's voice as he told them this. Oysters for the Oysters Rockefeller were from the all-but-depleted natural oyster beds of the lagoon. It would be some time before the new oyster farm began to produce. The spinach, baked stuffed tomatoes with sweet basil and the tiny new potatoes and fresh garden peas served with the pink, butter-tender steak were all grown on island farms. Even the crisp leaf lettuce for the salad had come from an island garden. The Crewes twins had picked the wild blackberries near the lagoon for the still warm cobbler served with clotted cream.

"It's a good thing we have Effie at Plantation House or I'd be up here first thing in the morning to steal your cook," Peg said, sitting up straight in a lazy but futile attempt to tuck in her naturally rounded and currently overstuffed stomach.

"Not a chance," said Burke with a laugh. "He only caters small private parties—preferably for no more than four."

"You wouldn't want him, Peg," said McGinnis. "It takes every dish in the galley for him to scramble an egg, and he leaves them all dirty. You oughta see the galley right now. If Ransome had to wash up after himself, he'd learn to consolidate everything in one pan like I do!"

Burke grinned amiably but didn't bother to reply as Allison turned astonished eyes on him. "You're full of surprises, Burke Ransome!" she said affectionately.

The evening seemed made to order, right down to the full moon lighting a silvery path across the waters of the lagoon as they leaned against the rail of the ship.

"I'd planned to give you an inspection tour of the

Ulysses, but I guess I'd better save it until tomorrow," Burke told her as they were about to leave. "Since McGinnis takes such a dim view of my galley, maybe I'd better polish up the whole ship before we put it on show."

That night marked the beginning of a new phase in Allison's relationship with Burke—a phase at once exhilarating and discouraging, frustrating and full of delights.

Late next day, as he'd promised, Burke took Allison on a tour of the lab ship, which he modestly declared was not as well equipped as Cousteau's *Calypso*, but for his purposes "close enough."

Awed though she was by the working lab and home-away-from-home Ransome had created out of the sleek, ocean-going pleasure yacht, she returned to the island feeling let down. Burke's manner was warm, affectionate at times, anecdotal and unhurried. But he kept them moving steadily along from lab to wheelhouse to engine room, explaining the functions of each as they went. They were alone on the small ship. The rest of the men were working on the oyster barge. Yet they continued on through sleeping and living quarters without a gesture or suggestion of intimacy.

What do you want of me, Burke, her heart continued to cry out in frustration.

Only once, in the well-ordered galley, did their eyes meet and hold. In the next moment they came together in a deep hungry kiss. But it ended quickly when the voice of McGinnis called out to announce he and Peg were boarding after her swimming lesson and did they want a cold beer?

Sometimes Burke took her away from Plantation House for an hour or so on strange junkets to familiar haunts from what he called his "Tom Sawyer years" on the island. He showed her the finger of marsh where he and Catfish Miller had once dropped a noose over an alligator's jaw and where he and his friend Esau had caught a wild razorback hog barehanded and tried to ride it. He showed her where his father had often taken him on clear nights to chart the stars when he was very young, and where he and Esau had set up a telescope and seen a man-made satellite in the sky for the first time.

It was as if Burke wanted to teach her the things he remembered about the person he'd been so she might better understand the man he had at last become.

She saw them both in almost perfect juxtaposition the day he took her out to the anchored barge to show her the Ransome's Cay Oyster Farm.

There for the first time she talked to the men who were Burke's boyhood companions—the boys he had gone to school with in his early years at the single-room schoolhouse that doubled as the island's church on Sundays.

She'd met them all at the fireworks party when she had been too busy managing the shore supper for more than passing sociability and they too joyous in their homecoming to notice her lapse.

They were all working on or around the barge—
Ollie Joe Fritter, Esau, Catfish Miller, Brick—each
eager to tell in his own words how Burke's sea-
farming project had changed his life.

"If it wasn't for Burke—" his friend Brick said.

But Burke interrupted brusquely, "Cut it out,
Brick. I couldn't have done it if you fellows hadn't
been willing to give up your job security on the mainland to take a gamble with me."

Brick and a crew of men were constructing an elon-
gated raft on the deck of the barge near a stack of
others. Three more were linked together afloat, anchored in the lagoon. Frames strung with wires to
which fragments of oyster shells were attached were
suspended from the anchored rafts. To these the free-
swimming oyster larvae, veligers, attached themselves, Brick explained, and stayed firmly fixed until
they were harvested as full-grown oysters.

"Maybe I don't make so much money, but it don't
cost so much to live here and I'm my own boss," said
Ollie Joe Fritter, a round, ruddy-faced man with
clear blue eyes. "I never figured I'd ever be working
for Ollie Joe Fritter."

"But I thought you all worked for Burke," Allison
asked, puzzled.

"Well, we do and we don't."

"I'm afraid I don't understand."

"I reckon I don't understand exactly myself,
ma'am, but Burke thought it up, so it's all right," the
tow-headed man declared with complete trust.

Esau, whom McGinnis was educating on the marine life of the lagoon and had made his protégé, came to the rescue. A tall handsome man with intelligent eyes and an infectious grin, he surfaced over the side of the barge in dripping wet suit and fins in time to hear Fritter's words.

"We're a company, ma'am," he explained. "The Ransome's Cay Oyster Farm. The workers own forty-nine percent of the business and Burke owns the rest. Until it starts producing, the money comes from Burke and the Ransome holdings on loan. When the company's in full production it starts paying back the loan. Eventually we'll have the option to buy Burke's share in the farm."

It sounded like a generous arrangement, almost noble in fact, but when Allison said as much to Burke on the way back to shore in the boat he turned it aside with a laugh. "You've been listening to Fritter and Esau and Brick," he said with a grin. "Fact is, I keep those characters around just to make me look good. Actually," he went on, "it's just an ordinary business deal. There's as much in it for me as for them."

"I don't see how," said Allison.

"For one thing a working oyster farm is the ideal adjunct to a research and study center," he said. "It may have helped us get the foundation grant."

"And..." persisted Allison.

"Well, taxwise it doesn't hurt. In the long run I expect it may turn out to be one of the better investments I've made. If everything goes well the company can buy out my interest in a few years and work out a lease arrangement for the farm's use of the lagoon.''

She couldn't see how letting himself be bought out just when the company was starting to make money was in his own selfish interests, but she let it go.

The young person he had been; the man he had become. From his boyhood companions and the Bunkers and Doc McGinnis she learned more about the man she loved with each passing day and in learning loved him even more.

She listened avidly, touched that he seemed compelled to reveal himself to her in these ways. She sensed Burke's feelings for her were as deep and overriding as hers for him.

Yet for some reason of his own he was not ready to commit himself. At times his deep sea-colored eyes would cloud over with some hidden thought and she wondered helplessly whether she really knew him after all.

And there beneath the surface of her mind, posed to spoil any chance of contentment, was the redoubtable question: *What do you want of me, Burke?*

If he loved her why didn't he say so? On the other hand, if he saw her role as manager and lover, didn't she have a right to know?

In either case the constraint he imposed on himself when they were alone together didn't make sense to her. Their nightly partings left her frustrated and touchy. When Peg encountered her on her way in and made an innocuous remark about her "suitor," Allison gave her a withering look and walked away, not trusting herself to speak.

It became a nightly routine for Burke to arrive at Plantation House on Cherokee with Godiva in tow, and Allison and he would ride off together bareback to race along the beach until dusk ended the game.

One such evening, when they had galloped in and out of the surf and splashed abreast through the shallows almost to the Plantation House beach, darkness overtook them. They pastured the horses and walked back to the house, their arms entwined, lingering in the shadows at the last minute like two teenagers to kiss and caress until it became near punishment. She felt the rise of his passion, matched by her own, and recognized the first reluctant signals that he was steeling himself to pull away from her.

Suddenly her own agonizing frustrations spilled over. "Burke!" she cried aloud. "This can't go on! Don't I have a right to know what this is all about?"

Burke gave a muffled groan and enfolded her in his arms. He held her there in tender silence for a long moment as if afraid to let her go.

He buried his face in her hair and said hoarsely, "My darling...oh, Allison...if I could only be sure it's not too soon."

"Burke," she whispered in bewilderment, but he touched his fingers to her lips in a gesture that beseeched her to say no more.

"No. Please wait," he insisted. "There will be time to talk. When the shadow of Tyler no longer hovers over your life. I didn't want to press my love on you until that ghost was laid to rest, but now you know."

The one word seared itself on her consciousness, filling her with an ecstatic tenuous hope. She dared not leave it. The nonsense about Tyler's ghost could wait. She had to hear it from his lips once more.

"Know what, Burke? Tell me! What do I know?"

"That I love you with all my heart," he said quietly. "The rest we'll talk out another time."

As her heart filled with a gladness that left no room for words, he bent and took her lips in a long poignant kiss. Then before she could find breath to speak he was off in the darkness, and though she called his name he did not come back.

In the first instant of her disappointment she was about to go after him. Then she realized that however swiftly she ran she could not catch up with him. She knew, too, that in the dark she could never find him unless he wanted her to, and from his parting words she knew he believed it was not yet time to talk things out.

Burke was gone. If he didn't come to her first she would go to him the next night, knowing he loved her. She would explain away his misconceptions about Tyler and tell him she loved him. They would talk about their love for each other until there was nothing more to be said. And then they would make love.

"Oh, Burke," she whispered softly aloud. In a sudden sweep of almost overwhelming joy she felt as if her whole body sang with life.

DURING THE FINAL week that Plantation House was a resort inn the launch had made only one trip from the mainland daily, and if there was no one bound for Ransome's Cay, it didn't come at all. With more than half the rooms empty by attrition, occasional random guests without reservations were brought by the launch simply to fill the empty rooms until the place was shut down.

The approach of the launch early the next afternoon brought a groan from Peg on the morning-room porch, where she sat with Allison finishing a sandwich lunch. "Drat!" she exclaimed. "Wouldn't you know someone would find the way here today. I hope it's a single and not a party of five. I've half a mind to turn them away. We can't start getting the rooms in shape again for the center if we keep renting them out to every stray who decides to hop on the boat."

"This one doesn't look like any stray," Allison said with a laugh as a blond-haired woman in white stepped down from the launch. A deckhand began unloading a pile of luggage beside her on the landing. "Either she's not one to travel light, or your party of five is still on the boat."

"There goes Max in a cart to pick her up," said Peg. "I'd better send Hoddy with another cart to bring up all those bags. They can't get them all on one cart." She darted inside to call her son at the carriage house on the house phone.

Allison lingered a moment longer watching curiously, unable to get a clear impression of the woman because of the distance between them. All she could establish was that she was slender and tall and carried a mountain of traveling gear.

Hoddy followed Max in a second cart to catch the overflow. From the porch Allison watched the impatient movements of the woman's hands and body as she directed the twins in loading her belongings onto the carts, making them arrange and rearrange the bags several times before she was satisfied. This one would be a difficult guest, she feared as she walked out on the veranda to greet the newcomer.

When the lead cart drew near enough for her to see the woman clearly she found herself looking at one of the most beautiful faces she had ever seen and at the same time one of the most dissatisfied. Every feature was perfectly proportioned. Her skin was flawless, her mouth a classic bow with a full sensual lower lip. Her eyes were dark—contemptuous and cold as ice. When she stepped out of the cart, Allison saw a body as sleek as a jungle cat's. Perhaps the woman was a high-fashion model, she thought, noting the oyster-white silk suit and peacock-blue blouse with plunging neckline.

"You and that other boy...see you take care with those bags, y'all hear?" the woman ordered in a petulant drawl.

Allison waited on the veranda with little welcome in her heart for this guest who seemed determined to make a nuisance of herself. Peg came through the door as the woman stepped up on the veranda, and Allison was glad to let her take over.

"Welcome to Plantation House," said Peg, extending her hand as she stepped forward. "I'm Peg Crewes. If you will step inside with me, I'll look after your registration while our young men take your luggage to your room."

"Look, I happen to be Margo Ransome so you can skip all that registration crap," the woman said haughtily, ignoring Peg's outstretched hand.

Peg appeared not to notice. Her face showed nothing but puzzlement, puzzlement that reflected the sudden confusion in Allison's mind.

"I beg your pardon?" Peg asked cautiously. "You're Margo *who*?"

"Ransome—Mrs. Burke Ransome," the woman snapped. "We own this place, don't you understand? Now will you kindly have one of those muscle-beach bellhops of yours take my bags to Burke's bedroom, and tell the other one to get a hustle on and go find my husband. Tell him his wife will be waiting for him in his room."

Standing but a few steps away, Allison reached out and grasped the back of a wicker chair with both hands to steady herself, as if she had been struck a physical blow. For a moment she wondered dazedly if she had cried out aloud. But when no face turned to look at her she knew the sound of her pain was all inside.

From somewhere far off she heard their voices drone on and on, the woman's haughty and unbending, Peg's grown formal and cold.

"Mr. Ransome doesn't stay at Plantation House," said Peg. "I find it hard to believe his wife doesn't know that."

"Well, I find it hard to believe Burke isn't staying at Plantation House. There's no other place on this godforsaken island that's fit for anybody to stay."

"If you are his wife, I should think you'd know where he is," Peg persisted, not giving an inch.

"If it's any of your business I'm his wife all right, and don't you forget it," said Mrs. Burke Ransome grimly. "We've been a little out of touch, you might say, but as of now we're together again."

"Well, bully for you!" said Peg.

"Let's cut the small talk. Have one of those boys go get Burke," Mrs. Ransome ordered imperiously.

"I told you, he's not here and never has been," Peg said in a voice that would cut glass. "I suggest you take yourself back to the mainland. Too bad the launch has already left. But I'll have one of my sons take you and your trappings over in our boat."

"Peg!" gasped Allison from behind her.

The answer was as shocking to Allison as a dash of cold water in her face. *Peg must be out of her mind!*

Pulling herself together, Allison stepped forward. "You can find your husband down at the lagoon,

Mrs. Ransome," she said in a cool steady voice that belied the terrible churning sickness inside her. "He has quarters in a mobile unit on the shore. Are you familiar with the lagoon, Mrs. Ransome?"

"I should hope so! I lived on this lousy island for an eternity," the woman said impatiently. "But a mobile unit? And why there?"

"Because of the oyster farm," Allison answered tonelessly.

"Oyster farm? Don't tell me old Burke finally got his oyster farm," his wife said with a brittle laugh. "It's mighty damn clear I didn't get here a moment too soon. Now get one of those boys to drive me down there to see my husband, miss. You can put my luggage in the suite that opens on the east balcony. They're Burke's rooms, and we'll be sleeping there tonight. You can expect the two of us for dinner."

"We have guests in those rooms already, Mrs. Ransome," Allison informed her stiffly.

"Well, get them out," the other woman commanded. "In the meantime I'll be with my husband at the lagoon."

Suddenly Allison could take no more.

"Mrs. Crewes will have one of our young men take you to the lagoon in the jeep," said Allison. "Peg?"

Sure that her voice would break on the next syllable, Allison turned away. Head high, shoulders squared, she executed a dignified exit with measured steps through the front door, into the house, across the great hall and up the stairs to her room.

Closing the door quietly behind her, she made a beeline to the bathroom and threw up.

CHAPTER SIXTEEN

UP AT THE LAGOON, Burke had spent the day transferring clouds of tiny larvae out of the spawning tank with its artificially warmed water. The previous week the seed oysters had exploded millions of eggs into the tank to provide the first crop for Ransome's Cay Oyster Farm. In the sheltered waters of the lagoon, warmed by the Gulf Stream, the mollusks would be ready for harvest in far less time than could be expected in colder water, Burke thought with satisfaction. With luck the first oysters might be ready for market in two or three years.

Casting off from the barge in the dinghy, Burke's thoughts turned back to Allison. He felt a quick pulse of anticipation. He would soon be with her for another of their evening rides. This time they would be together without the constraint of holding back his feeling for her. These interludes alone with her had become the shining hours of the day, warm, delightful, poignant—and sheer hell. He had come to look forward to them with both eagerness and dread.

Since the night of the storm he'd nurtured a growing hope that she was beginning to care for him in a deeper way... something beyond the intense physical force that drew them irresistibly together. Yet he'd dared not put it to test. He'd dedicated himself to making her forget Tyler before he admitted his own feeling for her, fearing that to rush her might be to lose her. Then the previous night, not wanting to, he'd blurted it out. Stunned by his indiscretion, he'd taken off into the darkness, not waiting to hear what she would say.

In the clear light of day he felt a deep relief. Maybe the time had come to bring his own feelings out in the open, whatever ambivalence she might harbor. Now that she knew, there was nothing left but to win her with whatever wiles he could command. That evening he would ask Effie to fix a picnic hamper. There was a cold bottle of champagne in the refrigerator at the mobile. They would go on down to Buttonhook Cove for a swim. He'd toss a magnolia blossom at her feet....

Once on shore, he was about to step inside the mobile unit that served as office and quasi-home when the sound of a jeep approaching through the near woods brought his head around to see who it was. The next moment he was looking into the cold acquisitive sloe eyes of a flawlessly beautiful face he hadn't seen in ten years.

As if thrown by the force of a blast, his body staggered backward and braced against the door behind him. For a moment he stared down at her, feeling nothing. Vaguely he wondered how he could ever have been under the spell of a woman with such a calculating insensitive visage.

"Burke, darling," Margo Ransome cooed up at him from where she stood. "Well, if you aren't still the sexiest man I've ever seen. I'd almost forgotten how utterly gorgeous you are." Over one shoulder she waggled her fingers in a gesture of dismissal at Hoddy, glowering at the wheel of the jeep.

"Run along, boy," she said. "You won't be needed anymore. My husband and I will be up at the house directly."

Hoddy didn't wait to be told twice. Gunning the motor, he turned the jeep in a wide circle and took off into the woods.

"Darling! You might at least come down those steps and give me a kiss," said Margo petulantly.

At last Burke found his voice. "What the hell are you doing here?" he demanded bluntly.

"Is that any way to greet your long-lost wife?" said Margo with a calculated smile.

Burke gave a derisive snort. "It won't work, Margo. You're not my wife. You got the divorce yourself."

"What makes you think so, silly? I've never had the slightest intention of letting you get away."

For the second time he felt as if he were in the path of a demolition bomb. With sickening realization he knew what she said could well be true. He had been so unnerved by what he'd seen that night at Plantation House he hadn't really the heart to take any action. For him the marriage was over. He moved out of the big house in Atlanta that had belonged to his father, where he and Margo had lived, and took an apartment. He closed his mind to everything but the family mills, where he worked at hard physical labor by day and dragged himself back to the apartment at night to fall into an exhausted sleep. He blocked from his thinking all that had to do with either Margo or Ty until his cousin appeared years later, wanting to sell his share of the island. At that time Ty told him Margo was getting the divorce at last so she could remarry.

Soon after, Burke left on the *Ulysses*. It had never occurred to him to request a copy of the divorce papers. He had taken it for granted that because he couldn't be reached at sea Margo had got her divorce by default and married her gambler.

Instinctively he knew at this moment that Margo's words were true. The irony of it was that he'd never believed anything Tyler had ever said to him previously. What had possessed him to trust him about something so important?

The morning after the Plantation House scene he should have filed for divorce himself and cleared the slate.

"To what do I owe this unexpected visit?" he asked coldly.

Margo lowered her long thick lashes, then blinked up at him with affected innocence. "I've decided to let bygones be bygones, darling," she said. "I'll forgive you for deserting me. You did, you know. Don't you think a reconciliation after all these years would be sweet?''

Burke's eyes were wintry, his voice like tempered steel. "My lawyer will start divorce proceedings in the morning," he said.

"I wouldn't be hasty about it, Burke," Margo responded, her voice as hard as his. "Face it, dear man. You don't have the grounds."

"Grounds!" Burke exploded. "You seem to forget that last night at Plantation House."

"Your corroborating witness is dead, so it's your word against mine," Margo said goadingly. "I don't think it will be much trouble to convince a judge that you're a wife deserter and I've been wronged. Not with Stoney Mansfield as my lawyer. You've seen Stoney's headlines, I reckon."

Ransome had seen the headlines—multimillion-dollar verdicts for clients against the rich and indiscreet.

"Those women weren't even wives," Margo gloated. "They were live-ins."

"Okay, Margo, we both know you don't want a reconciliation any more than I do," he said angrily. "Just what the hell do you want?"

"This island," she replied flatly.

Burke stared at her incredulously. "I don't believe it," he said slowly. "You've always hated Ransome's Cay."

"It's hardly my favorite place," she admitted

breezily. "But there's this California land developer I know who'll buy it for close to eight figures. Count that, Burke. That's a lovely bunch of coconuts! He wants to build another luxury complex like Sea Island and Hilton Head."

"His name doesn't happen to be Orrin Travis, does it?" asked Ransome grimly.

"How did you guess?" affirmed Margo smugly. "Now if y'all just sign over the cay, I'll give you an uncontested divorce. That way we'll both have what we want."

"You must be out of your mind!" exclaimed Burke. In spite of himself his fury and frustration were beginning to show through.

"Don't force me to turn it over to Mansfield, Burke. I promise we'll take you for half of everything you own. I might even end up with your precious island and a good chunk of the family mills to boot."

"Don't count on it. I'll see you in court." Ransome's voice was choked with controlled rage.

"When you've talked to Stoney Mansfield you'll see it differently," she predicted nastily. "Think about it. I'll be at Plantation House for a couple of days. You can bring me your answer there."

The very fact a Mrs. Burke Ransome existed was something Burke had fervently wished Allison need never know. He knew he must now tell her the whole story the moment he got Margo off the island. He had planned to tell her eventually, but he could see it would have been better if he had already done so.

He didn't dare contemplate the mischief Margo might engineer under the same roof with Allison for so much as an hour. It was too late to ship her out that night. There was nothing to do but keep her there in his quarters until morning, when he would call the company plane to deposit her in Atlanta.

"Okay, Margo," he told her. "If you insist, I'll think about your proposal until morning—but only if you spend the night here in my mobile unit. I think you'll find it quite comfortable."

Margo's brows shot up in surprise, and she eyed him with speculative pleasure. "I'm sure I will," she said coyly. "That's what I like about you, darling. You always were a reasonable man."

Burke moved aside for her to come up on the small porch and through the door. She climbed the steps and eased up cozily beside him.

"Umm," she murmured, tucking both hands around his arms and rubbing her cheek against his biceps. "Burke Ransome, you're about the sexiest man I've ever run across, I'd be obliged to admit."

Somehow Burke got her through the door and into the mobile without getting himself seduced, then went off to have Bunker bring her luggage from Plantation House.

He didn't return to the mobile unit. There was food in the refrigerator if she got hungry and television if she got bored.

At least he wouldn't have to explain her to Doc.

He was away temporarily, teaching a seminar at one of the coastal universities to the north.

Until well after midnight Burke prowled the deck of the *Ulysses*, stretching out at last under the stars to stare up into the night in insomniac torment as he considered the threat Margo posed to everything in the world he cared about. His wife! It was unbelievable, but there she was, and no *ex* about it. He'd check that out, of course, but when she'd said there'd been no divorce, it had had the ring of truth.

Shortly before nine the next morning he went ashore and aroused a sullen Margo, who appeared to be suffering a severe hangover.

"You can forget the hollow threats, Margo," he said when she opened the door of the mobile at his knock. "They won't work. I didn't desert you and you know it. The plane will be here at ten to fly me to Atlanta. You be ready. You're going, too."

She yawned sulkily. "It's practically the middle of the night," she complained.

Through the open door he observed the normally orderly unit strewn with garments. The champagne bottle intended for his picnic with Allison sat empty on a table near the unmade bed. He wondered if she'd spent the night trying on all the clothes she'd brought with her.

"What are we going to do in Atlanta?"

"I'm going to see my lawyer and file for divorce. You're going to the airport and taking the first plane out to wherever you came from. I personally intend to see you on that plane.'' Burke's tone was more reasonable and less hostile than he felt.

She slammed the door in his face, but when the plane landed she was ready to go. To his surprise she had little to say and mentioned nothing of the threat she'd brandished the previous day.

It was not until she was about to board the plane for Los Angeles in the Atlanta airport that she dropped the mask of indifference she'd worn since she stepped out of the mobile unit that morning. She gave him a hard level look.

''I'm going to get you *good*, Burke Ransome,'' she said, her voice filled with venom. ''You didn't win any points for yourself when you left me alone in that cracker-box trailer all night. You might have persuaded me to play nice if you'd stuck around. When Stoney Mansfield gets through with you, I'm going to walk away with a lot more than your crummy island.''

She started down the corridor to the plane, then turned back, her dark eyes glittering with malice. ''By the way, you needn't think I don't know you've been carrying on an affair while you're married to me,'' she said waspishly.

Burke stared at her blankly, not knowing for a moment what she was getting at.

''I have a witness to testify he saw you with your paramour on a recent overnight rendezvous right in this city. How'll y'all like the sound of that in court?'' With a triumphant toss of her head she walked down the corridor to the plane.

Orrin Travis! he thought sickly. *Allison!* Margo and Travis were going to try to make something of that night at the hotel.

As shock and anger subsided, the thought of how Margo's arrival must have affected Allison began to obsess him. Yet he dared not go to her as he longed to. He must first know for certain whether Margo was right. If indeed they were still married, he was in no position to present his case to Allison until he'd at least taken the first steps toward a divorce.

Why hadn't he filed for divorce ten years earlier, he asked himself grimly. But he knew the answer. He'd had no stomach for the inevitable ugly court fight over his property. It had been easier just to bide his time, replenishing Margo's personal checking account each month with the extravagant allowance she'd demanded early in their marriage. Sooner or later he'd expected her to find someone rich enough for her to give up the luxury of that monthly allowance and get the divorce herself.

He should have paid attention to the fact no divorce papers ever reached him during those last weeks when he was recruiting his people for the *Ulysses* and making it ready to sail.

From the moment he deposited the last check for Margo's monthly allowance the day before the ship embarked until the previous night when she arrived on his doorstep he'd thought of himself as a single man—a classic example of the wish being father to the thought.

Still, if there had been no divorce, why hadn't Margo kicked up a fuss when he'd cut off the allowance, he wondered suddenly with a flash of hope. How sweet it would be, he thought with a stir of excitement, if he could go to Allison and assure her he had not made love to her as the husband of Margo but as a free single man.

"I'm sorry, sir. There is no record of a Margo and Burke Ransome divorcing in Washoe County," the accommodating female voice at the clerk's office in Nevada informed him a short time later.

Burke thanked her and slowly replaced the phone, his last hope that Margo had lied to serve her own purposes dashed. This time she'd told the truth, he thought dully. Furthermore she'd hired Stoney Mansfield and was going to smear Allison publicly with the tar brush of Ransome follies.

He was sick with disgust—for Margo, for Orrin Travis, for his dead cousin, Ty, but most of all for himself, for not having cut all ties with Margo after the Plantation House charade. Allison was in jeopardy because of it, and the future of their relationship at stake.

BURKE'S ATTORNEY, Justin Collins, was sanguine about the forthcoming divorce until Burke told him who Margo had hired to represent her. "I don't like it," he said with a frown. "If Mansfield took it, he's got something up his sleeve. Mansfield doesn't handle a case unless he sees some way he can come through with a smashing verdict. He's given an ulcer to more than one lawyer in court.''

Stepping wearily into the plane for the flight back to Ransome's Cay the morning of his fourth day away, he was glad he had resisted a repeated temptation to call Allison and try to explain what was going on. The ugly story must be told to her face-to-face. He could withhold no dark secrets from her; she must be able to read the truth of what he said in his eyes.

He had purposely waited until Collins had actually filed for the divorce before heading back to Ransome's Cay. When he told Allison of the marriage he'd thought long since dissolved, he wanted to be able to say he had already taken the first steps in the divorce proceedings.

But would she believe him? How could he convince her that when he'd made love to her with all the fervor of a passionate heart he hadn't known he was a married man? The happiness of his future depended on making her believe. Knowing he *must*, he knew then that somehow he *would*—and was suddenly wildly impatient to get it over with.

He wanted desperately to see her again, to hold her in his arms, to tell her for the first time the full extent of his love for her—and to declare his intention to replace Tyler in her heart.

At the lagoon Burke waved the pilot off and headed for the mobile unit to drop off his bag. He was anxious to get to Allison and was glad Doc was still away at the seminar so he wouldn't be delayed by talk. Maybe the time had come for his friend to know the whole story of his marriage. But that could wait. At the moment Allison was the only person he wanted to talk to.

Stepping down from the porch of the mobile on his way to the pickup, he paused at the sight of a motorboat approaching the shore. As it drew near he saw it was a passenger charter boat from the mainland. Its sole passenger was Orrin Travis.

Involuntarily Burke's hands clenched into fists. Closing the door behind him, he came down the steps and across the sand to intercept the visitor before he reached the building. Travis came ashore, leaving the pilot waiting in the boat.

"Get out!" Burke ordered coldly when he was close enough to be heard without having to raise his voice.

Though Travis didn't venture to come nearer, neither did he leave. "Don't be so touchy, Ransome," Travis said across the short distance that separated them. "This time I got something you want. I came to do you a favor. I came to tell you how you can get that wife of yours off your back."

It was the voice of the snake-oil salesman, thought Burke, but what the man was offering held undeniable charm. "Not much you did," he relied bluntly. "You're in this together, but let's hear what you have to say."

"Not anymore, we're not," Travis declared. "You know Margo. We had a deal. Next thing I know she wants to steal me out of my socks."

Burke waited. Taking silence for assent, Travis continued. "Between Mansfield and her you can't win, Ransome. She'll get the island, and she'll get a healthy piece of everything else you own. But you're lucky. They're counting on me to give the case the pizzazz."

Still Burke watched him with a glacial eye as he listened to a rerun of Travis's previous offer to buy Ransome's Cay. The new figure he named made Ransome swallow in dismay. "Am I to understand that if I sell you Ransome's Cay for this astonishing amount of money you'll bow out of whatever suit Margo has in mind?"

Travis nodded.

"So what's in it for you?" Burke asked. "If Margo gets the island we both know she'll turn right around and sell it to you."

"That's where she and I part company. She says now she's going to sell it to the highest bidder, which means it would cost me half again what I'm offering you."

"And this 'pizzazz' you propose to give to the case?" Burke asked, his voice loaded with contempt.

Travis eyed him speculatively, then glanced quickly over his shoulder as if marking the distance to the waiting boat. "You don't have to give me an answer right this minute. Call Carlos Developers in LA. They'll know where to reach me."

Burke wasn't to be put off. "The pizzazz," he reminded him, a note of menace in his voice.

"Well, I'm supposed to testify you and Mrs. Hill spent the night together in an Atlanta hotel and you threatened to beat me up because I saw you. It's all true," said Travis as Burke took a step toward him. He began backing toward his escape, still talking. "With Mansfield on the case it'll make headlines, and if the tabs get hold of it they'll blow it up—'Rich island owner and paramour.' But maybe that doesn't bother you. Maybe you don't mind turning Mrs. Hill into a media event."

With those words Travis turned and puffed his way across the sand to scramble into the boat. Ransome, too, was walking back to the truck, his contempt for Orrin Travis so profound he wanted only to erase the miserable creature from his sight.

"WHAT DO YOU MEAN, Allison's gone?" he asked in a stunned voice a short time later, staring into Peg Crewes's disapproving face in disbelief. The two stood in the great hall at Plantation House.

Peg's manner was exceedingly cool. "Why didn't you tell her you had a wife?" she asked bluntly.

Burke shook his head as if to rid himself of a bad dream. "It never crossed my mind," he answered blankly. "I mean it, Peg. It didn't have anything to do with us."

Peg gave a snort. "And you're supposed to be the *good* Ransome!" she exclaimed with heavy sarcasm. "Your miserable cousin wills his half of the island— which was precious little for all he squandered of hers—then turns around and sells it to you. And now this!''

"Wait a minute," Burke interrupted. "That's the first I've heard for certain that Tyler squandered Allison's money, though knowing Ty I well believe it. Allison never told me. She's been very defensive about him, in fact.''

"I guess I'm the only person that knows," Peg replied. "I happened to be there when she discovered what a fool she'd been to put her inheritance from her folks in joint ownership with your cousin. He was systematically wiping her out. He would have gone through everything she owned in another year if she hadn't left him when she did.''

"They weren't living together when he was killed?" Burke asked in surprise.

"Allison happens to be one who takes marriage vows seriously, but it finally got too much even for her," said Peg resentfully. "She stuck it out long after she'd lost not only her illusions but her love.''

"What's that?" A spurt of something like hope coursed through Burke. "I thought she was still in love with Ty...Effie told me...I overheard something she said to Birch. I understood it to mean she was still in love with Ty, even though he was gone.''

"Just because she didn't bad-mouth Tyler?" Peg retorted. "Didn't wear a badge saying she hadn't loved him for years? Allison figured marrying your cousin was nobody's mistake but hers, so why talk about it. She just wants to get on with her life.''

"Thanks, Peg. You haven't any idea how much!" Burke burst out in an exultant voice. "Now tell me where she's gone."

Peg looked at him coolly. "Not on your life," she said.

"Come, Peg. I've got to know where to find her," he said impatiently. "I need her phone number and address."

"You won't get it from me." Peg's tone was adamant. "I like you, Burke, but not telling Allison you're married is the kind of thing Tyler Hill would pull. I'll be darned if I'm going to help you mess up her life again."

Burke stopped by to see Effie on his way out, but she could tell him only that Allison had gone to New York. She didn't have an address, she said, but she was sure he could get it from Mrs. Crewes.

Heading back to the lagoon in the pickup, Burke couldn't stay angry with Peg in spite of the frustration of her obdurate refusal to help him. She had lifted the burden that had lain heavy on his heart since he first realized how much Allison meant to him. That he would find her he did not doubt. It would just take a little longer without Peg's help.

Peg's prosaic declaration that Allison had neither illusions nor love where Ty was concerned had been like the trumpet to the walls of Jericho. They had knocked down the one barrier he'd feared would always stand between them. For Allison to continue to love Ty had seemed little short of neurotic. With that put to rest the other problems that had plagued his life the past few days suddenly seemed less important and no longer insoluble.

Yet it wasn't until four days later that he set out for New York to find Allison. His own unexpected absence while Doc was away had left the operation on the oyster barge without experienced supervision. By the fourth day, though, he could wait no longer. Confident the first emerging crop was in no danger, he made plans to depart. Early that morning he left Savannah for New York.

BURKE'S FIRST MOVE after he was settled in a Manhattan hotel facing Central Park was to locate Allison's friend Bob Birch by dialing each Robert Birch in the Manhattan telephone directory in the order listed. When he finally connected with the right Robert Birch the next morning, he met with a lack of cooperation as adamant as, though far colder than, Peg's.

"Look, Ransome, I don't know what's been going on down there at Ransome's Cay, but in my opinion Allison's well out of it," Birch said frigidly. "If she wanted you to know where she was, it's my guess she would have told you."

Burke put the phone back in its cradle and leaned his head in his hands, wondering where to turn next. He was determined to exhaust all possibilities before he called for professional help.

There was Herb Canby, of course. He'd had a casual acquaintanceship with Canby through the years, but in view of what he'd put her through with the will it was highly improbable Allison would call on him when she got back to the city.

To Burke's considerable surprise Canby knew exactly where he could find Allison and was delighted to be of help. It seemed he had run into her having lunch with Bob Birch at the Russian Tea Room a few days earlier. Allison had mentioned she was back in her old apartment in the West Seventies.

"Wait a minute," he'd said. "I'll get her address for you. I think I still have it in my files."

Given the address, Burke expressed his thanks and was about to hang up, but Canby seemed determined to apologize to the point of embarrassment for the trouble his carelessness in the matter of Tyler's will had caused.

Then unexpectedly Canby said, "By the way, Burke, I happened to run across some information about Margo that might be of interest to you."

"Margo?" Burke repeated, suddenly alert. "Something to do with the island?"

"Could be. She and that California developer she's sleeping with tried to sucker me on a deal a while back, and I had some investigating done on her. They've got their eyes on your island, Burke, and they'll try to get it by hook or crook."

"So what else is new?" Burke said disgustedly. "Listen, Herb, thanks for your help. I've got to be on my way."

"Suit yourself," said Canby. "I just thought it

might come in handy for you to know you and Margo were never legally married.''

He made a throwaway line of it, and it took Burke a moment to digest what he'd said. "What are you talking about!" he demanded.

"Margo was married to a fellow before she was married to you," Canby explained. "I talked to him. A pretty decent sort. They've never been divorced. She was in too big a hurry to hook you—and the poor devil still hopes someday to get her back. You can trust me on this, Burke, I swear. I've gone to considerable trouble and expense to make sure. It all checks out.''

Burke let out a low whistle. All that business about Stoney Mansfield was nothing but bluster! Margo had never even been to see Mansfield. She thought she could scare him into selling the island without a fight. That was why she hadn't screamed when he cut off her allowance. It all made sense. She was afraid if she created a fuss he'd start checking into her past.

Bigamy. So much for her desertion charge.

Once more Canby apologized for the foul-up with the will, clearly still shaken by the mess he'd caused for them all.

"Forget it, Herb," said Burke with quiet satisfaction. "You just wiped the slate clean.''

CHAPTER SEVENTEEN

AFTER THE FIRST SHOCK WAVE at the unexpected materialization of Burke's wife had passed that afternoon following Margo's unheralded arrival, Allison was left numb and dry-eyed. In her bathroom mirror the drawn colorless face looking back at her seemed that of a stranger. There was an ogre within her, precariously contained and poised like a jack-in-the-box to spring out and fill the terrible surrounding emptiness with the continuing echo: *He has a wife.... He has a wife.... He has a wife....*

She didn't dare let herself explore the emptiness itself, nor did she want to so soon. Instinctively she understood she must first discover how to live with it, or it would destroy her.

She washed her face and then washed it again. After that she spent a long time with her makeup. She took uncommon care to apply the exact degree of color that would make her appear at least superficially alive yet didn't scream out the truth that she'd painted her face to hide the pain lurking inside, waiting to break through.

When she could find no more to do for herself she

left her room and went downstairs. She avoided Peg's sympathy-flooded eyes. Like a sleepwalker she went back to the accounts they had been finishing when the visitor who was to turn her life into a shambles first appeared.

"We don't have to finish this right this minute, Ally," Peg said, noticing with concern her friend's set face as she thumbed impatiently through a sheaf of papers before her.

Allison didn't look up. "If you don't mind, Peg, I'd like to get this job finished today before we quit," she replied in a toneless voice that was harder to argue with than words.

And so they pushed on into the early dusk without a word about Burke or the woman up at the lagoon. When a grim-faced Bunker arrived in the pickup to carry the matched designer luggage away to the lagoon, it was Peg who directed him to the great hall, where she'd had the twins deposit it.

Allison kept her eyes and mind on the figures she was processing on the calculator, not daring to look away for fear that if she strayed once, she could never return.

As she worked the same questions rose to intrude as regularly as the crickety chirp of the calculator's total key. *Why? Why, Burke? Why did you let me find out like this?* For he must have known his wife was coming. Or hadn't he?

It was irrelevant. Instead of saying he loved her, why hadn't he told her he had a wife?

But these were questions to be stuffed into the Pandora's box of troubles locked in her head. *Not now,* that inner voice cried. *I can't think about that now. Later. Later. Later!*

Inevitably, after the final accounting was done and she'd bade a constrained good-night to Peg, her "later" came.

In bed alone and sleepless in the darkest hours of the night she at last faced the truth she had furiously avoided until that moment: In the final analysis Burke was a greater villain than Ty.

Even at the height of her schoolgirl infatuation for Ty she'd secretly guessed he was flawed, though for a long time she would not acknowledge it even to herself. Despite earlier misunderstandings she'd come to see in Burke a kind of nobility tempered with just the right measure of humor and human frailty to banish established guards.

She'd believed in him, trusted him, *loved* him. After he'd declared his love for her she had even let herself dream for the first time of spending the rest of her life with him. That he already had a wife was the last thought in her mind.

Disillusioned, ashamed and deeply hurt, she felt, too, a crisis of confidence in her own judgment of men. She'd blamed her youth for her disastrous infatuation for Tyler, but it was a mature woman who had fallen in love with Burke. She was mature, reasonably well balanced, coolheaded, for the most part—even sophisticated, she liked to think.

If he had only told her in the beginning he was married she would never have let the times they were together get so out of hand. The code was inviolable, however attractive the man. Apart from a strong instinct for self-protection and an empathy for the injured wife, Allison had a deep contempt for cheaters. Any flame she might feel was quickly snuffed out whenever she found herself being approached by a married man.

Why hadn't Burke told her? Was the conquest of a woman a chauvinistic game he liked to play? Or had his longtime dream of a Ransome's Cay Center become such an obsession he saw her as no more than a convenient tool for its realization. To keep her there running Plantation House was a means of paying back what she'd put into the house without having to postpone the center, and it also freed him to devote his full attention to the research and study program.

None of this explained why he had told her he loved her. But the *why* didn't matter. Only two things were relevant: Burke had made love to her, and he had a wife.

Sometime before dawn, her immediate future resolved in her mind, Allison turned on the light and pulled her suitcase down from the top of her closet to pack.

"IF YOU'RE GOING, the twins and I go, too," Peg declared hotly as she and Allison stood facing each other on the morning-room porch some three hours later.

"Please, Peg, don't," said Allison. "I've spent the whole night thinking this thing through, and I really hope you will stay at Plantation House—unless there's something you'd rather do."

"You know there isn't. If it weren't for that blasted woman—"

"Please, Peg!" Allison stopped her. It was the first mention of Burke's wife between the two since Allison had walked away from the veranda and Margo Ransome the previous afternoon.

After a moment's pause Allison continued as if Peg's last words had not been spoken. "As you know, most of my money is tied up here," she reminded her friend. "The agreement is that we're to operate Plantation House as our own and the rent normally paid the owner will be applied to what I have coming from him."

"The owner being Burke Ransome," said Peg sourly.

Allison ignored the remark. "The point is, Peg, if you pay me a certain fixed amount out of the proceeds every month, it will be like leasing from me. I'll get my money back as agreed, and the rest of the net income will be yours."

"I don't know anything about a study center," Peg demurred. "I don't know whether I can handle the place without you."

"Nonsense," Allison declared. "Of course you can. It will be the same as a resort, which you know how to run—only without a lot of the problems. Hire an assistant to give you a hand. Keep some free time for Doc.''

Peg frowned uncertainly. "I don't know about Doc," she said unhappily. "It seems to me he should have told us."

Allison turned and grasped her friend's shoulders to look into her face. "Stop that!" she ordered sharply. "Doc's a good man. Don't get him mixed up in this. It wasn't for him to report what Burke could have told if he'd wanted it known. If you care about him, and I think you do, you won't even mention it to him, Peg."

Peg's eyes were a confession to the question that remained unasked. "To tell you the truth, Ally," she said, "I really want to stay on here, but I think you're making a mistake. If it were me, I'd hire a lawyer and go after him for everything you put into this house, plus punitive damages—cash! I'd demand it be paid in full right now."

Allison walked over to the screen and looked out across the broad slope of lawn to the beach and the ocean beyond. With a deep sigh she turned back to look at her friend.

"No, Peg, you wouldn't," she said bleakly. "If I did that it would jeopardize what he's accomplishing down at the lagoon and the center, as well. He's doing good things with his money. I'm not out to make them suffer or to get back at him for his personal life."

In the kitchen a short time later Allison said goodbye to a tearful Effie and a grim-faced Bunker. The two kindly people seemed bewildered at her sudden departure and together tried to persuade her to stay.

"You're needed here," Effie told her, dabbing her reddened face with a tissue. "Mr. Burke's counting on you for the center, and that one won't stay more'n a few days. Pay no mind to what she says now. I promise you, she'll never stay."

"Listen to Effie, Mrs. Hill," Bunker threw in. "Stick it out. We all know that woman's hard to deal with, but I guarantee that before long she'll be gone again. Just be patient."

Allison heard them with a kind of dull astonishment. She'd supposed they knew of her feelings for Burke.

But Effie and Bunker apparently hadn't even guessed. They thought it was the woman herself who was driving Allison away—not the fact that she was married to Burke.

"Why didn't you ever tell me he had a wife, Effie?" Allison found herself asking in a strained voice.

Effie's face looked puzzled for a moment. "Reckon I never thought to. It was such a treat to have him back on the island without her, I liked to forget. Long as she stayed away, I didn't guess it mattered."

Max drove Allison down to the landing in one of the electric carts, followed by Hoddy and Peg in a second cart. The Bunkers stood on the veranda watching the procession with long faces. The twins loaded her bags onto the launch, and Allison kissed the Crewes family a suddenly tearful goodbye.

As the boat pulled away from the landing the sound of a plane heading out from the lagoon, low overhead, brought her eyes up for a moment. It was the Ransome company plane. Turning away, Allison wondered bitterly what pleasure excursion Burke was off to with his beautiful brittle wife.

Looking back on Plantation House from the boat dock, she took leave of Ransome's Cay in a silent goodbye that was as painful as a final parting from an old and gracious friend who had added to her joy in the best of times, given comfort in the worst and now would be seen no more.

"Don't go fixin' to settle in up there, honey, 'cause you'll be back," Effie had insisted as she'd kissed her goodbye. "It won't be no time before that woman's gone. Take my word for it."

And Peg, who knew better, had said, "At least you can come for a visit when they aren't here."

Allison had managed a doubtful smile and replied, "We'll see." But she knew as she'd uttered the words that she would never come back, even under those conditions. Just being on the island again would stir up memories she intended to banish from her mind. How could she chance upon the wooded glade bedded with mint where they had first made love without again feeling an overwhelming loss?

The boat rounded a bend in the shoreline, and Plantation House was lost to her behind its sheltering trees. Still Allison watched the land, remembering, sorrowing.

There they had galloped, the two of them, into the incoming tide. There one early evening they had stood together under a century-old live oak with Spanish moss draped about it like a canopy hanging almost to the ground. Beneath it they had clung to each other and kissed and made unspoken promises with their eyes—promises that meant nothing.

As one bites down on an aching tooth, Allison punished herself, taking a certain perverse solace from her agonizing reprise until the boat passed by Buttonhook Cove. She could not see the ravaged waterfall from the sea, but it blossomed in her mind as a metaphor for her love affair with Burke—beautiful while it lasted but fragile, destined to collapse.

For a moment she saw it as it had been the morning she had first caught sight of Burke, the crystal fresh water splashing out of a bower of sweet bay and cassina holly over the moss-grown ledge. She could taste again the sweet scent of honeysuckle in the air, see the waxy leaves of the magnolia tree shimmering in the early-morning sun.

She was there again, dipping a tentative toe into the pebbled basin with its border of maidenhair fern until she gathered her courage and ran all the way in, letting the cold water rush over her head and flow down the length of her bare body.

Then for a moment she saw him again as she'd seen him that morning—the perfectly carved head, the splendidly proportioned torso moving swiftly, surely, through the incoming surf, the rider on the swimming horse. On they came, splashing through the shallows to the beach, the horse rising up to paw the air, the man welding his muscular body and blue-jeaned legs to the bareback mount. And she saw the magnolia blossom at her feet.

A soft moan escaped her lips. She shook her head and pressed her hands to her eyes for a moment to drive out the apparitions. Eyes covered, shutting out all sight, she thought again of Buttonhook Creek as she had seen it last—fragmented into myriad trickles that meandered aimlessly across the slope to lose their way in the sea grass.

Stop it, she cried out silently. *No more!* The time has come to give up what she'd never had. Anything less than a clean break was neurotic. Her love affair with Burke was no more than a sweet lost illusion.

From there on she deliberately turned her head away from Ransome's Cay and schooled her eyes to watch the waves ahead. At that moment she made an earnest vow to close her mind to the past.

WHEN SHE REACHED NEW YORK in the early afternoon she took a cab from Kennedy airport to a midtown hotel, where she booked a room. From there she called her friend Karen, who had sublet her apartment when Allison had left Manhattan in the spring.

"You must have read my mind," Karen said when

the greetings were over and Allison had told her she was back in the city to stay. "I was going to call you tonight. I wanted to ask you if it would be all right if I found someone else to take over your place. A vacancy's come up in the building I'd like to live in permanently."

"How soon can I move in?"

"Tomorrow, if you like. The landlady has been holding the apartment for me until I could contact you."

Allison's next move was to call the familiar number of Edwin Barron, her former employer. She might have waited, since the afternoon was half over, but she made an appointment with his secretary to see him at 4:00 P.M. that day. If she could fill every minute, she could almost keep Burke locked out of her mind. Her biggest problem for a long time to come, she feared, was to keep her hours so busy there would be no minutes left in them for remembering.

Shortly before the appointed time she stepped into the elevator that took her up twenty floors to the accounting firm of Carston and Ames.

She wasted no seconds in getting to the purpose of her visit and was grateful for the tact that kept Edwin Barron from plying her with questions about her return.

"We're glad to have you back, Allison," he told her. "We can fit you into the company at about the same level you were at when you left us. Are you still considering becoming a certified public accountant?"

She hadn't thought that far ahead yet, but the moment he brought it up she saw it would fill a gap. If this was to be her career, it was high time she got on with it. With school and study there would be no empty spaces in her life for forbidden memories to come crowding in.

She nodded. "As soon as I get settled, I'll check on classes."

"Good," said Barron. "You won't regret it. Once you've passed the exam and have your certification I don't mind telling you there's a very good future here for you at Carston and Ames."

"Why, thank you, Mr. Barron," she replied, hoping she showed proper enthusiasm for what she recognized as a generous promise. She was pleased naturally. If her career wasn't to be at Ransome's Cay, as a second choice she knew this would suit her best.

"When would you like to start work?" asked Barron.

"I'll be settling back into my apartment tomorrow," came her prompt reply. "How about the day after?" *No empty moments, Allison. Keeping moving right along.*

As she was about to leave, Barron said, "Oh, by the way, I have an appointment with Bob Birch to go over some investments tomorrow. May I tell him you're back?"

The question caught her unawares. She hadn't even thought about Bob. It was through Edwin Bar-

ron that they'd first met. Bob was a good friend. Now
that she was here she supposed there was no reason she
shouldn't see him as long as he understood they could
never be more than friends. "No, of course not," she
said. "Give him my best."

She was not particularly surprised, then, when Bob
phoned and asked her to have lunch with him her first
day back at work. Nor was she surprised when Bob
was less easy to handle than she might have hoped.

"You could have let an old friend know you were
back in town," he said in an injured tone.

"Oh, Bob, things have been such a scramble," she
replied vaguely, knowing that wasn't true. Things had
moved more smoothly than she'd dared hope.

Nor was Bob willing to leave questions about her
return unasked, as Edwin Barron had been. Again she
parried with evasive answers about the wisdom of
leaving Peg Crewes in charge of Plantation House so
she could come back and pursue a career in accounting.

So troublesome were Birch's questions she almost
welcomed the appearance of the originator of her
woes when he arrived right after the first course.

"Allison! I couldn't believe it was you when I saw
you across the room. I had to come and see for sure."

It was Herb Canby, looking every inch the handsome young man-about-town, thought Allison dour-
ly, though she recognized a certain sheepishness in
his eyes. "I can't imagine why, Herb," she said
evenly.

"I suppose not," he said, for a moment not meeting her eyes. "I really want you to know, Allison—"

"That you're glad to see me back in town, I'm sure," she interrupted, catching his eye and giving him a warning look. "And I want you to know I'm glad you're glad," she babbled on, determined not to let Herb start apologizing and blat out the whole miserable business about her phony inheritance in the presence of Bob Birch, who was looking at her as if her eyes had suddenly crossed.

However careless Canby might be he was not dull of wit. He got the message. Changing his tone abruptly, he asked, "How long are you going to be in the city?"

Allison told him she was back in her old apartment at her former job and she was there to stay.

"I'd like to talk to you, Allison," said Canby. "I'll give you a ring." With an uneasy parting nod he backed away a step or two, then turned in retreat to join a companion at a table across the room.

All the old frustrations and anger roiled up in Allison, and for a moment she felt completely unforgiving, but she shrugged her feelings aside. She could hardly blame Herb because Burke had neglected to tell her he was married. Before that all other betrayals paled.

ALLISON HAD ALWAYS HAD a fondness for Manhattan, even during the time she had lived there under trying conditions with Tyler. Now as she settled into the unrelenting monotony of her new life the city for the first time seemed a cold and uncaring place.

Coming out of Gristede's, her neighborhood market, with a bagload of groceries one afternoon in her second week back, she felt tired and dispirited; alien to the honks and squeals and roars of Broadway traffic; foreign to the hurrying, pushing bodies in their endless comings and goings around her on every side.

The late-afternoon sun reflecting back off the pavement seemed harsh and unfriendly, unlike the golden effusion that bathed Ransome's Cay.

She welcomed the breeze off the Hudson that whispered up the cross streets as she left the hassle of Broadway and crossed over to walk the few blocks up to her apartment along quieter West End Avenue.

The day marked the twelfth since her return to New York City, her ninth back at her old office in a job not unlike the one she had left.

With the promise of something better to come she'd taken Edwin Barron's advice and registered for night classes that would not only prepare her for the crucial accounting exam but take up the day's dismal slack for weeks to come. The empty hours she saw immediately ahead brought a sudden regret that the new term didn't begin until the following week. It would help to have a class to go to this evening.

Without putting the point explicitly, Barron had made it clear that before his retirement he hoped to see her move into the company's executive framework and step in line to replace him when he left.

"There isn't anyone coming up in the organization with your potential, Allison," he said. "If you build up your training and experience in the interim, the board would follow my recommendation." Then, with a quizzical smile, he'd added, "You can do it, my dear—but only if you want it enough."

But did she want it enough, she wondered. Did life's fulfillment for her mean a vice-presidency in Carston and Ames?

She had to stop thinking like that, she ordered herself sharply. Things were going well. Her timing, for instance, had been perfect. She'd been luckier than she'd had any right to expect. The apartment, the job, Bob Birch waiting in the wings.

If she was so lucky, then why didn't she feel happy, she asked herself crossly as she trudged on up the street, hugging the heavy bag of groceries to her bosom.

She hated to go to the empty apartment.

She hesitated a moment, then turned and walked a long block out of her way. She crossed Riverside Drive to the park, a ribbon of green fronting the Hudson River sporadically from Seventy-second Street all the way up to Grant's Tomb some thirty or more blocks beyond.

At the edge of the park she set her groceries on the grassy slope and sat down beside them, staring absently across the river to the Jersey side. She was scarcely aware of the children, the dogs, the late-afternoon joggers. Her mind was on the people at Ransome's Cay and the long telephone conversation she'd had with Peg the previous night.

Peg had made the call. Allison knew from the moment she'd heard her friend's voice that she was calling with good news, and for a moment her pulse had quickened with a crazy hope that somehow that last nightmare afternoon at Plantation House had been a mistake—even some kind of a hoax.

"Oh, Ally, you'll never guess!" These were Peg's first words.

And Allison had said on a sudden held breath, "Peg, what is it?"

"Doc and I are going to be married!"

Her joy for her friend was lost for a second in the wave of her own disappointment. What had she expected, for heaven's sake?

Recovering, she said with genuine pleasure, "Oh, Peg, that's wonderful! Tell me all about it. I can't wait to hear."

Like a love-struck teenager instead of a nearly forty-year-old woman with two grown sons, Peg told her in a voice bubbling with happiness that Doc had arrived back from his two weeks' absence and come straight to Plantation House to propose marriage. The short time away had made him appreciate how important she'd become to him, and he'd wasted no time in telling her so.

"What about Hoddy and Max? How are they taking it?'' Allison asked, though she knew what the answer would be.

Peg's giggle sounded over the line. "I think I might have to marry him for the sake of the twins, even if I didn't think he was the dearest man alive," Peg told her. "I can't believe the change that has come over those two since Doc appeared on the scene. The scuba diving got them so interested in undersea life they've enrolled at the University of Georgia for the fall semester and are going to major in marine sciences.''

Allison laughed. "So much for my vagabond handymen. And here I am in an apartment with the world's most erratic plumbing!''

"Would you believe it?'' sighed their mother with great satisfaction.

Eventually Peg had brought the talk around to the subject Allison wanted most to hear about but would not let herself ask. "I don't know whether to tell you this or not, Ally, but I suppose you should know,'' said Peg. "Burke was down here a few days after you left, wanting to know where you'd gone. I didn't tell him.'' There was a pause. "I hope I did right.''

"Thanks, Peg,'' Allison said dully. "You did right. We've nothing to say to each other. Any business we have in regard to the center can be handled through you.''

"If I don't get fired,'' said Peg. "I was pretty cool to him. I don't think he'll be bothering you. I'm the only person he knows who has your address, and I won't even tell Doc if you say not to.''

It was so final! Allison had felt a swell of new loneliness at the full realization that she might actually never see Burke again thanks to her zealous friend.

"Whatever you think best," she'd managed to say. After a moment's hesitation she'd asked, "About Doc...what does he think? Have the two of you talked about...all this?"

"Of course we've talked," Peg had said impatiently. "We're human. Doc doesn't know much more about it than we do. Oh, yes, he was aware that Burke had been married, but he assumed there'd been a divorce. This Margo is from a branch of an impoverished but haughty old plantation family— sort of a latter-day Scarlett O'Hara. At least that's Doc's impression. Burke never really talked about it. Just bits and pieces dropped here and there."

Which should have been enough, Allison reminded herself, thinking back. But she hadn't been able to leave it alone.

"Did Doc say...what does Doc think of her?" she asked, not without a touch of malice, having seen the woman herself.

"He never saw her," Peg said. "The two of them—Burke and his newly reunited wife—had gone by the time Doc got back."

"Gone? You mean gone for good?"

"Well, Doc expects Burke back. Burke left him a note about the work on the barge saying they'd talk when he got back, but he didn't say when it would be.''

So that was that, thought Allison with a sigh, staring absently across the jagged, smog-shrouded line of the Hoboken sky. Burke's wife was very much in the picture, and it appeared they were on good terms. After all, they'd flown off together following that first night of reunion on what looked like a second honeymoon.

She hadn't the heart to point out to Peg that this might spell the end of Peg's days at Plantation House, as well as her own. If this Margo decided *she* was going to be chatelaine at Plantation House, it wasn't likely Peg would last long. Worse yet, Burke might even be persuaded by his wife to sell Ransome's Cay for the fabulous price the developers seemed all too eager to pay.

Across the river the transparent veil of smog picked up color as the sun lowered above the western bank. Allison gathered up her groceries and her roomy leather shoulderbag from the grass with a sigh and walked up Riverside Drive until she reached her own street. Her building, an old brownstone that had been converted into five floors of two apartments each, was just off West End Avenue.

The apartments, though charming and expensive, had minuscule kitchens and bathrooms and no doorman or elevator. Entry through the front door to the stairway could be gained only by buzzer or key, though salesmen or other unauthorized persons had been known to come in on the heels of a tenant on the pretext of a forgotten key.

Allison leaned against the heavy carved newel post to the stairway before she began the weary climb to the emptiness that awaited her five flights up.

On the landing of the third floor she stopped again to catch her breath. The stairs would take getting used to again. She remembered ruefully how she had been able to sprint to the top with a bag of groceries under each arm and reach her own door without puffing.

As she was about to start her last climb, she glanced up and felt a sudden grip of fear in her throat. There was a man up there on the landing in front of her door! She could see his legs through the rungs, and he was waiting . . . waiting for her to come upon him unaware.

For a second she panicked. Then she moved cautiously up the stairs and stopped again on the next landing, her heart pounding with apprehension. There she stood for a moment, finally stretching herself as far as she dared, hoping to see before he spotted her what manner of man he was.

"Who is it?" she called out cautiously at last, poised to go flying down to the manager's apartment. Her face was turned up as she strained for a better view.

Over the banister a flight above, under a thatch of sun-streaked hair, a lean strong face with two dark gold wings for brows smiled down at her. She was suddenly awash in the warmth of a pair of gray green, iridescent eyes.

She had no need to be told that the tailored business suit covered the splendid bronzed body she had first seen rising out of the sea at Buttonhook Cove.

CHAPTER EIGHTEEN

ALLISON'S WHOLE BODY went weak. Her arms and legs turned suddenly to rubber. The bag of groceries slid slowly out of her grasp and down the length of her body, spilling grapefruit, canned goods and bars of soap over the stairs.

But the instant of idiot joy that surged through her as she saw who it was was lost at once in a blaze of bitter anger. "What are you doing here?" she demanded hoarsely.

"I have to talk to you," Burke said reasonably. He gave a nod toward her apartment door. "I thought you might invite me in."

"Get out of here," she said in a cold level voice. "Leave me alone. Go back to your wife."

"That's what I must talk to you about, Allison," he said insistently, "but not out here on the steps. Could we...." He took a step as if to descend to her level. For a moment Allison felt as though she were on the edge of hysteria.

"Stop! If you come a step nearer I'll—" Just what would she do, she wondered in a kind of helpless fury. There he stood between her and her own door.

On the other hand, if he heeded her demand to leave, he would have to go around her on the stairs. Either way he need only take her in his arms and wounds that had not yet healed would be reopened.

She glanced wildly back down the stairs behind her, assessing her chances to escape that way. It was impossible. He could catch her before she had reached the next landing. Turning back, she was shocked to find him standing over her, looking down from two steps above. He made no attempt to reach out and take her, though certainly he was close enough, but the sea-colored eyes embraced her with a hungry passion as seductive as a pair of arms.

Oh, God, she moaned in silent desperation. *Why won't he leave me alone?*

Her voice frigid, she said aloud, "Please step aside so I can get into my apartment."

"Are you inviting me in?"

"No, and you know it," she snapped. "I suppose it's too much to expect you to do the decent thing and start walking down those stairs and out of my life."

"I have to talk to you, Allison," he said again quietly. "I won't try to force my way into your apartment, but I am asking for some place other than a public staircase where we can talk."

He stood so close above her on the stairs she imagined she felt the vibrant warmth of his body. Her nostrils were filled with his clean tweedy scent. For a moment she wavered. Then the echo of that brittle voice shrilling, "I'm Mrs. Burke Ransome, and don't forget it!'' ran through her mind and stabbed her again with the same lacerating pain. Nothing he could say to her now could heal that wound.

Didn't he realize it was too late for talk? The damage was already done. Where was his tongue when he might have used it to warn her he had a wife, she wondered bitterly.

"Why this sudden overwhelming urge to talk, Burke?" she asked scathingly. "You never felt any compelling need to tell me you had a wife!"

"I swear it was the last thing on my mind, Allison, after you walked into my life."

Appalled at the callousness of the reply, Allison stared at him in stunned disbelief. When at last she found words, she made no effort to conceal her contempt. "If I thought that was true—and I don't—I'd have to say I find it inexcusable. A man with any honor or decency doesn't simply forget he has a wife just because she doesn't happen to be on the scene."

She saw a muscle in his jaw tighten. The eyes that looked down on her were suddenly bleak.

"This is getting us nowhere, Allison. Can't we go into your apartment and talk."

There was an urgency in his voice, an almost pleading note that seemed so foreign to the strong, self-contained man she knew.

Allison felt her resistance begin to crumble. Still, the hurt was too new, too devastating. "I don't want you in my apartment," she said bluntly, her cold voice giving no hint of her inner turmoil.

"I see," he said, accepting it only to forge on. "In that case we'll have to find some other place. You're going to hear what I have to say, my dear. Then, if you're still determined to drum me out of your life I promise—"

"Yes, Burke?" she asked crisply. "Just what do you promise then? To stay away from me? To leave me alone and never come back?"

Gazing down at her, he gave a queer lopsided grin that set her heart pounding fiercely. From far below came the sound of footsteps on the stairs.

"No...I can't promise you that," he said. "I'll decide later. First you must hear me out."

There were voices now on the landing below. Unexpectedly Allison saw his patience end.

"Damn it, Allison, I'm not going to make what may be the most important statement of my life on a public staircase," he exploded. "I intend to make it with dignity and in private. If you're so afraid I'll contaminate your blasted apartment I'll take a suite at the Plaza. If I leave here you're coming with me and you're going to listen to what I have to say."

The sudden change of humor caught Allison by surprise. She was unhappily aware that Burke had taken over and she was no longer in control of either the situation or her own suddenly ambivalent emotions. She struggled for composure and words to make it clear to Burke her mind had not undergone any change.

"Well, what's it to be?" the velvet baritone above her demanded. "Your apartment or the Plaza?"

Allison drew in a shaky breath. She stood her ground. "Not my apartment!" she said. He stepped down beside her, his face a stern mask of determination, and slipped his hand under her elbow to nudge her down the stairs.

She was astonished to hear her own voice say coolly, "All right, Burke, since you're bent on making an issue of it, we may as well go up on the roof and have it out."

She slipped away from him as his grip on her arm relaxed and led the way across her own landing and on up a last short flight of stairs to a door that opened onto the roof. There, overlooking the Hudson River, a scattering of deck chairs and sun cots were arranged in a half circle behind a lattice-work screen that supported an espaliered pear tree.

Allison rounded the screen and crossed the small area where the furniture was clustered, taking a chair on the far side. She looked back to see if Burke followed.

Out of the shadows of the building's utilities structure he came, his long lithe body framed in an aura of light from across the Hudson where the late-afternoon sun turned the Jersey skyline into red gold splendor. The breeze off the river caught a swatch of tawny hair and brushed it down over his forehead as he strode across the rooftop with an easy yet somehow imperious grace.

Allison caught her breath. Her throat filled with a sudden poignant unwelcome longing. How splendid he looked! Whether fully clothed in a vested suit or stripped bare to the waist to ride the surf, there were moments like this when he took on for her the illusion of physical perfection, like some sculptured god of an ancient time. As she watched him approach, for a moment she forgot to breathe.

He let himself down in one of the faded canvas chairs a discreet distance from where she'd seated herself. The strong jaw and wide, sensuous mouth were set in a stubborn line.

Allison let her breath out in a soundless sigh of despair. How could she have forgotten for even that fleeting instant how deeply he had wronged her, she wondered in dismay, and she steeled herself resolutely for the ordeal that lay ahead.

"To begin with, let's get one thing clear," Burke said when he had jockeyed the light chair around impatiently until he faced her, compelling her to meet his gaze. "There is no wife—I am not married. Fact is, I never have been. But I'll take no credit for that. I only found that out myself today. I don't have a wife."

A flicker of hope sprang to life within her, then was lost. She wanted desperately to believe him. Yet, every fiber of her rational being cried out that it was not true. "You seem to forget that Mrs. Burke Ransome dropped in on us at Plantation House," she pointed out. Her voice was steady, though her tongue stumbled on the name. "In case your memory has failed you, her given name is Margo, or so she said."

"Ah, yes, Margo!" Did she detect a note of something akin to satisfaction as he repeated the name? "Margo is Mrs. *Somebody*, I'll grant, but she's not Mrs. Burke Ransome and never was. Unfortunately I didn't know this at the time. When she married me, Margo already had a spouse. It seems she'd neglected to get a divorce."

For a moment Allison's pulse raced in wild relief. Then it slowed dismally. If in his own mind Burke had thought he was married yet still made love to Allison, he was as culpable as if he'd actually had a wife.

"If you didn't know your marriage wasn't valid, that hardly changes the picture," she protested, the sound of lost hope in her voice. In spite of herself she leaned forward, waiting for him to go on. She was taken aback when Burke answered her new show of interest by pulling his deck chair forward until he was directly in front of her, so close his knees were almost touching hers.

Seizing her hands, he said, "You're right, and at the same time, you're wrong, my darling. I didn't know until today that Margo and I were never legally married, but I understood she'd divorced me long ago. For me she had ceased to exist. When it dawned on me how much you meant to me, the last thing in my mind was Margo. She was the folly of my youth. Until she showed up on Ransome's Cay that day we hadn't been in touch for years."

Listening intently, Allison was scarcely aware of the intensity with which he gripped her hands until a prickling sensation in her fingers reminded her. She pulled them gently away and touched his cheek. She drew a deep tremulous breath. "I should have known..." she murmured sorrowfully. "I've been wrong about you so many times. Oh, Burke..."

"No more than I've been wrong about you," he reminded her quietly. Retrieving her hands, he turned them over to kiss the palms as he pulled her toward him.

In spite of her own deep yearning to throw herself into his arms, Allison held back. There had been too much doubt between them in the past; shades of darkness in this man she loved must be brought to light if they were to move on together in trust. "Wait, Burke," she said. "Something happened between you and Tyler and I think I should know about it. I have this feeling about it—that it stands between us somehow."

There was a pause, and she was disappointed but hardly surprised when he sidestepped her question. "That was a long time ago and it no longer matters," he said after a moment. "I let it affect my life far longer than the business deserved, and I'd just as well forget it. Besides, it had nothing to do with you."

"Then why do you keep trying to get me to say I hate Ty?" she asked in a small troubled voice.

To her surprise Burke laughed. In a sudden buoyant movement he reached out to take her face in his hands and capture her lips in a long hungry kiss that further weakened her resolve.

She let herself be pulled into his arms. He made room for her on the chair, cradling her with his legs until she half sat between them, half leaning against his chest. He rained kisses on her neck until she forgot for a moment there were still enigmas to be unriddled.

At last, with a singleness of purpose, she managed to fend him off. "Why, Burke?" she persisted. "There was a time when I did come close to hating him, but I got over it. I realized it hurt me more than it ever did him. Now I guess I don't feel much of anything for Tyler except a lot of pity and a little contempt."

"Which is pretty much the way I feel about him now myself," Burke agreed thoughtfully. "Even when I was pestering you to renounce Ty it had nothing to do with what was between him and me in the past. I was really only trying to find out if you had some feeling for him that stood in the way of your loving me."

"Oh, Burke, there's been so much misunderstanding between us," Allison murmured, distressed. "My marriage to Ty was a fiasco and better forgotten, but if telling you the miserable details would help to clear anything up for you, I'll—"

His fingers came up to gently cover her lips. "I learned all I need to know from Peg," he told her.

"No questions?"

"I have no questions, dear one," he said. He turned her face until his eyes looked deeply into hers, studying her closely. "But it's plain to see you still have some."

He searched her face a moment longer before bringing her head to rest on his shoulder. From that oblique viewpoint she watched the fine intelligent face reflect a moment of inner decision, signaled by an uptwist of his mouth into a sardonic smile.

"What I'm going to tell you is about Tyler and me, but it's about Margo, too," he began, his voice dispassionate. "I've never felt the need to speak of it to anyone before, but maybe it's time to get the skeletons out of the closets. Maybe it's better you know, if only so we both can forget."

At last Allison heard from Burke of that fateful night when he had walked in on Tyler and his wife in flagrante delicto on the drawing room carpet at Plantation House. He related the episode tersely, without embellishment or bitterness, without self-pity. There was even a certain wry twist in the telling that said that at this late date he saw something ludicrous in the behavior of all three.

Not so with Allison. Listening, her anger and disgust for Tyler flared anew, this time there was a new dimension—the woman—Margo. How dared they carry on their sleazy escapade at Burke's expense?

By the time Burke had finished his brief account Allison's anger had turned inward on herself. What Tyler had done to her seemed nothing in the light of what he'd done to Burke. By her hypocrisy in defending her husband, even accusing Burke of cheating him out of a share of the Ransome inheritance, she had made herself accessory to a scoundrel against the man she loved. "Burke, if I'd only known," she cried out unhappily.

"You didn't," he said practically. "It happened a long time ago to another man. It has nothing to do with me—the man who loves you, Allison. It has nothing to do with us."

Leaving off words, he covered her lips in a great hungering kiss that filled her with such a swell of yearning she murmured his name in the warm cave of his mouth.

"Questions?" he asked hoarsely.

"No questions," she replied.

Then, when she imagined there were no more words to say, he uttered the ones that mattered the most. "I love you, Allison. Will you marry me?"

"Yes," she replied simply.

"Oh, God, how I love you," he murmured into her hair. "Sweet water maid! I want to crown you with magnolia blossoms. I want to take you to my bed."

The music of his words stirred the latent flame within her. In sudden sensuous awareness she thrilled to his warm breath, which whispered down the valley between her breasts.

An image exciting, beautiful, flickered into life in her mind, and she said it aloud with joy. "Centaur!"

"Centaur?"

"Never mind," she murmured. "It was just a way of saying I love you. Oh, Burke, I love you so much."

As she shifted her weight to bring herself in closer communion with him, the rickety chair collapsed, dumping them in a scramble of arms and legs on the floor of the roof. There they clung together, laughing helplessly.

Gradually Allison grew aware of an arousal in the body that supported hers and in the thrill of discovery felt an answering rise in herself. In the sweet hot pain of anticipation, she became conscious only of the new throb of yearning within.

Burke's fingers deftly unbuttoned her blouse and found their way under her bra, but, remembering where they were, she stopped his hand and pulled away. Rising to her knees she leaned over him. "Burke, darling, let's go home," she said, her voice muzzy with rapture.

"Home is Plantation House, love," he corrected. "Tomorrow we'll go home." His eyes lighted with a flash of amusement. "If I'm to take that as a belated invitation to your apartment, I shall be honored to accept."

They rose to their feet and clung to each other in a lingering embrace. Then, arms entwined, their bodies pressed together side by side, they crossed the rooftop and stepped inside to descend the stairs to Allison's apartment.

They were too preoccupied to notice the groceries that still lay strewn on the floor where Allison had spilled them earlier. Closing the apartment door behind them, they left the comestibles for someone with nothing better to do than pick them up.

HARLEQUIN
PREMIERE AUTHOR EDITIONS

6 top Harlequin authors—6 of their best books!

1. JANET DAILEY Giant of Mesabi

2. CHARLOTTE LAMB Dark Master

3. ROBERTA LEIGH Heart of the Lion

4. ANNE MATHER Legacy of the Past

5. ANNE WEALE Stowaway

6. VIOLET WINSPEAR The Burning Sands

Harlequin is proud to offer these 6 exciting romance novels by 6 of our most popular authors. In brand-new beautifully designed covers, each Harlequin Premiere Author Edition is a bestselling love story—a contemporary, compelling and passionate read to remember!

Available in September wherever paperback books are sold, or through Harlequin Reader Service. Simply complete and mail the coupon below.

Share the joys and sorrows
of real-life love with
Harlequin American Romance!™

GET THIS BOOK
FREE as your introduction to
Harlequin American Romance –
an exciting series of romance
novels written especially for
the American woman of today.

Mail to:
Harlequin Reader Service

In the U.S.
2504 West Southern Avenue
Tempe, AZ 85282

In Canada
649 Ontario Street
Stratford, Ontario N5A 6W2

YES! I want to be one of the first to discover
Harlequin American Romance. Send me FREE and without
obligation *Twice in a Lifetime.* If you do not hear from me after I
have examined my FREE book, please send me the 4 new
Harlequin American Romances each month as soon as they
come off the presses. I understand that I will be billed only $2.25
for each book (total $9.00). There are no shipping or handling
charges. There is no minimum number of books that I have to
purchase. In fact, I may cancel this arrangement at any time.
Twice in a Lifetime is mine to keep as a FREE gift, even if I do not
buy any additional books.

Name	(please print)	

Address		Apt. no.

City	State/Prov.	Zip/Postal Code

Signature (If under 18, parent or guardian must sign.)

Yours FREE, with a home subscription to SUPERROMANCE™

Now you never have to miss reading the newest **SUPERROMANCES**... because they'll be delivered right to your door.

Start with your **FREE** LOVE BEYOND DESIRE. You'll be enthralled by this powerful love story...from the moment Robin meets the dark, handsome Carlos and finds herself involved in the jealousies, bitterness and secret passions of the Lopez family. Where her own forbidden love threatens to shatter her life.

Your **FREE** LOVE BEYOND DESIRE is only the beginning. A subscription to **SUPERROMANCE** lets you look forward to a long love affair. Month after month, you'll receive four love stories of heroic dimension. Novels that will involve you in spellbinding intrigue, forbidden love and fiery passions.

You'll begin this series of sensuous, exciting contemporary novels...written by some of the top romance novelists of the day...with four every month.

And this big value...each novel, almost 400 pages of compelling reading...is yours for only $2.50 a book. Hours of entertainment every month for so little. Far less than a first-run movie or pay-TV. Newly published novels, with beautifully illustrated covers, filled with page after page of delicious escape into a world of romantic love...delivered right to your home.

What readers say about SUPERROMANCE

"Bravo! Your SUPERROMANCE [is]...super!"
R.V.,* Montgomery, Illinois

"I am impatiently awaiting
the next SUPERROMANCE."
J.D., Sandusky, Ohio

"Delightful...great."
C.B., Fort Wayne, Indiana

"Terrific love stories. Just
keep them coming!"
M.G., Toronto, Ontario

*Names available on request.

ROBERTA LEIGH

A specially designed collection of six exciting love stories by one of the world's favorite romance writers—Roberta Leigh, author of more than 60 bestselling novels!

1 **Love in Store**   4 **The Savage Aristocrat**
2 **Night of Love**   5 **The Facts of Love**
3 **Flower of the Desert**   6 **Too Young to Love**